NO MAN'

Barry England was born in London in 1932 and educated at Downside. He served as a subaltern in the Far East in the early fifties, then worked as an actor before starting a successful career as a stage and television playwright. His best-known play, *Conduct Unbecoming*, was a huge success in both London and New York.

Barry England's first novel, *Figures in a Landscape* (1968), was shortlisted for the Booker Prize. He is married to the actress, Diane Clare, with whom he has two children and lives in Oxfordshire.

BY BARRY ENGLAND

Figures in a Landscape
No Man's Land

Barry England

NO MAN'S LAND

VINTAGE

Published by Vintage 1998

2 4 6 8 10 9 7 5 3 1

First published in Great Britain by
Jonathan Cape 1997

Vintage
Random House, 20 Vauxhall Bridge Road,
London SW1V 2SA

Random House Australia (Pty) Limited
20 Alfred Street, Milsons Point, Sydney
New South Wales 2061, Australia

Random House New Zealand Limited
18 Poland Road, Glenfield,
Auckland 10, New Zealand

Random House South Africa (Pty) Limited
Endulini, 5A Jubilee Road, Parktown 2193,
South Africa

Random House UK Limited Reg. No. 954009

A CIP catalogue record for this book
is available from the British Library

ISBN 0 09 976561 6

Papers used by Random House UK Ltd are natural, recy-
clable products made from wood grown in sustainable
forests. The manufacturing processes conform to the
environmental regulations of the country of origin

Printed and bound in Great Britain by
Mackays of Chatham PLC

For Diane

The Outside

SAVAGE moved among the trees, soundless and insubstantial, as though he were a ghost bodied forth by morning mists. Ahead, the woman spoke again:

'I swear to God, I'll kill you.'

This provoked male derision.

'You don't want to say that.'

'You know you don't mean it.'

'I mean it.'

She sounded little afraid.

At the edge of the spinney, Savage crouched. The woman stood just beyond the tree line, at the periphery of the track, a shotgun levelled from the waist at three men who loomed with menacing imprecision in the fog. Each was armed and one materialised and dematerialised, as he moved to cut off her flank. She turned her weapon on him.

'You! Stay where you are.'

But the nearest chuckled and took a step closer.

'Why don't you give it up?'

At that, she raised the weapon directly to his face.

'You first.'

She had, Savage thought, correctly assessed leadership. He eased left to have a clear target of each man. The leader shook his head.

'You won't use it.'

Savage said,

'I will.'

He rose. The woman gasped and swung her aim uncertainly on him. Among the men was inhibition at the sight of his rifle. The leader said,

'Who are you?'

Savage said,

3

'Put down your guns.'

This gave rise to an obscenity.

'Do it now.'

The leader smiled.

'Alright.'

As he feigned to obey, Savage took first pressure on his trigger; the moment the other's muzzle began to rise, he fired. The man who had sought to circumvent the woman made to return fire, but he was betrayed by amateurishness and fright and Savage killed him. The third had thrown down his weapon and now put up open palms, as though in earnest of their emptiness.

'Don't shoot! Please!'

'How many are you?'

'What?'

'How many?'

'Three! I swear! Just the three!'

Savage fired again. At once, he moved to ensure that the fallen were dead, dispatching the one who was not. He then turned to the woman.

'You alright?'

She watched him.

'Yes.'

'Wait here.'

Although confident, from dusk and dawn sweeps, that there was no significant force in the vicinity, Savage ran lightly along his back track; dropped into the low ground east of the spinney; patrolled its perimeter northwards until he encountered the track again; crossed into the high ground on the other side (from which he had descended) and flushed the slopes back until he had completed his circuit. Visibility fluctuated constantly between a hundred yards and fewer than ten. When he was satisfied that, at least for a time, they would be free from interruption, he recovered his bergen from where he had cached it for combat and returned to the woman.

She appeared not to have moved, the shotgun clasped in her hands, an expression of suspicion in her face. Beyond her, a large pram was

4

slewed partway off the track, its front wheels in the coarse verge, where a bedding roll and other impedimenta were strewn about.

'You'd better get your things together,' he said. 'We need to get off the Main Route.'

'Who are you?'

'John Savage.'

'Are you the Army?'

'. . . Not exactly.'

It was a question to which he had no answer.

'What does that mean?'

'Look. There's a house. About three hours from here. To the west.'

He had found that civilians were less daunted by distance expressed as time rather than in miles. She said,

'House?'

She continued suspicious. He understood. He might, after all, have saved her for himself. He said,

'There are other women there. And a doctor.'

'A doctor?'

It was gall to her.

'Yes. Why?'

'Bad timing.'

'What?'

But she offered no explanation; said,

'I'm on my way to the Capital.'

'I'll take you there tomorrow.'

'*Take* me?'

'It's what I do.'

It was the simplest way to explain himself. She neither spoke nor made any move to prepare for march. He said,

'We're short of time.'

She stirred then.

'I haven't finished what I'm doing.'

'Quickly, please.'

He crossed to search the fallen.

Of their weapons, only the leader's was worth salvaging – a modern assault rifle which plainly had not been cleaned since having been taken (Savage surmised) from the same dead soldier as had provided the camo jacket which the leader wore and the bandolier slung across his chest. It was a weapon in need of constant preventive maintenance and Savage was disgusted by its condition.

He had just begun to strip it down when he heard behind him the *chic chic* of digging – the sound that had drawn him (and her tormentors) to the woman by dawn. She had been unlucky. She must inadvertently have bivouacked near to them the evening before. Movement at night and in the morning fogs was all but extinct, not least among the Scavengers.

As he rounded the pram, he saw that she was completing a shallow grave. Beside it lay the body of a boy of, perhaps, fourteen: he was not good with children's ages. The woman looked up at his approach and then continued her work in silence. He said,

'Yours?'

'No longer.'

From convention, he said,

'I'm sorry.'

'Why?'

Bleak.

'You want help?'

'No.'

He had seen sufficient grief to feel nothing for it now.

He cleaned and oiled the leader's rifle. Stripped and cleaned the magazine and reloaded it from his own stock. It was not that he anticipated trouble in the hills – but then, he had not expected to encounter anyone on this, his final sweep of his ground; and he had found the woman. She should at least be adequately armed.

He teased the bandolier out from under the leader's corpse. He would not trust the ammunition, but he did not mean to leave it for others.

When next he looked, the woman had covered all but her son's face (always the face last). She dabbled fingers in the features and mouthed something. Abruptly, she scraped over the remainder of the spoil and tamped it down beyond necessity. Then she looked at Savage.

'Are there any stones?'

'*Stones?*'

With an exclamation of disgust, she threw down her spade and

6

crossed to the ditch, where she rooted, presumably, for markers to the grave site. She was beginning to try his patience. With so great a superfluity of the dead veiled only by swags of fog, it seemed to him indulgent to make much of a single death. When finally she had set a stone at each corner and one at the head, he said,

'Have you finished?'

'Oh yes.'

She regarded him with revulsion. He said,

'Take this.'

He held out the newly-cleaned rifle, but she took the shotgun from where she had lain it across the pram.

'I prefer the shotgun.'

'No. The shotgun's no good. Take this.'

She returned his look levelly.

'With the shotgun, I can't miss.'

'With this, you get twenty shots. With that, two. Now – *take it*!'

He thrust the weapon at her with such violence that she was obliged to grip it. At the same moment, he tugged the shotgun from her grasp. She said,

'*Wait!*'

Her tone was compounded equally of anger and distress. She said, sharply:

'I don't know how to use something like this!'

'I'll show you.'

It was evident that the shotgun carried some burden of association from the past. Perhaps it had belonged to her husband. To ease her path, he said,

'I don't like to leave usable weapons for scum like that.'

She looked at the dead Scavengers and then nodded.

Before she could change her mind, he dashed the shotgun against the nearest tree, damaging it beyond repair. He disposed similarly of the unserviceable Scavenger weapons, hurling the remnants deeply into the copse.

The woman had turned her back and was transferring items from one rucksack into another. She and the boy, presumably, had divided their provisions against the possibility of separation or loss of the pram: he respected their planning. He said,

'Anything you want from the pram?'

7

He crossed to it. She looked at it as though from another time. 'No.'

The interior was well found. An intelligent selection of equipment and supplies, sensibly ordered, labelled, and protected from the elements by plastic bags and boxes. He was not surprised. She did not strike him as disorganised or supine. He said,

'Anything . . . personal?'

She smiled, bleakly.

'Not now, Mr Savage.'

As though she held him responsible for the death of her husband, her son and her pram. Without a word, she placed the second rucksack on top of the boxes and he drove the baby carriage into the densest part of the thicket. He did not mean to come this way again, but he saw no reason to provision Scavengers. When he returned to the woman, he said,

'Alright.'

The limits of responsibility eluded him.

'This is a modern, lightweight assault rifle. It has very little recoil. And the capacity for limited automatic fire. But you will never, *never* put it in that mode.' He showed her the selector lever beside the housing. 'That's the safety position. *Forward*.' He rotated the lever through ninety degrees. 'That's single shot. In the middle.' He completed the arc of travel. 'That's burst. To the rear.' He restored the lever to its original position. 'You will keep it here at all times. Check constantly. Whenever we stop, whenever we move.' Not least, Savage thought, because you'll be behind me. 'If you do have to fire, single shot only. And aim low. At the broadest part of the target. Is that clear?'

'Entirely, Mr Savage.'

As though even a child could not fail to comprehend. He doubted that her sanguinity was justified.

'Stay behind me. No more than thirty yards. Move when I move. Stop when I stop. If I go to ground, you go to ground. If you don't know what to do, do nothing. I'll come to you. Okay?'

She nodded.

'And watch our rear. That's your job. Left, right, behind. Left, right, behind. I count on you.'

8

This was a lie; nor did she appear persuaded, but she said, 'Very well.'

'Any questions?'

'No.'

'Put on your pack.'

He held it for her. It was greatly lighter than his bergen, which rarely weighed less than eighty pounds. He draped the dead leader's bandolier over her left shoulder and she tucked it under her right arm. He was happy to employ her as a mule. He said,

'Don't use the ammunition. I'll give you a spare magazine from my own kit.'

As they climbed into the hills, the fog dispersed and visibility expanded correspondingly.

To begin with, he looked back repeatedly. But it became apparent that she recognised his critical assessments for what they were and that she resented them. She returned his examinations with undisguised hostility.

It became evident, too, that she had a natural gift for tactical movement. She carried herself in balance and accommodated instinctively to the vagaries of terrain.

By the time they achieved the summit, he had come at least to accept her competence, if not to rely on it.

The plateau was not demanding. The dust-streaked grasses, the hummocks, hollows and ridges were not dramatically delineated, although sufficient to present many false crests. This was Savage's ground, yet he walked it with ingrained scepticism, ever watchful; heading west, to extend the gap between the Main Route and themselves.

The now familiar overcast was low and dense. He did not believe that the recently renascent sun, however feebly, would manifest today. Even such brief glimpses as they had been vouchsafed, in which a single weak beam pierced the caul and hung in their truncated day, seemed improbable. Indeed, the more he studied their altered sky, the more convinced Savage became that, no matter what the perturbation to the seasons, the Rains would break within ten days.

Time had become for him desperately short. He was in danger of

9

being trapped on his ground, his dilemma no closer of resolution. When they reached the house, he would impose his will.

After fifty minutes, he said,

'Rest now. Ten minutes.'

The woman would not settle. He said,

'Sit down. Take off your pack.'

She paid him no mind. Perhaps to move was less painful than to feel. In an effort at empathy, he said,

'Tiring yourself won't bring him back.'

She regarded him with derision.

'You're a psychiatrist, too, Mr Savage?'

'I'm a soldier.'

'But not of the Army. Exactly.'

'Sit down. Rest.'

He had chosen a modest eminence at the conjunction of two ridges, which offered a clear view in every direction and no possibility of covert approach. Nonetheless, he scanned the visible horizon ceaselessly.

The woman sat a pointed distance from him. It was evident that she disliked him as greatly as he was made uncomfortable by her. In a moment, she withdrew from her haversack a plastic cordial bottle filled, it appeared, with water. He said,

'Not yet.'

Without a word, she set the bottle down between her feet. He said,

'I don't know your name.'

Her use of his own name had brought the omission to mind.

'Anne. Paget.'

'Look, Mrs Paget –'

'Anne.'

It was not, he knew, an invitation to intimacy; rather, an acknowledgement of the reality that such soubriquets as 'Mrs' were out of time. As though in confirmation, she said,

'I have no family now.' And then, 'That's funny.'

He did not think it so. He said,

'Have you come far?'

'From Lulford.'

He envisioned the map.

'That's . . . a hundred miles north of here?'

'Approximately.'

'You've done well.'

'You think so?'

A reference, plainly, to her son's death. He said,

'Much trouble before today?'

'Usually we were able to take cover. But the last ten days . . .'

'The Scavengers are fleeing north, as the Army clears the Main Route.'

'I'm gratified to learn the Army is doing *something*.' She looked at him. 'I should thank you.'

'No. Why take to the road now?'

Given the supplies they possessed, it would have seemed logical, after fourteen weeks, to remain in situ until the Army reached them, as the broadcasts had instructed. She said,

'My son became ill. I hoped to reach the Capital.'

'What was wrong? Do you know?'

Nothing, presumably, deriving from the Event; not after this interval. The body, besides, had been of natural colour and consistency. She said,

'Unlike you, Mr Savage, I lacked a doctor.'

He would not pursue her account. It was no part of his job and, clearly, served merely to sharpen her grief and her tongue. He said,

'Here.' He habitually carried two water bottles in his belt kit, as he carried two bandoliers of additional ammunition for his rifle and ten spare loads for his Browning automatic. He withdrew one of the bottles from its holder now, unscrewed the cap and offered it to her. 'This may be fresher than yours.'

'Only if it was drawn this morning.'

'Last night.'

'Mine, too.'

From the same source, no doubt, since the East River ran contiguous to the Main Route at the place where they had met. When she tipped her bottle to her lips, he said,

'Sip, don't gulp.'

This earned him a rebuke.

'Even a woman knows that, Mr Savage.'

But it had not been her gender, rather her civilian status, that he had supposed might invoke ignorance. When she had finished, she re-stowed her bottle with a meticulousness that reflected his own.

They sat in silence. Silence did not trouble him. Nor solitude. Nor patience. In a little, she indicated the ragged green hills.

'Is there much of this?'

'Clear ground?'

'In a manner of speaking.'

Cleared of people, he took her irony to mean.

'I don't know. This stretch is about thirty miles wide. It extends approximately a hundred miles to the north, as you know. And as far as the coast, to the south.'

'Ah yes. To the *Capital*.'

She italicised the designation, as though not enamoured of her destination. He said,

'The East, as far as I know, is entirely Ashland.'

'Yes.' She looked in that direction, as though it held significance for her. 'Entirely.'

'West is the Desert. North and south of that is Ashland. What lies beyond the Desert, I don't know.'

This was not strictly true, but it was no concern of hers. She said,

'A comprehensive triumph, then.'

It was a relief to be on the move again. He did not relish the prospect of a trek south alone with this woman, even if only until they encountered Army units pushing north.

He angled as much north as west now. He was anxious to reach the valley over which his fortified house stood. The woman was maintaining pace and concentration, but he believed that by the third hour she would flag and then would benefit from the lane which ran the valley's length. There had been no serious contacts west of the Main Route for weeks and he judged the risk involved in quitting the high ground to be minimal.

Within an hour, the valley lay before them, the hills continuing on its further side and, at their feet, the scrub-girt shoulder along which the lane threaded its path to Savage's house at the western end.

The valley ran east-west. It was not possible, from their relative elevation, to discern the mild curvature to which it was prone – never mind the extreme northerly bias at either end; where, to the east, it joined the Main Route and the East River; and, to the west, its course was truncated by a massive prow of rock, which compressed it into a narrow, northerly passage and prevented it from giving naturally to the Desert.

These were topographical features of profound significance to Savage.

The lane led nowhere. Beyond Savage's house, it merely dissipated about the declining slopes and among the dead farms and flatland known as The Bottoms. As a consequence, it had played no part in the grim migration attendant on the Event and was free of the grisly artefacts by which all other ways were disfigured – although anyone who had surmounted a hundred miles of the Main Route, as the woman had, would be unlikely to need relief on that account.

When he told her the house was no more than five miles distant, she merely nodded. He did not think her weary, rather withdrawn. And as soon as they had set out again, he forced the pace. Whatever unresolved difficulties awaited him there, he was eager to reach the house without a further period of rest.

As it fell out, he would gladly have accepted the troubles he had above those that came on him.

The moment he saw the tower, he knew that something was wrong.

As they had approached the rise in the lane from behind which, for the first time, part of the house would become visible, he had set the woman to guard their rear and had himself taken to the drainage ditch. It was not that he had anticipated danger, but vigilance was ingrained in him. It would, besides, have been folly to have an alarm system and not permit it opportunity to function.

For the only occasion since their inception, the warning blanks were in place at the tower windows.

He cursed himself for having deviated, in the interests of the woman, from his standard approach procedure.

The lane receded from him over a distance of approximately twelve hundred yards, rising and falling gently as it did so. To his left, the ridge they had quit receded also, not merely in perspective but in stature, as it declined to the limit of its natural span. To his right, the valley was obscured by a desiccated hedge.

The house stood on the bluff to his left, some eight hundred yards ahead, from where it looked over the valley and down onto a farmhouse, stables and barn, directly across the lane. Ironically, much of this was hidden from Savage by a tangled copse, which rose from beside the farmhouse to the crest of the ridge – and which, for reasons of his own, he had done nothing to subdue. As a result, all he could see of the house was the stone tower which stood at its north-eastern corner; and, of the farmhouse, nothing. Not even the dissolving power of his binoculars had any impact, at this range, on the evergreen thickets with which the trees were salted.

Minutes of observation yielded nothing.

He passed through the hedge to view the target from the valley side. Now he could glimpse one end of the farmhouse – in that it stood athwart the shoulder rather than along it – with the foreshortened fluster of Low Wood beyond, from which the stumble of trees and scrub known as The Beard descended almost to the valley floor. But he saw nothing untoward; nor did any informative sound mar the unnatural quiet of their world.

He returned to the ditch.

He would not break radio silence unless convinced of extremity. There was only one force capable of penetrating the house and he knew of no reason why they would do so yet.

Too late to approach via an alternative route. He could do it on his own, but not with the woman. Nor could he abandon her here, remote from his sphere of influence. He would take her with him. As soon as he had determined the nature of the danger, he would harbour her, safe from battle yet within the compass of his protection, should it be needed. He signed her to him.

'We've got to close the house. Covert, silent.'

She simply nodded.

'I understand.'

They made good progress, returning to the lane whenever dead ground permitted, she exhibiting the instinct for terrain that he had noted earlier. From five hundred yards out, he identified the occupant of the tower room to be Martin. When they had come to within a hundred yards of the onset of the copse and with the last stretch of dead lane before them, he said,

'Flat out now. To the trees. Then into the ditch on the right.'

As they ran, Savage scanned the approaching trees repeatedly, seeking evidence of surveillance: but so little did he sense the probe of a reciprocal scrutiny that he became convinced they were unobserved.

The moment they dropped into the ditch, he lay against the bank – a formidable bulwark now, hunched up about the fringing trees – and brought his binoculars to bear once more. At less than eighty yards, the advanced focal plane liquefied the intervening trunks and branches and, except in two places, he was able to examine the farmhouse.

In that the building faced away from him towards the barn, it was the rear elevation that he scanned. He could see the windows of both storeys at either end. It was only in the middle, where double french doors led into the garden, that his view was baulked by the thickest of the evergreen. As they watched, the lower part of a male torso appeared at a half open upper window and a stream of urine was projected into the brush.

'Nice,' the woman said.

So. Someone had invaded the farmhouse. Scavengers? He had never encountered them this far from the Main Route (although current sanitary habits suggested otherwise). He shucked off his bergen and placed it between the woman and himself.

'Whatever happens, do *not* get involved.' When she made to speak, he lifted a hand for silence. 'You'll find everything you need to survive in here. If I don't come back – or you have reason to believe I won't – head south. Stay in the high ground west of the Main Route. You should meet the Army in about a week. Okay?'

She said,

'I can help.'

'No.'

She was angry.

'I am capable of pulling a trigger, Mr Savage.'

'I can't predict your actions. Nor you, mine. I need that, to do what I do.'

Her expression fluctuated between resentment and acquiescence in his truth.

'Very well.'

'Anyone who comes from me will know your name. Anyone else, start shooting. I'll come at once. Alright?' She nodded. He took her rifle, pulled back the charging handle and restored the lever to safe. 'You've got one up the spout now and the weapon's on safe.'

'I understand.'

'When I want you to come to me, I'll signal like this.'

He arched the fingers and thumb of one hand on the crown of his cap comforter.

'Right.'

She appeared primed but not afraid.

'Be calm. Stay alert. All will be well.'

Restored to a necessary solitude and glad to be, Savage ghosted along the lane, at peace in his milieu, tucked under the lee of the bank, which rose now on either side above five feet as though the trees, in growing, had hauled the earth up with themselves. Trunks danced by above and the farmhouse turned on its axis to meet him. Twenty yards short of the treeline, he flattened to the bank again. He was certain now that no sentries had been posted; that the urination had epitomised a slovenliness by which the invaders were characterised.

They had no scent of their impending death.

The french doors had been reduced beyond the requirements of mere entry; but, although sounds emanated from beyond them, Savage excluded those from his calculations: they carried no operational weight, other than to inform him that the enemy numbered more than one.

He crossed the lane and advanced to the edge of the trees.

Immediately beyond the copse, a service track turned left off the lane and ascended to the original front door of the house, located in its eastern end. As Savage leaned forward now, he brought this slope by degrees into view.

First, he saw the chicken's head and the burst of feathers. So they had lost livestock.

Then, the hanged cat. Strung up by wire from the small iron gibbet (which, according to Madge, had served in times past to hoist provisions from carts into the cellars below).

Like first days.

The coming of barbarism.

Then the graffiti of automatic weapons fire, etched in the stone walls. (So they had automatic weapons.)

He showed himself to Martin, in the tower above.

The moment eye contact was made, the big man began urgently to indicate the farmhouse. Savage acknowledged, but asked by mime if all was well within the house. Martin perfunctorily sketched the all-clear sign and again took up his gesticulation. But Savage persisted. What about the environs of the house? Same result, renewed urgency.

Martin was not given to undue alarm, but already once today Savage had made the mistake of presuming too much; he did not mean to make it again. He ran lightly up the slope, under the cat and past the imposingly-porticoed and now barricaded front door to the south-eastern corner of the house, where he crouched to survey the southern approaches. But these were so mildly expansive and so devoid of cover that covert approach was impossible. In a series of graduated glimpses, he scanned the rear elevation of the house and then ran along it, past their single functioning aperture (the ballroom entrance) to the far end, where again he crouched, looking along the ridge and down its declining slopes, until his view was baulked by the sheer rock wall, which so brutally truncated the western end of the valley.

Again, the careful check. Up the side of the house. The front facade clear. And forward to the rim of the bluff, where he lay among the grasses, looking down.

Conscious that he had come again within the ambit of Martin's vision.

And that he had been watched throughout by Other Force.

Patient and deadly.

The farmhouse, stables and barn formed three sides of a hollow square about a small yard, which fronted on the lane. From his

17

slightly oblique angle, Savage saw the front of the house, most of the horse boxes and the back of the barn. Nowhere was there the smallest sign of disturbance. He allowed his eyes to travel to the left, along the length of Low Wood, which rose up under the lane, and down the tangle of The Beard, which depended from its nearer end into the valley. In so far as he could penetrate the canopies of the trees, he observed nothing.

The evil, almost certainly, was confined to the farmhouse. But first he must sweep the stable yard.

Fleetly now across the face of the house, down into the service track and soundlessly over the lane to the gable end, where, ignoring the sounds from the garden room, he worked left under the frosted lavatory window to the first corner

Scanned the shrouded hulks and shadows in the open barn across the yard

Around the corner, stalking the kitchen window. The room empty, nothing visible beyond the part-closed door

The porch, door secured

To the second and third windows, but these were shallow rooms, the larger space on the garden side

Along the stables now, feinting and weaving

Tuned only to the prick of danger

Of which he felt nothing

Made liquid by light

Like a wolf, up the barn, around

After motion, stillness

Scan the trees. No contact. Along the rear of the barn, loping, to the corner. Check, test

And now, as though he were weightless, behind the stables, striving not to impress the leaves nor to force passage through the air

As though he moved down secret corridors of insubstantiality, become the state he sought and the place he inhabited

Not being

At the corner, check, test

Closing on the enemy, all energy constrained, to send no harbinger before

Sarah was naked.

What was she doing outside the house?

Three Scavengers had sufficiently divested themselves of motley to plunder her. One held her from behind. Another dragged down her face to where he had one leg cocked up on the sofa. The third appeared to derive pleasure as much from witness as from participation. Each was a target (Sarah below the line of fire) and they had abandoned their weapons fatally far from themselves.

How many upstairs?

Savage stepped through the hanging shards and fired three groups of two, each at a different target. He then moved at once to the stairwell, where he crouched to align on the turn in the stairs. He knew that his rounds had found their mark. From above, a man called:

'What's going on down there?'

For Sarah's ears, Savage murmured:

'How many upstairs?'

He knew that she must reanimate horrors, but he needed the information. The man shouted:

'Knacker? Maggs? What are you playing at?'

She said,

'One.'

The man:

'Answer me!' In a moment, footsteps began to descend the flight. Savage thought, Come on, show me a target. But at the last they faltered, short of appearance. 'Who *is* that down there?' A weapon inexpertly cocked. Savage waited. 'You'd best come up, 'cause I en't coming down.' You'll come, Savage thought. The footfalls retreated.

Savage returned to the french doors, from which he could cover both outside and in. The end, he knew, would come in the garden. For the first time, he looked at Sarah.

'You alright?'

She pushed at the fall of her fine fair hair.

'Yes.'

Her habitual air of self-possession persisted to a remarkable degree. It was as though, for all that she was flecked with blood, she had been wholly unaffected by what had happened to her. (Which could not be the case.)

She was not a woman with whom Savage had ever been at ease. There was between them a gulf of education and culture that he had been unable to bridge.

Even now, her nakedness made him uncomfortable.

Footsteps creaked across the ceiling. He thought, That's right. Check the window. Assess the drop.

Sarah coughed, as though irritated at the throat. Abruptly, she turned, pushed wide the kitchen door and went to the sink, where she retched. In a moment, she operated the pump handle with vigorous strokes and, when the spout barked water, began to wash herself with clinical disregard for modesty.

The man above had returned to the head of the stairs.

'Take her! She's yours! You want a woman, don't you?'

He began to describe in gross anatomical detail the delights that a body such as Sarah's might offer a man of Savage's discernment. Sarah came back to the kitchen doorway, her face hollowed by recollection, oblivious apparently of the spate from above:

'They've got Madge.'

Savage's stomach contracted.

'What?'

'And the children.'

'What children?'

Sarah brushed, as though at cobwebs. Savage wondered who else had disobeyed his orders that morning. She said,

'We saw these two kids, boy and a girl. Thirteen, fourteen. We thought we could . . .'

The man upstairs shouted:

'We didn't have to make her! She wanted it!'

Savage said,

'Where's Sammy?'

(In command when Savage was absent.)

'He went to The Bottoms, after breakfast.'

And Martin's job was to anchor the house, which he at least was doing. Savage said,

'Anyone else?'

She shook her head. The footsteps returned to the window. The man would notice the ledge now and that from it he could drop to the ground. When Sarah said,

'You mustn't blame Martin —'

Savage raised a hand.

'Not now.'

He listened intently. The muffled scrape of an attempt to raise a window without transmitting sound. Such niceties were impossible in their all but silent world. Sarah had followed the focus of his attention.

'You will kill him, John?'

'Oh yes.'

He had not heard belligerence from her before.

Had the man not attempted two actions at the same time, he might at least have posed the threat of an armed incompetent. As it was, in landing he sought also to run, measuring his length and losing contact with his rifle. Savage was on him in an instant.

'*Lie still!*'

'For God's sake . . .!'

'*Spread your arms and legs!*'

'Please, Mister . . .!'

'*Be quiet!*'

'Look . . .'

'*Silence!*'

'I beg you . . .!'

'*Total silence!*'

Savage imparted to his commands the concussion of blows. But in truth such artificial aids to dominance were unnecessary. The man was abject.

Savage searched him. No more weapons. Confronted him.

'You speak only to answer questions. For no other reason. Understood?'

'Yes, yes.'

'Where are you from?'

'The Track.'

The Scavengers, Savage knew, called the Main Route the Track.

'Why come here?'

'For food, and . . .'

The man looked away.

'And?'

'Women, but –'

'Why look for women here?'

The man frowned.

'Everybody knows about this place. And you.'

'Who's your leader?'

'Maggs, I suppose. Mordred, maybe. We en't really got one.'

'Which is Maggs?'

The man craned his head back to the farmhouse.

'And Mordred?'

'Gone ahead.'

'How many are you?'

'Fifteen, twenty.'

It was a large force to have banded together without a recognised leader; although the size might explain their boldness in attacking him. He said,

'Was that before or after this?'

The man paled.

'Before.'

Call it sixteen remaining. Sarah had come out of the house, in long skirt and jumper, her hair tied back with a scarf. She stood, arms clasped, watching without expression. Savage said,

'Where's the woman?'

'The woman . . .?'

Confusion.

'Which way did they go?'

'Oh. To the house.'

'What house?'

'Over there. By the river.'

The man nodded to where the rock wall, cleaving the valley, forced passage northward along a narrow creek. This was a dry water course which, four miles distant, gave to the bend of the northern tributary.

On the bend, a house was situated: MacKenzie's Farm.

Madge's home for many years.

She had been taken home.

Savage was puzzled:

'How do you know MacKenzie's Farm?'

'We went that way last night. Thought it were the right road. Come up the creek this morning.'

They had passed the unprepossessing reverse entry to his lane and had taken the next left by the river. Had their approach via the creek hidden them this morning? It should not have done.

'Are the kids in the same party?'

'Aye, unless . . .'

'What?'

'Taken north.'

'Who are they?'

'I don't know. I swear. We never saw them before this morning.'

'Will they wait for you at the house?'

'No.'

'Where then?'

'North. I don't know. *North.*'

He opened his palms, as though he knew the answer to be inadequate. Savage looked to Sarah. She nodded. He killed the man.

Having checked that the Scavengers in the farmhouse indeed were dead (as he already knew), Savage returned to Sarah.

'How long ago did these people leave?'

He knew that she must again resurrect horrors, but time was a factor now. She looked at her wrist. The watch she habitually wore was missing. He said,

'I'll recover it.'

He showed her his own. In a moment, she said,

'More than an hour.'

Alone with them. And for Madge, on the march. And children. By the time he set out, he would be more than two hours behind. He said,

'Better get up to the house.'

She nodded. But he sensed that she was as yet unready to face the others. Abruptly, she clung to him. Insofar as he was able, rifle in hand, he reciprocated. Deep sounds escaped her. But he had no capacity to comfort (this woman, least). He wished that Sammy were there.

23

Perhaps she sensed his awkwardness, for she straightened and said,

'I'm alright.'

It was plain that she was not. He said,

'I've got someone with me.'

'Yes?'

'Her name's Anne. She's just along the lane.'

'Well, fetch her, John. Fetch her.'

As though she were a hostess and he the host, derelict of duty. He crossed the lane to be sure that Anne could see him and put a hand to his head.

In normal circumstances, he would have alerted Sarah to the fact that Anne had just lost a son, for Sarah was their doctor. But it seemed at the moment inappropriate. Sarah had joined him.

'Oh, *do* give her a hand, John.'

Anne indeed was unbalanced by the need to carry his bergen. When he moved to help her, he found that Sarah had come with him.

'Hullo. It's Anne, isn't it? I'm Sarah. Have you come far?'

It was not just the bruises blooming in Sarah's face, Savage knew, which caused Anne to look at her strangely. Sarah, indeed, continued in hostess vein as they approached the house and Savage signalled to Martin to admit them. It was only when they passed under the cat that, for a moment, she hesitated and put a hand to her chest.

'Oh no.'

Savage said,

'I'll take care of it.'

At which, she smiled brightly and said,

'You take care of everything, John.'

Not quite everything, he thought.

Savage bumped the butt of his rifle on the massive steel, wood and stone plug which sealed their only functioning aperture into the house. It had been constructed by Martin and himself from materials either serendipitously acquired, or salvaged from the outbuildings that they had dismantled. It was immensely heavy and had been chamfered precisely to fit the opening left in the two foot thick stone walls by the removal of large double doors.

From inside now came the scrape of the retaining rails being lifted clear and then the grinding of the block being hauled up the metal runnels in which it rode. Savage was not a weak man, but he had never known anyone, other than the exceptionally powerful Martin, capable of drawing so great a weight without assistance. The pressure that he himself applied to the featureless exterior was, he knew, of little help, since the mass must be lifted as well as dragged.

The plug unblocked with an intake of air and a staccato release of chickens, accompanied by a volley of mild oaths from Martin. Savage said,

'Let them go. There's no danger now.'

The interior of the once ballroom, now their stable, was lit only by the wash of light that they had admitted and by a single butane lamp, which hung from a defunct electrical bracket. (All but a handful of windows had been permanently walled up and those that still operated would have been battened down by Martin in accordance with emergency procedures.)

The stocky frame and face of Alice were redolent of anxiety as she came to claim Sarah.

'Oh, lovey. Are you alright?'

But Sarah was distancing.

'I'm fine, Alice.'

'There weren't nothing we could – *he* wouldn't let me!'

This accusation was directed at Martin, but Sarah said,

'This is Anne, Alice.'

'. . . What?'

It was evident that Sarah's alienation was as bewildering to Alice as Alice's compassion was unwelcome to Sarah.

Martin dropped the plug back into position with a soft boom. In his improvised stall, Spartan snorted at the withdrawal of daylight (Sammy must be riding Noble) and those chickens that had missed their opportunity became mutinous. Savage said,

'Don't bar it. I'm off again.'

Alice seemed suddenly to grasp the significance.

'Where's *Madge*?'

'I'm going after her now.'

She stared at him.

'Oh God.'

'Take them to the kitchen, Alice.'

But abruptly she was vehement:

'Where were *you*?'

Sarah said,

'No man can be everywhere.'

But Savage was inclined to take Alice's part. Martin said,

'He told us what to do.'

With edge, Sarah said,

'Yes. Which, in fact, we didn't do.'

Alice glowered at Martin.

'Well, *we* did what we were told, *didn't* we?'

It was apparent that the normally stable Alice suffered profound shame at having remained in a place of safety (although that was her job) while her friends had been assaulted: and that Sarah was bitterly conscious of the standard operating procedures that she and Madge had ignored. To Alice, Savage said,

'You did the right thing.'

'It don't feel like it!'

Savage wondered whether it ever did. Sarah took Anne's arm:

'Come on. Alice always has soup on the go.'

She led the other woman towards the archway into the hall. Martin said,

'They need you, Alice.'

Sarah said,

'We can have baths, too.'

'*Baths*?'

Sarah chuckled at Anne's startlement.

'Oh, John is a miracle worker.'

Alice snorted.

'Some miracle!'

But she left. Savage was not disturbed. There was too much good sense in Alice not to see to the centre of things. He slipped off his bergen and, while recharging his magazine against the rounds that he had fired that morning, said to Martin:

'What happened?'

'I spotted these two kids, from the tower. Nine AM. Near the farmhouse. Boy and a girl. Fourteen, fifteen.'

'Where had they come from?'

'I don't *know*.'

The admission was painful.

'Go on.'

'I stood back, not to spook them. Told Sarah and Madge.'

'And?'

The big man's story came haltingly.

'It were obvious they was arguing. Whether or not to come up here. The girl was keen, but the boy were dead set against. In the end, Madge said they'd have to go down, or the kids would be lost forever. I said they should wait for you. But you know what Madge is like.'

Indeed, Savage well knew that Madge's briskly patrician assumption of authority, allied to Sarah's professional status, would have been too much for the straightforward Martin to withstand. Had it occurred in Sammy's presence, he would have had no compunction in overriding them both: but Martin would have been 'jollied' into it. Savage said,

'Did Madge go armed?'

Sarah, he knew, would never carry a weapon. Martin sighed.

'No. Wouldn't have me go, either. Said I could cover them from the tower. But you can't do that, can you?'

'No.'

You have to be close.

'And then these – *scum* were *everywhere*, Savage! I never even saw them coming!'

The man's agitation and shame were extreme. Spartan steepled up and, absently, Martin stroked his muzzle, as much to comfort himself, Savage thought, as to settle the animal. He said,

'Put a saddle on him.'

'Aye. Right.'

The familiar task steadied the big man and in a moment, he said,

'I didn't dare risk a shot, for fear of hitting one of our own. And then, in a bit, they left. Most of them.'

It was eloquent for being brief.

27

'Who did you relieve in the tower?'

'Madge. She had first watch after Stand-to.'

Had Madge's own ageing eyes betrayed her? It seemed likely.

'When did they leave?'

'About hour and a half. Bit more, mebbe.'

The gap grew wider.

'Some came up here?'

'Not really. Oh, they fired wildly at the house. But why bother with us? They'd already got what they come for, hadn't they?'

The bitterness of humiliation. Yet the big man had done his job. He had closed down the house and had even insisted on bringing in all but the stragglers among their stock, before the women embarked on their folly. It was they who had been at fault. And they who paid the price. Savage said,

'If you'd gone down, you'd have been killed.'

'I know.'

'If Alice had, she'd have been taken.'

'I know that!'

But it did not repair the self-esteem. Savage said,

'I'm going after Sammy now. Then Madge and the kids.'

The big man straightened.

'Will I come?'

'No.' Savage studied Martin. He stood a head and a half above Savage's all but six feet. Savage said, 'I don't know about Sammy, after this. Or Sarah.' The relationship between them was no secret. 'You must be prepared to take responsibility.'

'I understand.'

'No one in, no one out. The animals, only in accordance with strict procedures. Observe procedures at all times.'

'It will be done.'

'Alright.'

Savage decided not to take his bergen. He wanted to be swift and battle-ready: and he carried on (and in) his person, everything necessary to fight, to survive and to sustain those whom he meant to rescue, virtually for a limitless period. He said,

'Open up.'

By virtue of Spartan's height, Savage cut down Madge's cat and flung the corpse among the trees. He then put the horse at the southern slopes and Spartan flew the ground as though he were as relieved as Savage to be free of the emotional complexities of the house.

Savage wondered whether, by harbouring his people so far from the Main Route, he had blunted their perception of danger. Certainly it was the case that, for all his exhortations to vigilance, at the first test they had fallen.

There passed through the periphery of his consciousness, too, the possibility that, in the morning's events (however odious), might lie the resolution of his dilemma. This was a thought so treacherous that he put it from him.

He turned his mount along the rim of the heights and brought him to a walk, looking down into the narrow strait of track and abandoned farm buildings that lay between himself and the huge rock wall opposite.

He had considered using a horse during his recent work. But he could walk as far in a day and carry as heavy a load. And he was fundamentally a man of stealth. Of silence and shadow. He came and went and was not known. While the horse, for all its virtues, was not possessed of these.

Savage knew that Other Force watched. He wondered, not for the first time, what part they may have played in the morning's depredation.

The moment he sighted Sammy, he turned to place himself on the skyline, for he knew that Sammy, with his good habits, would spot him quickly.

From Savage's point of view, Sammy was the most valuable of the group. Having seen active service as an infantry commander, he had harboured basic skills and experience which, under Savage's tutelage, had developed so rapidly that Savage had promoted him from local defence to helping in the escort of parties of survivors which, between them, they had shepherded down the Main Route towards safety at the Capital. He was the one on whom Savage had most relied.

Until now.

For his feelings for Sarah were an Achilles heel.

Madge had said,

He is enamoured, John, and the lady, I venture, is not averse.
Indeed, I shall go further and predict the same outcome for Martin and
Alice. Now all we need is to find someone for you. If only I were
younger.

He expunged her twinkling mockery from his mind.

Sammy was a tall, narrow man, of deceptive musculature and
austere in the face. As his horse picked up the slope, he raised a
hand in greeting: and when he came level, he said,

'Good to see you back, Savage.'

Savage nodded. Perhaps it was the paucity of his response that
alerted Sammy, for the other regarded him keenly and said,

'What's wrong?'

The two horses butted up to one another.

'There's been an attack on the house.'

'Serious?'

'They've got Madge.'

'*Got* her? *How?*'

'She and Sarah were outside the house, when it happened.'

There was silence. Even now, Sammy's characteristic reserve
masked his emotions.

'Is Sarah . . .?'

'She's back in the house. I . . . found her.'

Sammy drew a breath.

'Who were they?'

'Scavengers.'

Savage waited. Sammy said,

'Was she . . .?'

'Yes.'

'How many?'

'With Sarah, four.' At that moment, anyway. 'Altogether, twenty-
odd.'

'Did you kill them?'

'Yes.'

Sammy nodded, smiled slightly.

'I don't know what we'd do without you, Savage.'

It seemed to Savage an ambiguous remark. He said,

'I must get after them.'

He dropped from his horse and handed the reins to Sammy.

'Do you want me to come?'

'I need you at the house.'

At least until I am certain you have not become a liability.

'Thanks for telling me, Savage.'

'Should be back before nightfall.'

'Good luck.'

He stopped briefly at the farmhouse, hauled out the bodies, searched them, recovered Sarah's watch.

Photographs of families. Too late to view Scavengers in such terms.

There were four weapons, two automatic, with ammunition. A high ratio. Yet these were the men who had claimed the top prize, Sarah, and probably were lead dogs in the pack.

He smashed the weapons on stone and hid the ammunition behind the prepared riser under the third stair.

Finally, he washed his hands at the sink, recharged his water bottles and put up his face under the stinging flow, savouring the deep waters. He wiped himself, retied his scrim about his neck and headed north.

He dropped down through the trees of The Beard and cut diagonally across the vast, sloping meadow beneath Low Wood. This was an area so perturbated, so humped by ridges and pocked by hollows, that progress would have been taxing had not Savage known it intimately. It was bounded by Low Wood above, by The Beard to the east, by the valley floor below and, to the west, by a deep, peripatetic fissure, which scored the hillside from the lane virtually to the valley floor, and whose course was flagged by a straggle of desiccated trees and brush. This was Savage's training ground, where he had raised Sammy to a high, and Martin, Madge and (a reluctant) Alice to a modest competence with weapons.

Sarah alone had declined.

He ran off the slope and across the valley, maintaining a controlled pace and constantly scanning for danger. In the lee of the rock wall, he turned right and entered the creek which led to MacKenzie's Farm.

In that it was a dried water course, two-thirds of its width was occupied by the dry channel itself, thickly grown up with sere grasses and scrub. Indeed, the 'towpath', to which Savage confined himself, was no less overgrown and he experienced no difficulty in tracking the spoor that his quarry had left.

In normal circumstances, he would have taken to the high ground. But he did not believe these people meant to fight him. Indeed, if they did not linger at MacKenzie's Farm, or if they separated, he would be hard pressed to complete his task before nightfall.

Already it was close to midday. MacKenzie's Farm lay four miles to the north. He meant to cover the distance in no longer than twenty minutes. As it came out, he made contact of a kind before then.

The moment he saw the shape, he worked up into high ground. He did not seriously entertain the possibility of ambush, but he did not mean to forgo a lifetime's experience to test it. Only when he was satisfied, from a visual sweep of the entire visible landscape, that no trap was involved, did he descend to the body.

He had known from the first what he had seen. The signature of death was unmistakable. The boy lay face down, inconsequentially sprawled, trousers about his ankles, one foot free. He had been kicked and beaten to death.

Savage crouched to read the surrounding grasses. A pair of pants, that could only belong to a young girl. A shoe. Jeans. Savage did not doubt what had occurred. Another assault had been attempted and the boy (with unimaginable courage) had sought to protect the women. The Scavengers would not otherwise have killed him and forfeited the pleasure that his living body represented to them.

Savage did not bury things. But he laid the boy in a hollow and covered him with lifeless rushes and scrub hauled up from the dead river bed. No need to concern himself with leaving sign in this compromised place.

He then gathered the girl's clothes as he found them, rolled them tightly inside the jeans, secured the bundle with paracord and attached it to his belt. He meant to return the garments to their owner and to mark her defilers permanently in the process.

He made good time. Within the designated period, as he approached the end of the creek, he moved up into the greatly diminished foothills to his right. By now, the once imposing rock wall on his left had declined to a series of individual stones, scattered about the camber of a bank so modest that, even from ground level, it had been barely sufficient to deny the view that he now enjoyed of the coarse flatlands by which the rim of the desert was fringed.

He settled to study his target.

The valley spread before him. From half left, the northern tributary flowed towards him over the rugged plain and then turned across his front to continue its progress to the East River. On the far side of the valley, greater heights rose up. MacKenzie's Farm stood on the bend, some hundred yards ahead and directly to his front. There was no other dwelling within three miles.

As he viewed it, the house stood between a barn and three outbuildings, to the right; and to the left, a small yard with lean-to shed, encompassed by a low stone wall. From immediately to his left, the dried water course reached out across the valley floor, only to dissipate itself in a area of broken ground adjacent to the courtyard.

It was his obvious line of approach.

Through his binoculars, he glimpsed movement in the downstairs room; the main room, away from the river.

To take advantage of the sun, John, when we had sun.

A skein of smoke was brushed from the chimney by the ever-present river breeze.

Sixteen was an awkward number. Hard to engage and guarantee the hostages.

But then.

He inserted himself into the susurrant cage of the trench environment and wove among the stalks as though he were a fish gliding between pillars of weed. The fact that he had detected no evidence of surveillance did not disincline him of the conviction that he should behave at all times as though the enemy were the best.

Partway there, he paused to scan the house from closer range; but learned nothing.

The next time he rose from his wicker river, he had come level with the house and, as his eyes broached the scruff at the rim of the cut, he saw first the low stone wall before him and then, above, the tilt of the shed roof and the single window in the gable end.

The bathroom. His intended point of entry.

He knew the house better than they did.

After a comprehensive sweep in every direction, he flowed from the trench, left along the wall and then swiftly to the conjunction of gable end and shed, which structures were not coincident in length. Here he paused, tuning in. The water rippled opulently by, not twelve feet from where he crouched. Carefully, he scanned the river elevation of the house and the revealed section of valley.

Nothing.

He turned back to stalk the leaded pane in the side of the shed, feinting under sightlines from the bathroom window. The glass was broken, the interior reduced again to shambles. He had reluctantly brought Madge here, when the first days of looting and destruction had subsided; but nothing of utility had remained – other than, from pride, to restore some order, which they had done.

No longer.

He passed across the doors to crouch beside the rain barrel, which remarkably had not been overturned. Craning, he surveyed the southern elevation.

No one.

He returned the way he had come and, on soundless feet, moved under the windows on the river side to clear the barn and outbuildings at the further end. All were deserted. Satisfied that no nasty surprises could strike at him from the outside, he moved back, glancing into downstairs rooms as he did so. Wanton mess. But no useful intelligence.

Returned to the shed, he moved up onto the roof, experiencing a *frisson* of exposure from the increased elevation and visibility. Knowing it to be unreasonable, nonetheless he checked. Then, flat against the gable end, he peered into the bathroom.

34

It was empty. Nor was anyone visible in the passage beyond. He drew his knife, inserted it between the cross pieces and slipped the catch. As silently as he was able, he then raised the window, stepped inside and at once closed it behind him, not to betray entry by an infusion of fresh breeze from the river – although, to judge from sounds below, no one would be alert enough to apprehend it. The room stank of faeces and urine, Scavengers having used the system, knowing they could not flush it. He moved to the doorway and again paused, tuning in.

He stood at the threshold of a narrow corridor, which ran the length of the house. To the left, two windows, at intervals, which looked out onto the river. To the right, four doors, which led to bedrooms. Anyone in these must be killed with the knife, so as not to reveal his presence, nor to leave enemy at his back. In fact, all were empty; and by the time Savage had reached the small landing at the end of the corridor, he was convinced that he was dealing with a force of fewer than sixteen; perhaps no more than half that number.

Further pursuit was inevitable. From a pouch, he withdrew prepared lengths of paracord, draping them around his neck and down the front of his smock. He would need prisoners to interrogate.

From the right, the landing gave to an open stairway, which descended diagonally across the end wall of the room below and turned at the bottom about a stout, vertical beam which formed the newel post. Its open side was guarded by a handrail, supported by occasional uprights.

Savage lay prone and lowered his head down the stairs until he was able just to see under the sill of the ceiling below and into the full length room beneath.

First, he counted his enemy. Two, at this end. Four, in the middle. One at the far end. Then, weapons. Five. All but one gratifyingly distant from their owners. The nearest two were eating and swigging from a bottle which could only contain water. The four in the middle were wholly occupied with a young girl, whom they had spreadeagled on a table top. The one at the end was cleaning his rifle and regarded his companions with undisguised contempt.

He would have to die first.

No sign of Madge.

Savage drew back, took a breath and stepped down onto the stairway.

He fired methodically; it was over in moments.

He then projected himself drastically into the room, determined by force of personality to dominate the two whose lives so far he had spared.

'*Stand still! Stand still!*'

In the case of the younger, it was unnecessary. He was already broken, hands raised, on his knees.

'Oh God, Oh God . . .'

But the older, stockier man, implied potential yet.

'You! *Get down!*'

At that moment, the girl, relieved of her tormentors, precipitated herself between them with a cry and scrabbled into the fireplace.

The man went for a weapon, but he was irresolute and Savage subdued him with rifle butt and boot.

He turned to the younger man.

'Up!'

The girl was quicker. She was at the young man, clawed nails in his face.

'Wait!'

And he, as though jolted by electricity, came upright and fell back against the wall. Savage shouted:

'Not yet!'

She did not hear him; and it was impossible, in her naked, slick and crazed condition to take hold of her with only one hand.

'Wait!'

Fortunately, the young man was preoccupied with defending himself, but Savage was acutely conscious of the vulnerability that confusion can bring; of the unknown capacity of the older man to recover; of the untested status of the fallen.

He seized the girl by the hair and bumped her hard against the wall.

'Not yet!'

As she flailed wildly, he transferred his grip to her throat and pinioned her to the stone.

'*Soon*! Not yet! Soon!'

At last, a glimmer of comprehension. The young man said, 'Please, Mister . . .'

'Shut up.'

Scanning rapidly, left, right, behind.

The girl focused on Savage. She followed the line of his arm to the rifle he held and to the young man, cowering in its thrall. Savage said,

'Not yet. In a minute.'

She nodded. He released his grip, seized the young man and marched him back to the staircase, where he lashed him to the uprights, hands and feet bound and a cord tight about his neck. The young man said,

'Please, don't kill me . . .'

Savage hit him. He had no wish to nurture false hope.

'You speak when I tell you.'

He hauled the older man, now coughing to consciousness, to the newel post, where he tied him, in a seated position, to the base of the beam. Sometimes, it was an advantage to have two to interrogate, although in this case Savage already had doubts.

The girl ran lightly across the floor to sit back on her heels before the young man, hands folded primly in her lap, her eyes fixed on him as though they would not shift until he were dead.

Savage moved among the fallen, killing the one who lived. He lingered a moment over the man at the end, whose rifle indeed was in excellent condition. He took it up and placed it on the table where the girl had lain. He said,

'A minute.'

He went outside and swept the landscape in every direction.

When he returned, the girl had not moved.

There were, between her putative breasts, tracks as of snails. She had a raw, underwater look, her cropped-straw hair plastered to her scalp. He said,

'You alright?'

She appeared not to hear him. He remembered her clothes. He cut the roll from his belt and, having sliced the cord that bound it,

37

dropped it beside her; but it merely uncoiled slightly, without the smallest sign of awareness from her. The young man said,

'I didn't mean anything. I'm sorry. I –'

'Shut up.'

The older man laughed wearily:

'You did her as fine as I did.'

'Don't *say* that!'

As though words might save him: the older knew better.

'We're dead.'

'No!'

'Look at him. Look at *her*. We're dead.'

'No – *Please*!'

Savage hit the young man again. He did not believe in imposing terror any more than he believed in torture (of which he had direct experience). He simply wished the matter ended. To the older man, he said,

'You, too.'

But the man laughed.

'Or what? You'll kill me? Go ahead. Have done. What matter now?'

It was not, Savage recognised, defiance, but a weariness beyond death. The man had had enough. To the younger, Savage said,

'How long have you been with these people?'

'Only a few days.'

As though time would make a difference.

'How long have they been together?'

'I don't know.'

Not long, or Savage would have known of them.

'Who was the leader?'

'Mordred.'

He was very positive.

'Which one's he?'

'At the end.'

He craned his neck to be helpful. The one who had chosen weapons maintenance above rape. Savage wondered whether he had been a leader, come too late. He said,

'Did he attack the women?'

38

The young man shook his head. But he had done nothing, Savage thought, to prevent it.

'Whose idea was it to attack the house?'

'All of them. Maggs, Mordred, all the older men.'

'To get women.'

'And to get you.'

'Me?'

'They hated you. All of them. They wanted to kill you.'

Savage considered this.

'Where do the weapons come from?'

Five, three automatic. A number of bandoliers. This could have been a formidable force.

'Soldiers and . . .'

Other Scavengers. They turned on one another as the noose tightened.

'Where's the other woman?'

'. . . They took her on.'

'Which way?'

'To the bridge.'

'Which bridge?'

'. . . Where the little village is.'

'The first bridge.'

'Yes.'

Old Ford. Just over twelve miles.

'Is that where they're crossing the river?'

'Yes, sir.'

'When did they leave?'

'. . . I'm not sure . . .'

'Did they stop here, or go straight on?'

'Straight on.'

'How many are they?'

'. . . Seven or eight, I think.'

'Are they on foot?'

'Yes. Well, the old lady isn't.'

Old? Madge was sixties, looked fifty; a handsome woman. He would not think.

'How is she travelling?'

'They're carrying her.'

39

'How?'

'On a ladder.'

A *ladder*!

No point in rage at the youth. Savage looked to the older man, but he had nothing to offer other than ennui.

'How are they armed? Same as these?'

'Yes.'

It was over. The young man knew it at once.

'Please. Don't kill me, please.'

Savage drew his Browning and jacked the action. For the first time, the girl stirred. The young man said,

'I didn't want to, they made me do it!'

'You could have said no.'

'They'd have killed me!'

'But you could have said no.'

Unexpectedly, the older man said,

'Aye.'

The young man said,

'Please!' He looked directly at the girl. '*Please.*'

Savage wondered how many times the girl had pleaded. Or Madge. Or the boy in the gulley. The girl said,

'Now?'

He reversed the automatic and handed it to her, butt first.

'Now.'

The youth said,

'They did it to me, too!'

It was probably true. Savage aligned his weapon to deliver a swift coup de grace, if necessary. In fact, the girl carefully fired four shots into the young man and six into the elder. She then discharged the remaining two rounds into the nearest bodies and continued to squeeze the trigger as though, by the sheer intensity of her yearning, she might impel further destructiveness from it; until he touched her bare shoulder and said,

'Enough.'

She stared at him as though trying to place him – and herself – in a context. He said,

'Give me the gun.'

He put out a hand. She hesitated and then, looking beyond him, saw (he realised) the rifle he had left on the table. At once, she pressed the Browning into his palm and hurried past him. But he outpaced her to the table top, clamping a hand on the weapon as she sought to lift it.

'Wait a minute.'

She fixed him with stubborn eyes, declining to relinquish her grip on the weapon. He said,

'You know who I am?' He meant to be certain that she had grasped the fundamentals of friend and foe in their situation. She appeared unsure how to respond. He said, 'You know I'm not one of them?'

At that, she nodded vigorously.

'Alright.'

He lifted the weapon, so that they held it between them.

'Know how to use one of these?'

She nodded. He supposed her to mean a shotgun.

'How come?'

'My brother showed me.'

She spoke as with a rusted voice.

'You know he's dead?'

Again, she nodded. He set down his own rifle on the table top and demonstrated the action of the selector lever on the other.

'*That* is the safe position. You will leave it there at all times, unless I tell you otherwise. Understood?'

'Yes, sir.'

'And you will *never* waste ammunition again, like you did just now.'

'No, sir.'

She was both steely and meek. He became conscious again of the muck by which she was disfigured.

'Let's get you cleaned up.'

He gathered the roll of her clothing and handed it to her.

'Outside.'

'You can use this.' He riffled the water in the rain barrel. 'It's good clean water. Unless you prefer the river?'

She stood on the low stoop, rifle in one hand and clothing roll in the other, seeming rapt in contemplation.

'Here.' He took from one of his pouches a bar of soap in a plastic bag, and a small hand towel, which he had taken to carrying, in addition to the items in his pack, for the immediate benefit of survivors. 'Use these.'

He was obliged virtually to place the soap into her hand, which she then clutched involuntarily, as though she were an automaton. Of the towel, she appeared wholly unconscious; he draped it over the verandah rail.

'Wash yourself.'

Perhaps, if he moved away, the observance of modesty would enable her to begin. But when he looked back, she had not moved.

He was at a loss how to help her.

He had dealt with many rapes; but the victims had been older, or other women had been present (or the children dead). This child woman bewildered him. He had no idea how to free her of the maleficence by which she was confined.

Frustration turned towards anger. He looked at his watch. To have any prospect of overtaking Madge before nightfall, they should leave now. Yet he knew in his heart that, with barely three hours of daylight remaining . . .

When next he looked at the girl, at least she had set down rifle and clothing, but appeared to have fallen into abstraction again. Seeing the handle of the scoop protruding from under the verandah, he crossed to take it up and, with no purpose in mind, dipped the bowl into the rain barrel.

'You use it like this, see?'

On impulse, he tipped the contents over her head. She gasped when the water enveloped her, but did not otherwise appear released. He pressed the scoop to her.

'Take it.' And when she had, 'Use it.'

The next time he looked in her direction, she had put the soap to her chest, but was not moving.

And then, in the moment it took to look away, exasperated, and to glance back, she had fallen into a frenzy of self-ablution.

Scrubbing with her palms. Dousing. Scrubbing again. She washed out her mouth, her eyes, her hair.

It was painful to watch.

He thought that she would never stop.

42

And then, as abruptly as tumult, came stillness. Absorption. It was a moment before he realised that she was probing herself, for what private damage may have been done her. He did not think it right for him to see.

When next he ventured a glance, she had taken up her underpants and, suddenly conscious of his regard, she turned her back to step into them.

He felt a surge of hope that she should again see herself in terms of dignity; and then anger, that she could thus affect him. As soon as she was dressed, he said,

'Come on. We've got to get after the other woman.'

Inside, the girl stopped abruptly, looking at the dead Scavengers.

'What?'

'I want to burn Simon's clothes.'

'When we come back.'

She nodded.

'Alright.'

He knew that he would be held to account. He said,

'Have you eaten recently?'

'I'm not hungry.'

He did not think, having seen her body, that she had eaten properly for a long time. But, in that it suited his purposes, he acquiesced.

'Later. Let's have a look at you.'

Stout enough walking shoes. Socks. Jeans. Check shirt. Sleeveless sweater. No jacket; but nothing on the dead would be acceptable.

'Here.'

He divested himself of bandoliers, belt kit and combat jacket. Underneath, he wore a garment tailored to his own specifications: an adapted cargo vest with many pockets, in which he carried spares of as much personal equipment as viable, other than armaments. It was reasonably warm and had grip cuffs to the sleeves. He took it off and held it out for her.

'Put this on.'

Although it was utilitarian and hung on her like an overlarge pelt, she touched it as though he had dressed her in cloth of gold.

'Oh, thank you,' she said.

'Don't touch the stuff in the pockets.'

'No, sir.'

He looped a short bungee cord about her waist and hooked it at the front. Finally, he took off his cap comforter and pulled it down about her ears.

'Now you look something like a soldier.'

'Thank you, sir.'

But she was not a soldier. She was a child. He experienced a sharp unease.

Mordred's rifle and magazine being in excellent shape, he refilled the magazine from his own stock. He then recharged his own rifle and Browning automatic. He ruined the other weapons in the house and temporarily hid the bandoliers, of which there were four. When he had fully reaccoutred himself, he said,

'We're going to set a stiff pace. I want to overtake the other woman before nightfall.'

'Yes, sir.'

Privately, he no longer believed it to be possible.

'Cover our rear. Twenty yards back. If you see anything, or can't keep up, tell me at once.'

'Yes, sir.'

'Let's go.'

They walked through a world of perpetual twilight. It would remain like this, Savage knew, for the next hours, until extinguished by sudden night. It was as though the river to their left, the hills, the overcast, the air they breathed, were made of pewter.

The girl exhibited no difficulty in keeping pace. She was a rangy creature, whose stride devoured the track as though he were going too slowly for her. She scanned the landscape with fierce vigilance but without fear. She must, of course, have performed the same function, of back marker, for her brother. And they, Savage realised, must have been on the outside as long as he had himself.

When they came to the first of two small villages which lay between themselves and the bridge at Old Ford, Savage drew the girl to a small rise beside the lane.

'Wait here. Cover our back track. I'll clear the houses.'

But she said,

'Can't I come with you?'

'Why?'

'To help, you know.'

'Help by covering our rear.'

'It's just . . . I . . .'

She was unpersuaded; he, baffled.

'You think I'm going to leave you?'

'No, of course . . . I . . .'

He saw that this was precisely what she did fear.

'Do what you're told!'

He fled among the trees to which the river gave rise. The village was deserted. When he returned to the lane, to signal the child to him, she arrived with a velocity which argued relief rather than obedience. He said,

'Look. We've got to trust one another.'

'Oh yes. Oh yes.'

As though a contract had been drawn between them. He sighed.

'Come on.'

The second village, too, was empty, as he had feared. They were now no more than two miles from Old Ford, with darkness at best forty minutes away. He led her to the water's edge.

'Time to darken up.'

'Darken up?'

'Camouflage.'

'Oh.'

Although he carried camo cream, he rarely used that alone, preferring to become the place where he was. And when he offered it to her, she opted for the same process as himself, gouging up mud and daubing it about her face in addition, in imitation of him. He said,

'What's your name?'

She hesitated.

'. . . Cassie.'

'Where are you from, Cassie?'

A much longer silence.

'. . . A place.'

'Alright.'

He understood reticence. It was deeply in his own nature.

When he leaned down to rinse his hands, the river was choked with human soup and lamentation wailed up about him and he snatched back his hands to wipe the paste on his smock. The child, watching him, smiled uncertainly. She looked, in her dirt, like an urchin.

Responsibility oppressed him.

They lay side by side on a modest rise, looking down onto Old Ford. It was not yet full night. They could make out the ribbon of the river and the hulks of buildings, rapidly declining into insubstantiality.

Old Ford was little better than a hamlet, with a dozen or so dwellings on their side of the river and four on the other. One structure was slightly larger than the rest; the old Tollmaster's House (latterly an inn). Immediately beyond it, the arched stone bridge straddled the river. At the downstairs windows, glimmers of light were visible and the air was sour with a reek of burning; but, through his binoculars, Savage could see that the shutters were in place. He turned to the girl.

'I'm going to have a look around. You –'

'Watch our rear?'

She sounded pleased with herself. He said,

'Do it.'

He ghosted down among the trees. Immediately after dusk, there was a period of faint luminescence in the overcast (there being no moon or stars) which barely touched the ground and was followed by a darkness so absolute that it exceeded all experience of the past. But although Savage carried night vision equipment, he rarely used it, preferring, as now, the shadowscape to which, by nature, he was so perfectly attuned.

He feinted past the inn to check the other buildings, which he knew to be empty. When he returned, he stalked the most promising window.

There were iron bars set in the stonework, with strapped wooden shutters beyond (both of which had survived, Savage suspected, because they had proved too obdurate or too defensively comforting

46

to the relatively few vandals who had fled via this route). But the glass panes had been broken and there were cracks in the shutters. By tracking his head from side to side, he was able partially to scan the interior by means of the travelling vertical slit thus presented. It availed him little. The fire was dying. He could not locate Madge nor any but two of his enemies. And eavesdropping on their desultory conversation yielded only that they were elated by their capture and keenly aware of the need to escape rapidly in the morning.

He moved around the building. All shutters were secured, high and low. He well knew, besides, that although he could break in, to fight an unlocated enemy, in a confined and unfamiliar space, in virtual darkness and with one prisoner, above all, whom he wished to survive, was simply not viable.

He returned to the girl.

'We're going to cross the river. Sleep on the other side. Take care of business in the morning.'

They patrolled through the trees, past rotting wharves which must, in time, have served their turn, under the inn and across the bridge, from beneath which ripples liquesced against the piles. Nowhere was the smallest indication that they had been observed.

On the far side, a deteriorated track crossed the valley floor until it encountered the heights, where it turned east along them and ultimately north up a shallow draw (by means of which the Scavengers hoped to escape pursuit). From the heights, a series of low fingers of ridge reached towards the river, some extending directly from the hillside, others erupting spontaneously over a short distance and subsiding again. The track passed between two such; and it was to the lefthand of these that Savage now led the girl, up onto the crest and along the spine until they came to a natural hollow in the rock, where they might harbour for the night and where (Savage judged) they would find themselves in an excellent firing point for morning.

They were a bare thirty feet above the track and some hundred yards from the river. He said,

'Wait here. I'm going to make a sweep.'

This was not terrain entirely unfamiliar to Savage. When he had been demarcating his ground – which was bounded by the northern tributary, the Desert, the Main Route and the Southern Forest – he had patrolled beyond the limits. Now, as he swept out in a wide arc, he allowed his body to remember or to learn, his senses patiently to absorb, a milieu he could not see, until he knew the ground and could fight over it. Satisfied that it held no secrets, he returned to the girl.

'We lie up here for the night. Undo your belt, get comfortable. We eat, then we sleep.'

In that the luminescence had all but faded, he was barely able to discern her presence. He took from his kit a small item, which he hung by paracord about his neck. It was a beta light. There was a spare in the cargo vest that she wore and, releasing it now, he hung the second about her neck. Only then did he open the flip cap on the small rubberised holder to reveal the glowing light within.

She was entranced.

'What *is* it?'

'A beta light.'

'How does it work?'

'Glowing crystal.'

Tritium, he thought.

'It's *beautiful*.' She danced the faint emanation before her eyes. 'Does it last for ever?'

'Not quite for ever.'

But then, he thought, neither do we.

'It's like a firefly. Or a glow worm.'

Savage did not disagree. The tiny lamps yielded light without maintenance for some fifteen years – sufficient to permit close-quarter work without compromising security. He was not a man to abandon any piece of kit in which he had faith. He uncapped his own and said,

'Find one another in the night.'

'Yes. Thank you.'

But this was not the true reason he had issued them. He believed that she would need a light in the darkness when the horrors came.

48

He opened an emergency ration pack and handed her two squared blocks.

'Here. Eat these first.'

'What are they?'

'Biscuits.'

She examined them by nose and beta light.

'I'm not hungry.'

'You'll eat. You go down quicker than you think.'

He broke a strip of segments from a bar and said,

'Then this.'

Again, she scrutinised the offering; and then, with disbelief:

'*Chocolate*?'

'After the biscuits.'

In a moment, she said,

'Simon would have liked chocolate.'

'Eat it for him. But eat the biscuits first.'

He set aside two boiled sweets and, having satisfied himself that he had shed no packaging, restored the remainder of the rations to his pouch. The girl bit into a biscuit.

'It's *disgusting*!'

'Eat it.'

'It tastes like soap.'

'Nobody said it was caviar.'

Savage was not without sympathy. The biscuits often tasted, at first, over-chemical; but they were designed for survival and became, in his experience, addictive. He said,

'We'll have a proper meal when we get back.'

'Back?'

'To the house.'

'Oh.'

She knew which house. He said,

'There are other women there. Including the one with the long hair.' Sarah. 'One of them's a terrific cook. They'll be pleased to see you.'

After a moment, she said,

'But I'm with you now?'

'. . . They'll know how to take care of you.'

Someone of your age and sex. She said,

'But I'm with you now?'

He was not sure what he was being asked.

'Sure.'

Why not? It was a small lie and soon to be in the past.

'Good.'

When they had eaten, they drank, she taking controlled sips.

'Who taught you to drink like that?'

'Simon. Never too fast. Never more than you need. Never waste. That's what he said.'

'Good for him.'

Savage mourned again the boy in the creek. She said,

'He tried to stop them.'

'I know.'

He gave her the boiled sweets. She recognised at once their twisty, confectionary nature.

'*Barley sugar?*'

As though now he had taken his legerdemain to ludicrous lengths.

'One now, one if you wake in the night.'

Which she would.

'I haven't tasted barley sugar for ages.'

'Give me the wrapper. Never leave behind you sign of your passing.'

'No, sir.'

He rose.

'We'll have the ladies just along here, the gents the other way. Bring your rifle. Never be without it.'

He led her only a short distance south along the ridge, to where a re-entrant offered more than sufficient cover. He chopped out a scrape with his knife, heaping the spoil beside it.

'When you've finished, put some of the earth in. Should be enough for morning.'

'Yes, sir.'

'I'll wait at the harbour.'

When she returned, he rose, moved north along the ridge, cut out a scrape for himself and used it. He remembered finally that he had not told her his name. Seated before her again, he said,

'My name's John Savage.'

'Oh. How do you do, sir?'

It was a moment before he realised that she had put out a hand. He took it. It was bony and chill.

And there passed from it into him a recollection of horror so absolute and suffocating that it was all he could do not to fling her from him.

Sweat pricked out on his skin.

But in that moment she released him, and he was able surreptitiously (and ungovernably) to wipe his hand on the front of his smock.

'Best get to sleep. You can leave your light open. It's quite safe. I'll do the same.'

'Yes, sir.'

Her ember descended to ground.

'Thank you for saving me.'

But he had not saved her yet.

Savage had come to an accommodation with his demons and with sleep. So long as he slept no more than thirty minutes in any hour, they would not come.

Unless they came.

Or to touch him in the day.

He was content. Such ordered sleeping sorted well with the disciplines of an eternal vigilance, which had become for him the expression of his soul.

Sometimes, in one of his hides, in the ground as though he were already dead, he slept longer; but these periods did not bring the peace that he found at the rim of perpetual watchfulness.

And so he cleaned her weapon and his own; and watched over her; and waited.

The moment she began to scream, he was beside her.

'Cassie! It's alright! Wake up!'

Catching at flailing limbs.

'Cassie! You're safe! It's me!'

The wash from his dangling light faintly flushed her rictus, her whited eyes.

'It's your friend, John Savage! Wake up!'

She came suddenly bolt up, her breathing fricative in his face.

'You're safe! It's alright. You're safe.'

But she lay back no less rigidly than she had risen, one hand clawed on his, the other clutching her beta light as though it were salvation. He said,

'Cassie, it happens . . .'

She jerked her head violently from side to side, issuing grunts of resistance.

And indeed, what could he say? That the horrors pass? His had not.

He offered the only gift that he possessed.

'I'll sit here with you. We'll stand them off together.'

And so he sat, with her hand in his one hand and in the other his rifle, for all the world as though he could vanquish her demons with a gun, when he could not vanquish his own.

And wondered what harm he might have done her.

Stand-to.

Savage carefully extricated his arm from where the girl lay on it and waited out the dawn – such as it was. For the overcast was so low, the billows off the river so dense, the valley floor so beset by vaporous rolls, that he could see little other than a soiled, grey gloaming. There would be small improvement, he knew, for the better part of an hour.

The girl still deeply asleep, he melted into the ghostscape, down to the river and about in a wide sweep: but there was nothing to find and, at the Tollmaster's House, no indication of activity, the building itself only peripatetically visible, even from directly across the water.

There being no reason in the pervasive miasma not to make a brew, he lit his small hexamine cooker and made tea. Then he woke the girl.

'Cassie. Time to make ready.'

For a moment, she was puzzled. Then, memory returned, her eyes tipped inward, she rolled onto her stomach as though, from that posture, the more effectively to withstand its assault. He said,

'Here. Drink this.'

Her eyes glazed on the metal cup, the cap comforter slid from her butter hair, and she said,

'In a minute.'

She scrambled to her feet and, unbelievably, turning back for her rifle, hurried to her scrape; he supposed, to vomit.

When she returned, he proffered the tea again, but she was not yet exorcised of the past. She knelt before him.

'Simon's dead, isn't he?'

'Yes.'

It was confirmation, not question. She looked away. In a little, she said,

'One of them. Did to him, you know. What they did to me. After he was dead. They thought it was funny.' She looked at him. 'How could anyone do that?'

'I don't know, Cassie.'

There were questions, he knew, that could not be answered.

She did well with breakfast, getting biscuits, chocolate, tea down her throat. Being strong. In that she was a child, she shamed and troubled him.

'Better use the latrine now.' He handed her folded tissues that he carried. 'Make sure you bury them.'

He would not know what damage she had suffered until he could get her back to the house. She nodded, took her rifle with her.

In a sense, she epitomised the very destiny that he was determined to defy.

A destiny, ironically, first put on him by Madge.

He would not think of her.

When she had said,

Only show us the way.

And

What if we don't want to go in?

And

What will you do, John? Climb back into your box, like a good little soldier boy? I don't think so.

He would not think of her!

They did not know what they sought, these people.

Well, perhaps they had learned now.

He would be alone.

When he returned from the latrine, he said, not without misgiving,

'Let's see what you can do with a gun.'

By now, the nearer cottages had begun to peep through the drifting shrouds, as though they were creeping forward and back again, and the ridge opposite to their position, across the track, was visible above the thinning gauze between.

He had the child hook up her belt, pull on the cap comforter again and lie prone with her weapon facing the track.

'Your firing point will be here.'

He indicated the cleft before her in the natural parapet of their hollow.

'I'll be here.'

He patted the place some six feet distant where already he had set down a spare magazine on the shelf.

'I want you to go through the motions of firing a single shot down onto the track.'

He removed her magazine. She could fire dry. He would issue her own weapon later.

'Where should the lever be?'

Without looking, she set it from safe to single shot. He jacked the charging handle.

'Go ahead.'

What she did was correct, but lacking in intuition. She handled the rifle as though it were a club, rather than an instrument.

'Again.'

And again.

'Alright.'

He would not badger her. She had a clear grasp of the fundamentals. Besides, he did not mean, in any sense, to put her at hazard. But the mere fact of a second rifle's firing, noisily, if not effectively, should do much to unhinge an already demoralised foe. He withdrew a second magazine from his kit.

'I'll show you how to change magazines.'

She said,

'I know how.'

'. . . Oh? Show me.'

Again, her hands were bossy, unsympathetic, but undeniably informed.

'You had a rifle like this?'

She looked away.

'We found it.'

Found? Stole? Killed for? Good for them. The boy had done all he could to ensure the girl's survival. Savage would not do less.

'Get a chance to fire it?'

'Ten times. We couldn't waste ammunition. I'm a good shot.'

If true, even a single kill would be a bonus.

'Okay. Relax. Look.'

He pointed past her. The Tollmaster's House had begun to emerge through the fading wraiths that twisted off the river. Three figures stood in the lane, facing towards MacKenzie's Farm. He said,

'Looking for their friends.'

'Will they wait?'

'No. They'll come soon.'

'Good,' she said. 'I'm going to kill them all.'

Savage wondered whether he should intervene; prevent it, even. Her youth troubled him profoundly. But then he thought, Who better entitled? A battle is fought to be won. This was no moment for doubt. He said,

'They'll come in single file, over the bridge and along the track. If they're not in single file, I'll issue different orders, at the time.'

'Yes, sir.'

'When they get to here, directly below us, we open fire. You kill from the back, I kill from the front. Take your time. Make every shot count. One shot, one kill.'

She nodded.

'Don't forget the other woman. She'll probably be on a litter. Don't fire near her. Leave that to me. And when I go down there, you cease fire. Cover our flanks. Only fire at anyone aiming directly at me.'

Which he believed would no longer be possible.

'I understand.'

'Now we wait.'

'Here they come.'

As he had hoped, the unevenness of the terrain on either side of the track discouraged them from spreading out and they maintained the single file they had adopted on the bridge.

He counted them. Eight. Four weapons. Two bandoliers. This was the least favoured segment of the force. Beside him, the girl stirred.

'Not yet. Don't bring up your weapon until you're ready to use it.'

'Right.'

They came jauntily on, stepping to the killing ground. The two who bore the ladder, fore and aft, had inserted their heads between the end rungs, so that the weight rested on their shoulders; they would be gratifyingly haltered when the fire came down. There were three before the litter, three behind, two weapons in each group.

Madge lay along the ladder, face dipped to him, as though she were meat on a pole.

'When you're ready, open fire. Don't wait for me. I won't wait for you.'

'Yes, sir.'

'Good luck.'

She nodded, fixed on the killing ground as though already it were peopled by the dead.

Savage settled to his own firing point, cradled his rifle to him, became one with it. He would give no more thought to the girl. If she made a contribution, well and good. He would kill the front and back markers. Then anyone else who was armed. Then anyone.

The expanse between the two ridges was the perfect killing ground, devoid of cover (and now of fog); the further ridge too distant for even the fleetest of foot, given the time that would be available; nowhere to hide.

As the ragged column processed across their front, Savage tracked onto the lead marker, drew breath, allowed his finger to find the trigger.

In that moment, he sensed the girl tense beside him and it was she, by a fraction, who fired first.

Then him.

The lead man reeled out of line. As Savage corrected to his

second target, he saw at the edge of vision how the back marker plunged off under the impact of the girl's first shot.

He fired again. Number two foundered, spilling his rifle. Savage traversed right, for targets to the rear of the column. The girl fired and missed. Savage took down the one next after the litter – and at once switched to the next again, who had crouched, rifle to shoulder, and was scanning the ridge for a target.

Savage and the child fired together.

The man flung up and –

All weapons down.

Savage traversed back along the decimated column. The one still unscathed from the head was running for the far ridge. The rear bearer of the litter, having tipped off his load, fled for the river. The front bearer was bowed half back, yoked by the unexpected weight and struggling for release.

Time enough for him.

The girl was aiming at the river runner.

Savage took the further refugee; aimed; fired.

The man lunged forward. The girl fired.

The river rat lurched sideways under the impact but humped on, arms spread, as though he were a crow struck hard by shot in a high wind.

Savage rose.

'Stay here! Finish him!'

He ran off the ridge, determined to close the enemy as rapidly as he was able, to extinguish even the faintest possibility of mischief – although, in truth, there was before him only devastation, the little motions of dying, the charade of flight.

The lead bearer, at last unencumbered, fell backwards over a corpse.

The further runner, up again, tumbled once more, going nowhere.

The Crow flapped on, tatterdemalion.

Finish him, Savage thought.

Someone was firing at him!

The lead bearer, prone behind a corpse, in a panic, firing wildly.

The rounds spiking up over his head.

Savage crouched; fired once.

The silhouette slumped.

Even as he rose, the girl fired from almost beside him – not ten feet away.

'Go back!'

The Crow was down.

But as he ran on, Savage knew that it was not in him to dismiss anyone so utterly committed to the battle.

And then he was into the column, working brutally along it, flinging weapons aside, ripping rags in pursuit of hidden arms, of which there were none. Near the end was one still alive, who, when Savage rolled him onto his back, murmured:

'Please. Help me.'

Savage searched him and turned away. The Crow, unbelievably, staggered on. The further runner made the lax articulations of a swimmer doomed by too great a sea.

When the girl approached, he said,

'Finish them.'

Why not? Who better entitled?

He devoted himself to his (too rarely acknowledged) friend.

Madge lay as she had fallen, face down, still lashed to the ladder. He released her and carried her a short distance off, to be apart from those who had defiled her.

She looked wasted; aged. It was hard to see the robust woman in this crone. Her eyes were pinched shut and her mouth gaped. He took one of her flaccid hands and advanced his lips to her ear.

'Madge. It's me, Savage. You're safe.'

The *crack* of a shot behind him drew his attention. The girl had dispatched the Crow and was advancing implacably on the Swimmer. He bent to Madge again.

'It's John. Madge, it's John.'

Her eyelids flickered.

'You're safe.'

She exhaled words of which he heard nothing. He put an ear now to her lips.

'Say again.'

She said,

'Finish me.'

This he could not accept.

'Madge, listen to me. It's over, you're –'

'*Finish me! John!*'

'Madge . . .'

'*Please! Finish me! John! Finish me!*'

She clawed into him, her eyes fixed madly where he was not.

'*Please! Finish me!*'

'Alright.'

'*Now! Please!*'

'Yes.'

'Finish me!'

'I will.'

'*Now!*'

'Yes, now.'

She lay back. The pit of killing slid open before him and he stepped inexorably in.

He drew his Browning, released the safety catch and jacked the action with drained hands.

Her lips were moving again but, when he bent, it was not to him that she spoke:

'. . . heartily sorry for ever having offended Thee.'

He wondered for what sins she could possibly require forgiveness.

He put the weapon in and pulled the trigger twice.

Double taps.

Her head flung off, grossly evacuated.

And then he was possessed by a grief so powerful that he rose and stumbled under its weight and heard the cry driven from him.

He knew that the dead watched.

And then he saw that the girl had paused in her progress to look at him. And he raised up his armed fist at this outrage. And she started and turned away. And he realised that she was closer to him than she was to the Swimmer and must already have disposed of that item.

He put away his Browning. No one left to kill.

He wondered whether the dead mocked or merely waited in patience for his inevitable coming.

Then he took up his friend and carried her to the mountain top.

Partway along the ridge, where it erupted again out of the plain to ascend to the heights, he found a hollow in the rock and here he laid her down.

Closer to the sun.

I'm sorry, Madge, I failed you. But I did not forget.

When he returned to the killing ground, the child came to him.

'We killed them all.'

She appeared complacent.

'It's nothing to be proud of.'

Her face closed as though he had slapped her. He moved to the captured weapons and began to break them on rocks. In a moment, she said,

'She was your friend.'

As though to exonerate his rudeness. He said nothing. She came beside him.

'Would you like me to help bury her?'

'No.'

She was at a loss.

'I'm sorry. For what you had to do.'

He sighed.

'There's this place. She told me. India, I think it is. They don't bury their dead. They strip them. And they put them out in this, like, bowl in the mountainside. In the rock. And the vultures come and eat them. In the end, there's nothing left except bones, picked clean.'

And very happy vultures, John.

'It's what she wanted for herself. Practical, hygienic and environmentally efficient, she called it.'

I want to lie in the sun and feel the wind blow through my bones and be thin again, not rot in the ground and be eaten by worms.

'So that's where I put her. Closer to the sun. Except that we have no sun.'

The child said,

'We haven't got vultures, either, have we?'

'We've got people.'

'Yes, people.'

That, she understood.

When he was satisfied that all items of their personal equipment had been accounted for, he said,

'Change magazines.'

And then:

'Here, you can carry these.'

He draped the two captured bandoliers criss-cross over her chest. She appeared gratified by the task. He never left ammunition. If he could not deep bury it, he took it back to the house for disposal. The rivers were more pure than ever they had been in his lifetime: and although there was much dust yet to be flushed through them, he would not needlessly invoke pollution. The child said,

'Did I . . .?'

'What?'

She looked away, shyly:

'Nothing.'

He contemplated her.

'How old are you, anyway?'

'Nearly sixteen.'

In a pig's ear. Nearly fourteen, maybe. Well, he had been places the whores were six. He said,

'You did well.' She flushed. 'Let's go. Cover our rear.'

And so they left the place of ambush.

Of ambushes.

Savage resolved that he would not again fall victim to the second.

For the truth was that Madge had been more than a friend.

(Whose friendship he had been reluctant to acknowledge.)

She had been a conduit to an humanity without which he was the more comfortable. By declining to accept him at his own purely military valuation, she had sought to reclaim him for a lost self.

Well, no more. He meant to take advantage of her death to be free again.

To be himself again.

At MacKenzie's Farm, they set briskly about their business: burning the boy's clothes (no jacket, Savage noted); depositing the bodies into the dried water course, from which, soon enough (with all other detritus) they would be taken. They did not otherwise cleanse the house, since Madge would not return and his own last call would be fleeting.

They recovered the hidden bandoliers and set out along the creek.

When they came to the place where the boy lay in his reliquary of weeds, Savage said,

'Do you want to bury him? Say goodbye?'

She shook her head and in a moment smiled wanly.

'The vultures can have him.'

But he was immune from expropriating appeals.

'Best get on then.'

But she knelt and reached out a

hand

hand

hand

As though it were an extensible mechanism

slidey and slick

And he thought

Enough.

The House

SARAH was outside the house. He could not believe it. He had given specific orders. Her image skidded as he deflected his binoculars up to the tower room. (The new woman on watch, he thought. Anne. No alarm blanks posted.) Then back to the two figures, more than a hundred yards along the ridge. Sarah. And Martin, presumably standing guard.

Savage was furious. It seemed to him not merely disobedient but stupid.

He returned to the child in the creek; and, although he believed there to be no danger, he led her out across the valley, taking every advantage of the scrub and gulley at the foot of the rock wall until, unseen, they had achieved the opposite slopes, where they worked up the humpback terrain, through the coarse spillage of underbrush from the western end of Low Wood, into the main body of the trees themselves. Here, they ascended with no less caution, mounting towards the lane and peering up through the canopy overhead for a sight of Sarah on the ridge above. The moment she came into view, Savage stilled the girl.

'If you can see, you can be seen.'

'Yes, sir.'

He studied Sarah through his binoculars; but although her face was turned to the north, it was apparent that she looked inward. Martin was nowhere visible, being further back from the modest cliff edge.

Savage drew the child on to a natural bower between tree trunks, where she could settle, just below the lane, amid the roots and spoilage of the wood.

'I shouldn't be more than fifteen or twenty minutes.' Her face clouded at the prospect of being left alone. 'You got a watch?'

She shook her head.

'Here.' He lifted off the spare G10, which, along with identity discs and morphine, he carried on paracord about his neck – another item of personal kit, like the beta light, to be reclaimed as soon as decently possible. The child assumed the watch as though it were an award.

'Thank you.'

'Anyone comes from me, they'll know your name. Anyone else, start shooting. I'll come back at once.'

'Yes, sir.'

She gripped her rifle with purpose. She looked, he thought, like a babe in the wood.

He moved rapidly through the trees to the place, just short of the rear of the barn, where they yielded finally to the farmyard – and from where, he knew, he could show himself to the watcher in the tower.

It was Anne.

A brief, soundless colloquy passed between them:

Is all well in the house?

Yes, but – She pointed along the ridge.

He nodded. And the environs?

She pointed now behind her, to indicate some further untoward element outside the house.

Probably Sammy. Savage issued visual commands. Stay where you are. Keep watch.

He moved along the lane, in the lee of the bluff, and turned up the service track. Sammy, standing stag on the skyline, saw him coming. They met at the high corner.

'Thank God you've come, Savage.'

'I saw. What's happened?'

'She spent the entire night in the tower room, waiting for you. She seemed more normal this morning, but she slipped out with the animals and she won't come back. She won't listen to me. I am, it seems, the last person she'll listen to.'

His habitual reticence was under siege by pain.

'I'll deal with it. Tell Alice I'm bringing in a girl, thirteen, fourteen. We'll need baths, a hot meal and clothes. She was raped.'

The tall man nodded.

'It's all in hand.' And then: 'Madge . . .?'

'No. Nor the boy.'

'I'm sorry, Savage.'

'Tell her.'

There was a cart track which ran like a scar diagonally up the face of the bluff, from the lane to the crest. As Savage and the child attained the summit, Martin stirred, in evident discomfort, and Sarah, as it seemed to Savage, having glanced at him, fixed the girl with a look of unmistakable animosity. When they drew closer, she said,

'We expected you sooner, John.'

As though he were a guest late to a party.

'I was held up.'

She contemplated Cassie, restraining with one hand the trails of hair which the ridge breeze cast across her face.

'And this is . . .?'

'Cassie. You . . . saw her yesterday.'

When your attempt to rescue her led to the bruises on your face. Neither woman spoke. Savage said,

'This is Doctor Sarah.'

'How do you do?'

Sarah ignored the introduction. She said,

'Madge . . .?'

'Gone.'

Martin made a sound of regret. Sarah said,

'And . . . the other?'

In a sharp tone, Cassie said,

'My brother's dead.'

Sarah said nothing. Plainly embarrassed on her behalf, Martin reached in a hand:

'I'm Martin, Cassie. It's good to see you.'

'How do you do, sir?'

'No, you call me Martin. That's best.'

Watching Sarah, Savage said,

'Cassie had a bad time. Like you.'

But if he hoped to engender empathy, or mere professional sympathy, he was misguided. She said,

'Indeed?'

And turned her face to the wind. Martin said,

'Will I take you up to the house, Cassie . . .?'

'No!' The child attached herself to Savage's arm. 'I'll stay with Mr Savage.'

Savage was beginning to be annoyed.

'You were told to stay in the house.'

Martin said,

'It were my fault, Savage . . .'

'Nonsense!' Sarah was imperious; but for once Martin was stubborn:

'It were my responsibility.'

'Nobody is responsible for me, except myself!'

Savage said,

'And you knew better.'

She looked away.

'. . . I needed air.'

The fact of her rape was unarguable. He said,

'You want to go in now?'

Sarah looked at the child.

'No.'

At once she turned her back. It was inconceivable to Savage that the insult could be deliberate, yet he could put no other interpretation on it. Martin said,

'Why don't you come and meet the others, Cassie? Alice'll be that pleased to see you . . .'

Savage expected the girl again to resist this suggestion, but she seemed to sense his predicament.

'Do you want me to?'

'. . . It might be best.'

'If you want me to.'

Sarah said,

'You have an *admirer*, John.'

The girl flushed and stalked off towards the house. Martin said,

'Don't fret, I'll look to her.'

And made good his own escape. Savage said,

'There was no need for that.'

'*Sorry*.'

68

'She's a child.'

'Do we honour such concepts now?'

'Why not?'

Yet it had been he who had taken the 'child' to war; who had maintained that such distinctions were now out of time. She said,

'You're a romantic, John.'

He had never known with her (as he had always known with Madge) when he was being chided and when mocked. And then she said,

'How many times did you tell us? Never go out unarmed. Never without backup. Observe procedures at all times. Trust no one. Trust nothing. Is there a single precept I didn't break?'

'You're a doctor.'

He meant that he understood her resistance to killing and even to training; but she said,

'I know better.'

He was at a loss how best to proceed, when she said,

'I did this to myself.'

'That's nonsense.'

'If I had listened to you . . .'

'It was them, not you! Don't blame yourself for this, Sarah! You did nothing wrong!'

He hated to hear victims blame themselves for the depredations of predators; but she said, in a cutting tone:

'Don't pretend to be more tolerant of stupidity than you are, John! I shall not, I assure you!'

'Don't do this, Sarah! Don't get clever about this!' There was, he knew, no comfort behind the rampart of intelligence. 'Stick to what you know is right.'

'*Right?*' She looked at him then, amused. 'Happy the man who knows what is right. Or wrong, for that matter.'

He said,

'Don't do this to yourself.'

She smiled.

'Poor John. How many of us have you had to deal with? Thousands? Tens of thousands?'

'What?'

'Victims.'

'Not so many.'

It just felt like it. She said,

'And every one written in your face. Madge saw that, I didn't.'

'You want to go in now?'

'You carry our sins, John.'

'Oh, for . . .!'

Suddenly he wearied of her game, which was not a game. She said,

'Well, they say only the sick doctor heals. I wonder whether your Cassie would agree?'

'I doubt it.'

She was not his Cassie. Sarah came close to him.

'You'd give anything to be free of us, wouldn't you?' She put up a hand to touch his cheek, but instinctively he drew back. 'Oh dear. Well, don't hope for too much, John. I fear I lack your generosity of spirit.'

She walked past him towards the house.

Perhaps she did not mean to patronise him, but it always felt as though she had. Nor was he impressed by the method she had chosen to fight her demons (although he knew of none better). At least it implied defiance. But it would make what he must do the harder.

All the same, he would do it.

Inside the house, he found that Cassie had progressed no further than the hall, a lofty space washed with light from a single window at the top of the stairs. Indeed, from the egregious nature of Alice's smile, it was apparent that an impasse had been reached. She said,

'We were just telling Cassie here about the baths and the bedrooms . . .'

The girl came to Savage.

'Where do you sleep?'

'. . . In the tower.'

'I'll sleep there, too.'

Alice said,

'There's just the one room up there, lovey.'

Sarah murmured:

'Hallowed ground.'

Savage said,

'It's like a lighthouse.'

'Well, is there a room at the bottom?'

Martin, coming from sealing the entrance, said:

'You don't want to sleep there, Cassie. The main rooms are much nicer.'

The accommodation immediately beneath the tower was the original servants' quarters. Savage's people occupied the principal suites on the floor below. But the child said,

'I'll sleep where I choose.'

Sarah said,

'Certainly, you shall, my dear,'

As though amused by the group's antics. Savage said,

'Come on.'

As far as he was concerned, the child had earned the right. They had fought a battle together: he would not have her beset by adults now. At the foot of the stairs, he said to Alice:

'Bath ready?'

'Aye.'

'Clothes?'

She nodded. Martin said,

'I'll look to the pump.'

Partway up the stairs, Savage remembered.

'Cassie.'

'Yes, sir?'

'Someone ought to . . . have a look at you. Make sure you're alright.'

She was wary.

'I'm fine.'

'Still . . .'

Unfortunately, the logical candidate was out of the question: indeed, when Sarah said, in a dry tone:

'I don't suppose it would be any use, my offering my services?'

Cassie said, with great vehemence:

'*No!*'

Alice said,

'Would you like me to, lovey?'

Cassie looked to Savage:

'You can.'

'What?'

'You can.'

It was not what he had had in mind. Her youth and gender daunted him.

'I'm no doctor . . .'

Sarah was impatient:

'For heaven's sake, it's not the most complicated procedure in the world. Look for any obvious tears or signs of damage. Anything internal will hurt or bleed. You can do it to yourself, with a small hand mirror and an ounce of common sense.'

She quit the hall, the personal relevance of her words heavy on them all; except for Cassie, who said,

'Mr Savage can do it, then.'

He nodded. But at the last, from motives obscure even to himself, he motioned to Anne to follow them.

The bathroom was situated along the broad, lushly-carpeted main corridor. It was a preposterously ornate room, much given to mirrors and onyx and gold, which glowed now palely by the light of two softly-exhaling butane lamps, which Alice had placed in scalloped niches. Cassie said,

'Crikey! Is this where you live?'

'You're kidding.'

He crossed to the bath, thereby drawing her attention to it.

'A *round* bath!'

She set down her rifle on the nearby vanity top and knelt to spread her palms on the marble surround. He said,

'Let's fill it.'

He actuated gold levers and there sputtered from the mouths of arched dolphins both water and steam.

'*Hot water!*'

The provision of a hot bath in their changed world was not quite the miracle it seemed to Cassie.

Whoever had owned the house had everywhere preserved in it the old along with the new. So that there was in the kitchen, besides the useless electric ovens and fridges, an old-fashioned cooking range, with rack and pinion spits, which had been meticulously maintained and blacked. And in the cellars, alongside the defunct oil-fired burner, an ancient brute of a solid fuel boiler (which hated Savage but which, for Martin, purred with combustion, whatever he put into it).

This was the old heart of the house and when it burned, as now, the place reverberated with remembered life.

Nor had it been any great matter to adapt the cat's cradle of plumbing to their purposes. They had introduced into their truncated system a hand-cranked pump, which delivered well water to the storage tank in the roof space. And they were able, by the short-run use of one of Savage's portable generators, to drive the cannibalised central heating pump, thereby circulating hot water through the heat exchanger of a previously disconnected cistern.

It gratified Savage that, while the artefacts of his own time passed so rapidly into history, the house now functioned by virtue of technology built into it more than a hundred years before. It had been the availability of this technology, allied to fresh water supply, strategic location and defensive potential, that had led Savage to choose the house in the first place.

Such secrets as he had later uncovered had been pure bonus.

Cassie riffled the water.

'I haven't had a hot bath for *ages*.'

'Well, get in. It's me next, and I don't want it cold.'

She grinned.

'Sorry.'

As she divested herself, he reclaimed his cap comforter –

'Can't I keep it?'

'No.'

– His cargo vest, beta light and watch.

The items of his personal kit were significant to him. He had chosen them. He trusted them. They were part of him. Not to be relinquished unless they failed; and certainly not to the whim of another.

Her disillusionment was profound. He said,

'Look, as soon as we finish up here, I'll give you kit of your own.'

She brightened at once.

'Really?'

'Yeah.'

'Exactly like yours?'

'Sure.'

More or less. Much cheered, she hauled sweater and shirt over her head. He said,

'You'll need it for the journey.'

Immediate suspicion.

'What journey?'

'To the Capital.'

'Is that where we're going?'

'Yeah.'

'Together?'

'That's right.'

She asked no more and he offered none. When she pulled off jeans and underpants, he said,

'Here. I'll give them to Alice for boiling.'

She hesitated.

'. . . I haven't got anything else.'

'There's plenty coming.'

In the early days, when survivors had been recovered on a regular basis, he and Sammy had harvested all dwellings (and many bodies) for useable garments and other items. The girl said,

'Alright.'

He rolled her clothes at once, as though they were of no interest. She stepped into the bath and, with a luxuriant wriggle, crouched to let the water get to her.

'Oh, that's *gorgeous*.'

'Soap's there.' Heaped in an oyster shell dish. 'Use any towel you want.' They hung, Savage thought, like minks on the rail. He took up the captured bandoliers that she had brought in, but when he made to leave, she said,

'You don't have to go. You've seen me bath before.'

But that had been in the field. Here, in a domestic setting, it seemed to him inappropriate. He said,

'A lady is entitled to her privacy.'

'. . . Alright.'

But again she stopped him:

74

'You won't go far?'

'Just in the corridor.'

And when he sought to draw the door to, she said,

'Leave it open, please.'

Fortunately, Anne had had the good sense not to intervene in the bathroom, but waited now along the corridor, where daylight flushed through the open doorway from the adjoining bedroom. Savage set down the captured bandoliers, including those he carried, for later disposal and joined Anne. At once, she said,

'She needs to be examined by a properly qualified physician.'

'Tell me something I don't know.'

He saw no blood in Cassie's garments; the girl called, in an anxious tone:

'Who are you talking to?'

Anne said,

'It's me, Cassie. Anne. I'm a new girl, like you. Still trying to find my way around. Sorry to disturb you.'

'. . . That's alright. Alice said.'

They heard the renewed plashing of water. The woman's confidence had conveyed itself to the child. Now she looked to Savage again:

'Well?'

The desirability of a doctor?

'What do you expect me to do about it?'

She considered this.

'Would you like me to examine her?'

'Not without her agreement.'

'Well, shall I *ask*?'

She had a hectoring manner which aggravated him.

'Not yet.'

But she, plainly as exasperated, said:

'Then why did you ask me to come up, Mr Savage?'

'I don't know!'

Finally, he had found an answer that seemed to satisfy her. She nodded, as though in comprehension. A sound behind him caused him to turn. Alice had come to the head of the stairs, clothing in her arms. In a voice clearly intended for the child, she said:

'I've brought the clothes for Cassie.'

The girl called:

'Mr Savage can take them.'

'Right you are, lovey.'

Alice stood her ground. Evidently she needed to speak confidentially. When Savage joined her, he found that Anne had come with him. Alice said:

'Sarah says to be sure to ask about bleeding. That's important.'

Anne said,

'She's taken up the practice of medicine again, then?'

Alice gave her a hard look, but placed the clothes she was carrying into Anne's outstretched arms. Savage said,

'I'll ask.' He handed Cassie's clothing to Alice. 'Show these to Sarah. Then boil them, don't burn them. She may want to keep them.'

Cassie called:

'I'm out.'

'Okay! And take the bandoliers down to Martin. Tell him they're for disposal.'

'I'll do that.'

As they walked back, Anne said,

'Where?'

She hefted the clothes in her arms. He pointed to the open doorway.

'Bedroom.'

'I'll be just across the corridor, if you need me.'

He knocked on the bathroom door before he entered, much to the child's amusement.

'Come in.'

She was swathed in a large blue towel and rubbed her hair vigorously with another. He said,

'We're in there, when you're ready.'

'Where?'

'Through the door.'

'What door?'

Of course, she was right. The door was just a mirror among

76

mirrors. When he turned the onyx globe and stepped into the bedroom, she said,

'Like magic.'

The bedroom was substantial, with a four-poster bed but otherwise modern furniture. It had been Madge's room and smelled of her. There was a modest fire in the grate and the single functioning shutter had been opened to daylight.

It had been Madge who had persuaded him of the importance of daylight. *People need it, John. They're like flowers. Without it, they die.* And so he had selected three apertures to be left unsealed (other than those in the tower) and, with Martin's help, had constructed and installed three heavy-duty shutters, which swung on crude iron hinges and could be barred securely at night.

For himself, he did not miss light. He was at ease in the dark, where others were ill at ease.

Anne had separated the clothes roughly on the dressing table: Jeans, dresses, sweaters, underwear. Socks. Behind him, Cassie said,

'I'm ready.'

She appeared childlike and apprehensive.

In the event, examining her did not prove embarrassing. She lay on the bed and opened herself for him. But it did make him angry. It was not the indignity of her posture. Nor yet the evidence of damage done to her body. It was the almost total absence of it. Apart from a nail scrape along one flank and a small bruise to the opposite thigh, there was nothing. Yet, given the evil done to her, he felt with rage that there should have been.

In a small voice, she said,

'Am I alright?'

'Yeah, I think so.'

She pulled the towel across herself again. He said,

'Any pain?'

'My bottom's a bit sore.'

'Yeah. That, what they did, that's . . . not right to do, you know.'

He thought, What I am saying? She looked away.

'I know.'

He remembered Sarah's admonition.

'Any bleeding?'

'. . . Not bleeding.'

'Something?'

'Stuff.'

'Stuff?'

'. . . Sort of stuff.'

'I mean . . . What sort of stuff?'

'Thick. And slimy.'

He was at a loss. Such medical training as he had acquired did not cover this eventuality. He said,

'Still? Now?'

'Yes.'

Then he remembered the proximity of Anne.

'. . . I'd like to ask Anne, if you wouldn't mind.'

'What?'

'I mean, she's a woman, you know.'

And thereby, what? An expert in rape? He was doing everything wrong. But the child said,

'Alright.'

He crossed to the door.

'Anne.'

He expected her to come from the corridor, but in fact she came from the room opposite – maintaining, he supposed, the fiction that her presence was by chance.

'Yes, Mr Savage?'

'I wonder if you'd have a look at Cassie?'

'Of course.'

She came into the room, exhibiting the same confidence that she had before.

'Hullo, Cassie. How are you?'

'Fine.'

But there was a fear on the child. Savage said,

'She's got this . . . stuff coming out of her.'

Anne nodded.

'Vaginal discharge.'

Her tone was matter of fact.

'. . . Right.'

She crossed to sit on the bed and took the girl's hand, as though it were the most natural thing.

'How long ago did the attack take place, Cassie?'

It was a moment before the child could work it out.

'Yesterday.'

Much of yesterday, Savage thought. Anne said,

'Have you started to menstruate?'

'Of course.'

'When?'

'Ages ago.'

Anne smiled.

'How many ages?'

'. . . Eighteen months.'

As though unconfident of belief.

'How old are you, Cassie?'

'. . . Nearly sixteen.'

Anne was placid, plainly untroubled by inconsistency.

'Or nearly fourteen?'

Cassie said nothing, but she did not take her hand from Anne's. Anne said,

'Were you a virgin, before the attack?'

Savage was shocked.

'Of course she was.'

'Please, Mr Savage.'

'What kind of a question is that?'

'*Shut up.*'

But she took the edge from the command with a humorous look to Cassie – who, to judge from her reaction, shared the belief that his was the compunction of a man, rather than of a woman. She said,

'Yes, I was.'

Justified, Savage said,

'You see.'

But they paid him no attention. And when next he looked, Anne was stroking Cassie's hair in a gesture that seemed to him both agelessly and ineffably maternal. She said,

'It's nothing to worry about, I promise you. It'll stop soon. Perfectly normal.'

'You're sure?'

'I'm sure.'

Indeed, the child plainly was comforted at a level beyond Savage's compass. Anne said,

'Any other worries?'

'Will I get pregnant?'

This fear had not even occurred to Savage. Anne said,

'No.' She looked up at him. 'I don't think it can happen at the moment?'

He shook his head: he had seen only spontaneous abortions; no successfully retained pregnancies.

'Anything else?'

'No.'

'Good.'

They continued to communicate in a manner which excluded him; and then, as though at a mutually-acknowledged cue, they drew apart. He said,

'I'll have my bath.' As he crossed to the intercommunicating door, he said to Cassie: 'There's a pile of stuff on the dresser. I expect to see you in something really elegant when I come out.'

She swung her legs from the bed.

'Yes, sir.'

Anne said,

'This pink looks gorgeous, Cassie.'

But the child, suddenly cold, said:

'I can choose for myself, thank you.'

'Of course you can. I'll leave you to it.'

But Savage, if only for his own purposes, thought it undesirable that they should become alienated. He said,

'Maybe Anne could help . . .'

Anne said,

'Cassie is more than old enough to choose for herself, Mr Savage.'

– In a tone which implied far greater annoyance with him than with Cassie. But the child appeared now confused by her own rudeness and anxious to take her lead from him:

'Of course. If you . . .'

He said,

'Anne had a son, about your age.'

Even as he spoke, he knew that he had blundered into error. Cassie said,

'Oh.'

In an acid tone, Anne said,

'You are a wizard with words, Mr Savage.'

Cassie flared:

'He was only trying to let me understand!'

Savage thought, I am defended by children. Anne sighed.

'I know.'

– as though, indeed, the depth of Savage's ineptitude was imponderable. He said,

'Do what you like!'

He slammed the door behind him.

He cursed her roundly.

A wizard with words!

He cursed her again.

And then he thought, Get rid of them. The lot of them. Take them to the Capital. Be done.

Think of nothing else.

He would not let her anger him again. The angry die.

He lay back in the bath.

A moment of respite.

Then he washed himself with the same meticulous attention to detail that he applied to the cleaning of his weapons. Beyond the closed door, he heard them laugh together. No doubt, at him. He did not care.

Remain alert at all times. Concentrate. Be switched on. Never relax. Dominate your environment. Command yourself.

This was his life and he was not ashamed of it.

When he had dried, he set about shaving, a lamp on the vanity beside him, his rifle at the other hand. In a little, came a knock at the door.

'What is it?'

'It's Cassie. Can I come in?'

He sighed.

'Wait.' He tied a hand towel about his waist. 'Come.'

He thought for a moment that a stranger had entered the room. She wore a plain pink dress with a scooped neckline and no sleeves. Across her forehead was a gold band. She looked new minted; on the brink of her first grown-up party. She said,

'Is this elegant enough?'

She spun – and in the interplay of many mirrors, a thousand Cassies turned before him. He said,

'You look . . .'

He stepped forward – and at once she was beset by predators (that all were him). She smiled:

'What?'

'Like a fine young woman.'

He drew back, unbeleaguring her. From the doorway, Anne said,

'She *is* a fine young woman, Mr Savage.'

He wondered whether the woman had engineered this revelation. But Cassie, now that she had his approval, examined herself in the mirrors and shrugged:

'It's alright.'

Anne said, in a dry tone:

'We chose a practical outfit, too.'

'Sweater and jeans.'

'Good. Soon as I finish here, I'll show you where you sleep.'

He returned to his shaving, hoping that they would take the cue: but Anne said,

'Wouldn't it be more sensible for Cassie to sleep in here?'

She indicated the room behind her.

'If you wouldn't mind, Mr Savage?'

'Why would I mind?'

'Your friend, you know.'

The room had been Madge's.

'It should be used.'

'Thank you.'

Again, he thought to have dismissed them, but Cassie said:

'But you will kit me out, like you promised?'

Anne said,

'Oh, I think we can count on Mr Savage for that.'

And Cassie agreed heartily, as though Anne had praised him.

Savage contemplated himself in the mirror.

And remembered how, in mass, he had seemed to menace Cassie.

He looked more tired than once he had. More marked by battle.

He thought that soon he might die.

He cleaned and dried and stowed his shaving kit with care.

When he crossed the room, there sprang up about him again a multitude of images, receding in graduated slices, as though they were halls of the dead.

And he thought, Be patient.

Clad only in hand towel, cargo vest and combat jacket, with belt kit and bandoliers loosely about his neck, soiled clothing in one hand and rifle in the other, Savage bunted the door and pushed through.

'I'm going up to the tower room, won't be long.'

Cassie said,

'Can I come?'

He regarded her finery.

'Where's your rifle?'

She ran into the bathroom to fetch it. For the first time, he noted that Anne had changed from the corduroy trousers of yesterday into a skirt and heavy sweater. He said,

'Where's yours?'

'In my room.'

'Carry it with you always.'

'In the *house*?'

'Always.'

She flushed and turned away. But she would not again, he knew, offer a ready occasion for rebuke.

As he mounted the circular, stone stairway, Savage recognised, from the asynchrony of footfalls behind him, that Anne had joined them.

Sammy was on watch in the tower (Savage suspected, to avoid Sarah).

'Take a break.'

Sammy left them.

The tower room was hexagonal in shape, with three broad windows which, between them, commanded a three-hundred-and-sixty degree panorama of the surrounding landscape – except immediately to the east, where, by virtue of Savage's deliberate failure to thin the copse, the proximate terrain was partially obscured. Each window was guarded by a steel shutter, installed by Martin and himself.

In any event, the tower could only be stormed by Special Forces troopers. And Other Force would not intervene yet.

The room contained a camp bed, with a single, folded blanket. A slatted, adjustable wooden armchair. A plain deal table. And a low chest, with eight shallow and two deep drawers, which had been designed (so Madge had told him) to accommodate an architect's drawings and impedimenta; and in which he kept a standby rifle and automatic; spare magazines; clothing, emergency ration packs, first aid kits, maps, batteries, compass – the entire capacity to resupply and to fight, without recourse to his main armoury and stores in the cellars below.

It was onto the top of this chest, where Martin had placed his bergen, that Savage now set down the items he was carrying.

The room had become 'his' by decree of Madge, who had seen at once that, if Savage was to spend any time in the house at all, he must have a place where he could be alone.

It had been here that he had planned his secret foray to the west, which had done so much to harden his intentions for the future.

Even so, he came only briefly to the house and rarely stayed the night. When obliged to, he prowled the shadows until morning. If he tried to sleep, the horrors came.

He did not feel justified.

Cassie spoke for a second time. He said,
'. . . What?'
'You've got a lot of scars, haven't you?'
He had slipped off cargo vest and smock and she was surveying him critically. Anne said,
'Cassie.'
He said,
'Mistakes.'
He pulled on clean underpants under the towel and, the

84

exigencies of modesty having been served, dressed rapidly in clean singlet, shirt, socks and trousers. At a window, Anne said,

'I must say, even I appreciate the military excellence of your location, Mr Savage.'

He said,

'Don't show yourself. Don't offer a target. Do nothing direct. Approach the window obliquely. Only gradually enlarge your field of view. Seem not to move. The less you move, the more you see movement. The less you show, the more you see.'

Anne said,

'Is there some point to this lecture?'

He returned to her.

'What?'

The point, he thought, was survival. She said,

'Shall we be here long enough to benefit?'

'Depends.'

'On what?'

'How well you do on the training ground.'

He began to lace up his boots. She said,

'Are you joking?'

'You think I'm going to take you on the Main Route, without satisfying myself that you've grasped at least the fundamentals of movement and evasion?'

'We've managed well enough so far.'

'Have you?'

But he had intended no reference to her dead son, nor to the circumstances in which he had first encountered her, or Cassie; and he said,

'Look, the Main Route's more dangerous now than it's ever been. The Scavengers are on the run. The Army's butchering them. But these aren't front line troops, they're rear echelon scum. They're killing for pleasure. It's a *hunt*. I'm not going to put you into that until I'm sure you'll survive the experience. Me, too, if it comes to that.'

In a moment, Cassie said,

'What about the others?'

Immediately, he was wary.

'. . . What about them?'

Anne said,

'Will they be coming with us?'

He wondered whether she meant to embarrass him, or merely was ignorant of the implications. He said,

'It's up to them.'

Anne said,

'I'd heard differently.'

Cassie said,

'You can't leave them here, can you?'

He was pondering how best to respond to this, when Anne said,

'Perhaps, when you return.'

He saw Cassie stiffen.

'. . . You're coming back here?'

He found himself reluctant to lie.

'I don't know . . .'

At once, she said,

'I won't stay at the Capital without you.'

'Cassie . . .'

'I won't do it.'

Anne said,

'Cassie, we don't know anything about the Capital –'

The child turned on her.

'*This has nothing to do with you!*'

It had the viciousness of a blow in the face. Anne grew still. The child looked at him.

'You said we were together now.' Betrayal pricked at her eyes. 'You said that.'

'. . . Yes, I did.'

He had not expected to be called to account so soon. She said,

'I won't stay there without you.' She moved away. 'I'll go on my own. I've done it before. I'm not afraid.'

They were not the threats of a child. Anne said,

'Cassie, listen –'

But Savage said,

'I won't leave you – anywhere you don't want to be. Not against your will.'

She fixed him with a straight look.

'You promise?'

'I promise.'

She nodded.

'Alright.'

Anne turned away, as though only now understanding what she had done.

In the kitchen, Alice looked up from where she was gutting rabbits at one end of the table; at the other, Sarah sat, eating what was, presumably, her first food of the day. To Cassie, Alice said,

'Well, don't you look nice!'

Behind her, coppers simmered on the range, giving to the daybright room steam and the sweet savour of cooking. Being the centre of their habitation of the house, the kitchen had the largest (and best-protected) functioning high window. Cassie said,

'What's that delicious smell?'

'Steak and kidney.'

'Steak and kidney?'

The child had not lost her capacity for wonder. Sarah said,

'Savage provides.'

He said,

'It's just standard Army rations.'

He (later, with Sammy) had freely plundered the Army dumps under the Southern Forest. Alice said,

'Would you like some now?'

She began to wipe her blood and fur-flecked hands, but Savage said,

'First, the armoury.'

'Give her a chance. She's only just got here. What do you say, lovey – ?'

Savage said,

'We kit out first.'

But Alice persisted:

'I bet you en't had any breakfast, have you?'

The girl said,

'Mr Savage gave me breakfast.'

'Oh, aye? What did that consist of?'

'It was very good.'

'I'll believe that when I see it.'

87

Savage was puzzled as to the cause of Alice's intransigence. But Sarah said,

'You should learn to fight, Cassie.'

She spoke as though the concept were entirely abstract and in no way connected to herself. Cassie said,

'Mr Savage is going to train me.'

Alice protested:

'She's just a child!'

Savage said,

'Nobody's a child any more.'

He had barely time to register the irony of his own words before Alice said,

'Not with you around, they en't!'

She turned angrily to the range. He wondered whether in this were his clue: that the lone child, prettily dressed, had recalled for Alice her own children, whom Savage had killed. Anne said,

'Where do you want these?'

She hefted the unused clothing, which she had brought down. Sarah said,

'I'll take them.'

She rose, assumed the burden and left the room, in the manner of one remote from all of their concerns. Alice said,

'I didn't mean that, what I said.'

'It doesn't matter.' He indicated the archway which led to the service hall and to the cellars. 'Through there.'

As he followed Cassie and Anne, Alice said,

'When do you want to eat, then?'

'Normal time.'

'It'll spoil. It's ready now.'

'It'll reheat.'

She made a gesture, as though there were no speaking to him. He wondered whether, in Alice's bad temper, in Sarah's abstraction and Sammy's avoidance of her, lay the seeds of the disintegration of the group. It would be no bad thing if it were so.

The cellars consisted of a series of vaulted brick and stone chambers, linked by passages, which extended under the entire length of the house to form a honeycombed netherworld, the ambience of which gave Savage much satisfaction. As he led the way down the steps, under a lamp hung by Martin from an iron bracket on the wall, he savoured the deep dry smell and the tang of fumes from the early-morning generator run.

The boiler was situated in the second chamber. It was used only for the provision of hot baths. For all other purposes, water was heated on the range and either employed in situ or ported to where it was needed. The range, too, supplied such heating as the house enjoyed.

From this chamber now came the sound of Martin raking out. As soon as the boiler had cooled sufficiently, he would relay the fire box for immediate action. This was significant routine.

For the second chamber contained also Savage's 'hidden exit', of which he was certain by now Other Force was aware; and access to his 'trap door', of which he was certain they were not.

(If he was wrong, he was dead.)

In the first chamber was Savage's armoury and store, where weapons, clothing, equipment and supplies were housed on shelving and duckboards cannibalised by Martin from the wine racks and bins with which the cellars had been furnished. Food was stored in the pantries above.

In other chambers were items of interest to Savage.

As he crossed to the trestle table in the main storage bay, on which Martin had placed a second lamp, Savage called:

'Martin!'

The big man came to the connecting archway. When he saw the women, he said,

'I'm about finished here. I'll top up the tank.'

He meant that he would hand-pump water to the roof space, to replenish what had been drawn. Savage set down his own rifle on the table top and told the women to do the same. When Martin reappeared, he looked at Savage.

'That problem.'

'Yeah?'

'I reckon I've solved it.'

This was good news.

'Later.'

With Martin gone, Savage said to Cassie:

'You first.'

She stood to the counter with the eagerness of a shopper at a sale.

Singlet.

'You can wear your own clothes underneath, it's just the top layer –'

But she said,

'No, I want to be exactly like you.'

Anne was dry:

'Not exactly, surely?'

'Why not? Don't you?'

Savage thought he would not stay for Anne's answer. In any event, the more they looked (and acted) like soldiers, the less likely they would be to be fired on by those who would shoot first and question after. He dropped the singlet onto the table top.

At once, Cassie hauled up her dress, spilling the head band in the process. Anne stooped to retrieve it. Savage was no longer embarrassed by the child's nakedness, finding it no different now from his own trade's lack of inhibition in the field.

Shirt and sweater went on over the singlet.

Socks.

'These need to fit. Trousers, too.'

Cassie sat on the flagstones to try on the socks. Anne said,

'Don't sit on the floor, Cassie. You'll get piles.'

'What's piles?'

This time, Savage thought the answer might be worth waiting for, but the woman merely said,

'Very painful.'

The socks fitted snugly. The trousers deployed some slack in the seat and about the waist, due to the child's spareness of frame; but the waistband at least could readily be adjusted by means of tab and buckle fastenings and he could do no better.

Boots.

'You live and die by these. If they don't fit, you're gone in twenty minutes.'

The child nodded solemnly. But Anne said,

'Surely, an exaggeration?'

'No.'

Shutters dropped over her eyes and lifted again, but she did not speak. To Cassie, Savage said:

'What size do you take?'

'Six. I've got enormous feet.'

Not enormous, long. As he guided her into the boots he had chosen, there came resistance and then the soft rush of a foot bolting home. He knew at once they had a fit.

'Wiggle your toes.'

He palpated the upper against the ensuing movement. Satisfied, he laced the boot.

'Flex your ankle, bend your knee.'

'It's *soft*.'

'Jump up and down. Run on the spot.'

This, she did with abandon.

'And *light*.'

'They're jungle boots. Lightweight, flexible, weatherproof, tough. Hardly need wearing in.' In fact, he had pre-eased a number of pairs, against some such eventuality as this. He said,

'Just like mine – see?'

'Excellent.'

Anne said,

'If they're good enough for Mr Savage . . .'

'Exactly.'

The child missed the irony. He said,

'Let's try the other. Feet can be different.'

They were not. She was shod.

'Camouflage netting.'

He showed her how the scrim could be worn as a scarf about her neck, or shaken out and draped over head and shoulders to form a porous veil. Again, she said,

'Excellent.'

Anne muttered:

'*Most* ingenious.'

Her sly mockery was beginning to aggravate Savage.

'Combat jacket.'

The child received it as though it were the *pièce de résistance*, murmuring in appreciation when he demonstrated the double-fastening of the pockets, reacting luxuriantly to the drawing up of the hood.

'It's so warm.'

The fit was close enough.

'Belt kit.'

This was a modified version of his own, with two pouches and two water bottles – and easily adjusted to her waist size. The pouches contained emergency rations, medical kit and like supplies. He said,

'Look; but don't open the packets.'

She said,

'Will I have one of those things that I wore before?'

Cargo vest.

'No, you'll be carrying a small pack; that's all you'll need.'

In fact there was, on the shelf beside him, a set of packs, already provisioned.

Brusquely, he said,

'Cap comforter.'

She pulled it down over her butter hair. He took an empty pack, put into it spare singlet, socks, shirt and sweater; fatigues for training; and then, having adjusted the straps on her webbing, he said,

'That's it for now.'

She said,

'Do I . . . get a light?'

A beta light. After a moment, he said,

'Haven't got a spare. Sorry.'

She accepted this with resignation. Then he remembered:

'Got a watch, though.'

This was one implied promise that he could keep. He had three spare G10s, which he kept permanently wound and corrected, and half a dozen other high-quality time-pieces, harvested from the dead. He gave the girl one of the G10s, buckling it on himself.

'Thank you.'

She admired it extravagantly, as though it were an engagement ring. Anne said,

'You look quite the soldier, Cassie.'

The child agreed. Savage did not know what else he could do, other than to prepare them for what lay ahead. He said,

'You next.'

She stood, sceptical, before him. He said,

'I don't know how far you want to take this – the outer layer, presumably?'

But she said,

'Oh, all the way, by all means, Mr Savage.'

The mockery, then, had not ceased.

When he placed singlet and shirt before her, she seized the hem of her sweater and began to haul it over her head.

There came at once to his mind an image of Cassie baring herself.

And of Anne.

She had paused and was watching him.

And he knew that the image had communicated itself to her, that she had seen into his mind.

He turned away.

Bitterly angry with himself, for having fallen below his own standards.

And angry with her for . . .

Whatever it was she had done to humiliate him.

He heard the sweater pass over her head.

'You don't have to try them on.'

'I'll have to try the trousers on.'

In fact, the first pair of trousers was too tight; and having struggled for some moments to accommodate them to her hips, she said,

'You have a kind eye, Mr Savage.'

And pulled them down.

He found himself obliged to turn away again.

But he was not so foolish as to suppose that she was being provocative.

Indeed when, shortly thereafter, he had to adjust first her waistband, then her belt kit, then the straps of her pack, she endured the intimacy as one turned to stone. Finally he said,

'Watch.'

And gave her a G10. Then:

'Weapons.'

He issued to each a new assault rifle, taken from a rack on the end wall. These were weapons which he knew, from test, to fire true from a fixed stand over two hundred yards. They could be zeroed later. He said,

'These are yours now. Personal. Memorise the number. Take care of them. Cherish them. Practise with them. Carry them with you always. Your life depends on them.'

The child was impressed:

'Yes, sir.'

But Anne was droll:

'You will be instructing us in these dark mysteries, Mr Savage?'

Suddenly goaded beyond patience, he said,

'*Right now.*'

Cassie stirred, pleased:

'Good.'

But he said,

'Anne first.'

He knew that the dry challenge in her face reflected the intransigence in his own. Then she said,

'You can put on your *real* clothes again, Cassie.'

The child said,

'I want to keep these on. I want to practise like Mr Savage said.'

The woman smiled at him.

'You have a recruit, Mr Savage.'

Two, he thought. You'll find it's two.

He took her to the training ground, she now dressed in fatigues and carrying one weapon; he, two. Partway down the slope, he turned her along one of a number of modest shelves, which traversed the meadow from one side to the other and by which the rugged hillside was divided into segments, as though by gentle steps. Between, was much perturbation of ridges, fissures and hollows and a fierce acne of coarse vegetation. Some sixty yards below Low Wood and a third across the meadow, he said,

'Stop.'

The second rifle that he carried was an earlier model than the assault rifles, although of similar weight and dimensions, with a hand-operated bolt action. It was his 'concentrator'. It taught good habits.

But first, the modern assault rifle.

He took her through the procedures for loading and mounting a magazine. Cocking the weapon by means of the charging handle. Simple field stripping and maintenance, by use of the concealed kit provided. It was not that he expected her to become expert, but he wanted her to be intimate with the weapon, to make it her own.

And it became apparent quickly that she had for the rifle the same instinct that she had for movement. Her hands were fleet and apt to their purpose. Unlike Cassie, she apprehended the weapon intuitively.

It became evident, too, that her palms were badly blistered – from burying or wheeling her son, presumably. But if she did not complain, he would not.

'Aiming and dry firing.'

'*Aim low*. Always aim low.'

She lay prone on the shelf, her profile closed to him.

'I have grasped the concept, Mr Savage.'

'We'll see.' He crouched beside her. 'Another thing. You've got to pull the weapon in *here*.' He seized the butt and thrust it into the meat of her shoulder – and felt at once her resistance to this unwonted familiarity. But he persisted: 'This weapon may not have much of a kick, but others have. And if you let it ride up here . . .' When he touched her collar bone, he was shocked by the violence with which she recoiled, as though she had been scalded; and angered, too, for it was no part of his purpose to affront her. He said, 'You'll *hurt* yourself. And you'll die from not wanting to hurt yourself again.'

After a moment of contemplation, she said,

'I understand.'

They would find out soon enough.

'If you have to use this weapon on the Main Route, it'll be under pressure. People don't stand still. You won't be aiming at a stationary target. They move. They fire back.'

Sometimes they stand still, he thought.

Sometimes they die for that.

He said,

'So you have to have a drill. That you practise *every time*. Take a breath. Release. Take aim. Aim low. *Squeeze* the trigger. Good habits. That's what guarantees you live, not him.'

She watched him without comment and he ventured a further step:

'Sometimes, you have to do it with your . . . spirit. Let the weapon find the mark. How can it do that, if you haven't got good habits?'

She looked at him then with curiosity and he wondered whether, after all, he had said too much.

'Let's try it.'

'First, with this.'

She accepted the exchange of weapons with suspicion but without demur. He said,

'This is a bolt-action rifle. You have to cock the weapon after each shot.' He demonstrated. 'You can do that.'

Indeed, within moments, her good hands manipulated the mechanism with a facility that any trained man should envy. He said,

'Okay.' He attached a full magazine. 'Look down the hill.'

There was, some seventy yards down the slope, an outcrop of rock, with a chalk white 'face' and a frizz of tufted 'hair', which gave the impression over distance of a startled man bobbing in a coarse green sea. Savage said,

'That's your target. Fire when ready.'

The woman settled to her firing position with none of the laboured earnestness of Cassie. But she forgot the placement of the rifle butt.

He did not warn her.

She squeezed the trigger.

He glanced down the hill.

The shot clipped the hairline.

He looked back to the woman. The hammer of recoil on bone had shocked her, but her face was locked against giving any of her pain to him. A faint flush betrayed her. He said,

'Again.'

This time, she cradled the weapon correctly and contained the recoil to far greater effect. But missed.

'Again.'

A perfect shot.

'Again.'

Dead centre.

'Again.'

Left and low.

'Rest.'

She rubbed her elbows where, in forming a bipod for the rifle, they had scraped in the rough, but did not touch her shoulder. He said,

'There's no merit supporting the rifle, if you don't have to. There's a perfectly good firing point there. Why don't you use it?'

She looked to where, eight feet along the ledge, a low mound offered cover and support; and then back to him, with undisguised contempt.

'You are right, Mr Savage. How unobservant of me.'

He was justly rebuked; for, in submitting to training, she had relinquished independence of action temporarily to him – and he had afforded no encouragement to do otherwise. But he said,

'This isn't a game. It isn't fair. Cheat. Use everything to your advantage. The object of the exercise is to kill, before you are killed.'

In a little, she nodded; and he wondered whether, for the first time, the nature of what they were engaged in had entered her mind.

He took her some twenty yards along the shelf.

'This time, start from a standing position. I want you to find the nearest cover, get behind it and get your shot off. I'm going to count you down. But *don't rush*. Go through your drill. I just want you to have a sense of how long you're taking. Alright?'

She nodded, her face expressionless.

'*Go*. One. Two. Three.'

After the briefest appraisal, she moved to the mound he had already pointed out to her – and he was truly impressed: for it was

97

the best and nearest cover; and she had chosen the tactical
advantage over the desire to better him.

'Four. Five. Six.'

She melted to the ground, took aim.

Forgot the butt.

He declined to warn her.

She squeezed the trigger.

The weapon bucked.

Dead centre.

This time, the effort to overmaster pain was cringingly apparent.
He said,

'Again.'

She dug down, found the resource (probably in rage) to fire.

A hit.

'Again.'

He led her up and diagonally across the slope, in the direction of the
deep fissure which marked the western perimeter of the training
ground, until they came to the next shelf above, little different from
the one they had quit. He said,

'Movement. You're good at that. But you can't move over ground
if you don't know it.' Her face gave nothing. 'You've got to be able
to read it. Close to. And distance.'

His eyes quartered the hummocks and hollows by which they
were sequestered.

'Close to is . . . observation. Concentration. Seeing the ways. The
cover. Like an animal. Knowing where you're safe. Becoming where
you are.'

Seeing that he had her attention, he said,

'The earth is your larder. Your hide. Your hunting ground. Your
. . .'

The word he sought eluded him.

'*Place*.'

She said,

'I see.'

He looked across the valley.

'Distance is . . . knowing what lies ahead. Seeing what you can't

see, from what you can. The high ground. The dead ground. The
dominating position.'

'Dead ground?'

'The place where he can move, and you can't see him. And you
can move, and he can't see you. That's your way. Your advantage.'

She said,

'I understand.'

He wondered. He said,

'You have to see without seeing.'

She said,

'I understand what you're saying, Mr Savage.'

Antagonised, he said,

'This isn't something you can *understand*! You have to *feel* it!
Sense it! Just – *know* it!' Seeing her expression, he wondered
suddenly at the nature of his own insistence. Yet he could not quite
abandon the hope which he found (unaccountably) he had in her.
He said,

'Look down the hill.' She did so. 'Our friend with the white face
has got a friend of his own now.'

Some fifty yards to the left of the first target was a second, cruder
of physiognomy but more imposing in size, which formed the
western end of the minor ridge by which the two were conjoined.
The woman said,

'So he has.'

She sought, Savage knew, to mask her surprise at the extent to
which the hillside had been reconfigured by their modest change of
location. (It would hold more surprises yet.) He said,

'If you crouch now, which will you see?'

She looked at him, as though to confirm that the question were
serious. Then she glanced briefly into the terrain below.

'The one on the right.'

'Check.'

Again, a look; but she crouched. Partway down, she laughed.

'Neither.'

'Go in that direction.'

For a moment, he thought she might refuse; but she walked away
from him along the shelf. He said,

'Diagonally up the hill.'

As she accommodated to the change of direction and inclination, he was struck again by the grace with which she found her centre. When she had achieved the third shelf, he called:

'Try now.'

Once more, she looked into the ground with too little interest.

'Both.'

'Check.'

The part crouch, the half laugh.

'Neither.'

'Walk directly down the slope.'

In short order, she came again to the shelf on which he stood, although some forty yards from him.

'Try now.'

At last there was an effort at concentration in her, if only, he suspected, because pride had entered the equation. In a little, she said,

'The one on the left.'

'Check.'

She had barely begun to stoop, when she laughed aloud.

'Another bullseye, Mr Savage.'

Enraged, he shouted:

'*It isn't funny!*' She glared at him. 'You can *do* this!'

She spread her hands.

'Evidently not.'

'. . . Come back, then.'

He turned away, disillusioned. He had, it seemed, been mistaken in his instinct of her. Yet when he looked back, there was on her, he thought, a reluctance to acquiesce in defeat; and on impulse, he said,

'Try now.'

For the first time, there was humility in her appreciation of the ground. After a considerable period, she said,

'Both are visible.'

He thought it unlikely, but he said,

'Have a look.'

Her head dropped.

'Only the left-hand one.'

'You were half right.'

'I was wrong.'

Sharply, as though she had been patronised. He said,

'It doesn't all come at once.'

But in one of her (he believed) ability, it came quickly or not at all. He said,

'Look.' He met her on the ground between. 'Suppose there's an enemy on the left-hand head. How will you get at him, without being seen?'

He moved away, not to oppress her; nor, indeed, did he look in her direction, until she said,

'There's high ground on that side.'

'Yeah.'

In so far as there was any lateral bias to the meadow at all, it declined very slightly from The Beard on their right, rising again to the crude hedge which marked the progress of the fissure down the slope to their left. This placed the hedge marginally above the left-hand position. She said,

'There's dead ground around the foot of the head.'

To anyone in the hair, undoubtedly this was the case. She glanced briefly to the right, but found nothing of interest there. Sensing that she was beginning to founder and, not wishing her to lose prime, he said,

'How will you reach the dead ground?'

She looked along the shelf.

'I could go through the hedge, work down behind it.'

'Show you something.'

He ran lightly up the slope, high and left, until he had placed himself on the skyline between the sparse trees of the hedge. He called:

'Am I a good target?'

She studied him from below.

'Yes.'

'Why?'

'I see you against the sky.'

Now he ran to the right, under the mass of Low Wood, where his frame, he knew, could be glimpsed only fleetingly against the deeps of the trees. Abruptly, he crouched:

'Now?'

She shook her head.

'No.'

He ran on, angling slightly down towards The Beard, until he came to a modest declivity which, although unemphatic in itself, would be hidden from her position, he knew, by the (unapparent) confirmation of the hillside. As he flowed into it, he stopped. To her, he would seem to have melted into ground.

'What about now?'

She called:

'No.'

'I'm standing *upright*!'

As he dinked down the slopes, he chose, off each shelf, the most revealing face. When he stood before her again, she said,

'See yourself from his position.'

'*Yes*! Go down there – in your mind. *Feel* it out. *Sense* it out. Find the way. Make it *yours*.' He struggled to express further. 'It's – *different* down there.'

She nodded.

But he felt that he had failed utterly to say what he wanted to say: that person and place (and moment) are one and cannot be divided; that if you cannot find – accommodation, you fail.

But he had not words.

She said,

'These . . . ledges are like giant steps.'

She was looking up the hill.

'Yes.'

'I can't use them without being seen.'

'On the forward slopes, that's right.'

She looked down towards the left-hand position.

'And if I come through the hedge, there are – forward slopes there, too.'

She handled his terminology as though with tongs.

'That's right.'

For the first time, she turned her attention seriously to The Beard. She studied the trees.

'But if I go in there, the same applies.'

'So?'

It was as far as he was prepared to go, by way of prompting.

At last, she looked *into* the ground before her. It took a moment, but then her eyes paled, as at the passage of light. She looked at him, frowned, crouched, peered into the ground again. Abruptly, she rose and brushed past him, as though he were of no account – and he recognised that in discovery she had found the impetus to seize the initiative for herself. Along the ledge, again she crouched, fiercely abstracted – and freeing herself, he knew, of the constraints of physical geography. In a little. she rose and, in a still voice, said:

'There *is* dead ground down there.'

'Oh yes.'

For all that, from their elevation, the training ground would appear to her uninitiated eye to be rugged but no more than routinely disrupted, it was in reality a place of vicious perturbation, with all of the treachery and contradiction attendant thereon; and it was in the relatively level stretch between The Beard and the low ridge in which the 'faces' were located, that hidden ways were concealed. They were all but unamenable of merely sensory perception, yet she had found them out (and was, indeed, still charged by the experience).

He was pleased.

It was precisely in such unregarded thoroughfares that men could be wraiths and impossible aims accomplished. He said,

'How will you get there?'

She returned from revelation to reality.

'I'll have to . . . draw back off the ledge. Find the way. Creep down, as you said . . . Like an animal . . .'

Her eyes tracked her course.

'And then?'

'Sneak round the back, I think –'

He interrupted her.

'*Do the impossible!*' She stared at him. 'Go like the wind! Be where you *can't* be! Strike from where you *can't* strike! Do the *impossible*! *Nothing* is impossible!' The intensity of her gaze drew him on. 'Be like air! Like water! *Flow* through the ground!' She watched fixedly. 'Never be what you *seem* to be! Never be *where* you seem to be!' He reached for some ultimate explication. 'You've got to – *change*! *Disappear!*'

It was then that he saw in her a look of infinite distance.

As though indeed he had ceased to be.

He was shocked by a sense of his own destiny.

And then – something happened.

The light went out in her.

It was as though some jolt of recognition had stilled her.

She turned away and he knew that he had lost her.

But he did not know why.

And then, when she again looked into the ground, he saw that she did so with a kind of yearning; and he realised that it was not the spark that had been extinguished, but that something had come between her and the will to burnish it.

And he was all the more frustrated.

For to have the gift to imagine perfection and not the urge to seek it, was to Savage unimaginable.

To be the best.

He said,

'Let's get on.'

'We're going to move down the hill. Tactical movement over ground.'

He thought, Why am I doing this? To a woman; a civilian? But he was more than ever certain that he was responding to some quality innate in her. He said,

'You'll come under fire, left or right. When you do, move to the nearest good firing point, get your shot off.'

She nodded.

'Take this.'

He restored to her the modern assault rifle, accepting the other in exchange. At once, her hands moved about the weapon with an instinctive grace which made his frustration the greater. He said,

'Go.'

She advanced into the ground below, well balanced and seeming to scan the terrain with fierce attention. Yet when he called: 'Under fire! Target left!' she went down too gingerly, lingering at the half crouch for a final sweep of the slopes. He shouted:

'Stop! Get up.'

She rose and turned to him.

'This is *yours*.' He struck the earth with the flat of his hand. '*Make* it yours.'

She nodded.

'If you have to take a last look round, you're not doing your job. *Know* where you'll go – where the cover is – *all the time.*'

Again, she bobbed her head.

'Move on.'

She had taken barely three paces when he called:

'Under fire! Target right!'

This time, she moved swiftly and with intent, at one point rolling (the weapon protected in her body, as he had shown her) to the nearest (and best) firing point, where she missed with the first shot, realigned and struck with the second.

'Better. Keep low. Move on.'

She would find soon enough how coming ground would confound her.

While they were still in forgiving territory, he called her to account twice more. On the first occasion, she was undone by posture.

'Get your *bottom* down! Stay flat!'

He was not one to accept the peculiarities of the female form as excuse for incompetence (nor, he suspected, was she). On the second occasion, she did well: scorning the bait of a false crest, perceiving that she must move to the right in order to engage the target to her left – although she clipped the rim twice before she struck it plumb.

'Don't snatch at your shots.'

She nodded in acknowledgement.

'Move on.'

Now the terrain deteriorated slyly and he resolved to press her harder, to test what resource she had. He watched to see how long she would take to realise that she was among ditches and cracks; and the moment he was certain that she had spotted the ditch to her right, he called:

'Under fire!'

But he did not designate a target location.

She crouched to assess her situation. She was confronted by a dilemma. There was, on either side, a viable firing point, but she did not know from which direction she was under attack. In a moment, she wormed to the right – having discerned, presumably, that from that quarter she would have the better shot on either target. Then she remembered the ditch that lay in her path. She hesitated. He shouted:

'Move! You're under fire!' He counted loudly: 'Five! Six! Seven! Eight!'

She refused to be flustered. From rapid reassessment, she calculated that she could not, after all, cross the ditch without being seen. At once, she accepted the inferior firing point, moving left towards it. Whereupon, he shouted:

'Target right!'

He fancied he heard her snort at his awkwardness, but she found the correct firing position and struck the target with her first shot.

'Good. Move on.'

Now she uncovered her error. For the ditch, which undoubtedly she had thought to leave behind her, turned sharply back across her front beyond the next crest, spreading claws deeply into the face of an unexpectedly steep slope.

She drew back to consider her options – and brought herself immediate relief. For she quickly saw, Savage noted, that for all its implied exposure, she had come to the one place where she could leap the five-foot span of the ditch without being seen. She gathered herself to spring. What she failed to do was sufficiently to examine the terrain on the other side. While she was still in the air, he shouted:

'Under fire! Target right!'

Again, he thought he heard her snort. But then, in coming to ground, her boots skidded in scree and she plunged her left knee into the rock beneath. Seeking to cushion the impact, she jarred her elbow also. He shouted:

'*Move! Move!*'

He did not want her to yield to pain, by which for a moment she was possessed.

'Under fire!'

She must have seen to what extent the inviting firing point had betrayed her, skeletal as it would prove to be from her altered perspective.

'Target *right!*'

She thrust off venomously, scrabbling through the spoil and scrub –

'Don't put up dust!'

– her every action vivid with the rage she was experiencing. At the firing point, she took aim, the rifle butt too high: and for all that the recoil would be nothing to the earlier model, it should deliver a chastening jolt to an already bruised area.

He remained silent.

She squeezed the trigger, struck the target, dipped her head in anguish. He shouted:

'Under fire! Target left!'

She swung about, although fully exposed (which was correct) and fired repeatedly in rage (which was not) – four shots, dead centre – until he called:

'*Cease fire.*'

'Stand up.'

Her face was pinched and her breathing stiff when he came to her.

'Never waste ammunition. All you've got is what you carry.' She said nothing. 'Use your anger, don't let it use you. Lose your temper and you lose the battle.' She remained closed to him. He shouted: 'Nothing hurts! *Nothing!*'

She looked at him then and he turned away.

Why did she *anger* him so greatly?

Well, if she did not give up, he would not.

'Move on.'

At once, he said,

'Stop.'

Again he approached her.

'How many shots have you fired?' She recognised the significance immediately. 'How many rounds left in your magazine?' She looked inward, plainly vexed with herself. 'Always count! Maintain your maximum fire potential at all times.' He did not expect her actually to count, but a basic principle was involved. 'Change magazines.'

At once, she crouched, as he had taught her, in patent defiance of his overbearing manner. He admired her for it. Then he saw how newly-skinned palms were tacky on gun metal. He said,

'We could stop now.'

She looked at him.

'Why?'

He escalated the pressure on her drastically, switching targets, driving her onto fragmented ground, shouting:

'Target *lost*!'

– seeking at every turn to confound and disorient her, falling silent for longer than a minute, suddenly shouting:

'Target *behind*!'

But to every challenge she responded with dispatch, imagination and a mounting conviction.

Until she grew tired.

Mistakes crept in. She drummed her knee again, forgot her collar bone.

He pressed harder.

'*Move, move*! You're *under fire*!'

To emphasise the point, he fired rapidly into the ground not four feet from where she lay. She drove herself on, the struggle no longer between her will and his, but between her will and herself.

Until at last she foundered.

And he knew that he must bring the training to an end, for she never would. And he sought only that she should find what she could do, not what she could not. Failure now would be his.

He ran before her down the slope, savouring with what expertise she accommodated to the ground. As he traversed the front of the low ridge, he shouted:

'Target right!'

And then, flitting across the second face:

'Target left!'

He knew at once when the rifle was directed at him. All of his sensory acuity clamoured alarm. It cost him much not to go to ground and to respond in kind. He turned to look up the hill. She fired four shots within close range of his feet and then dispatched two rounds into the chalk face at his side. He shouted:

'Get up! Move on!' But the moment he saw that she had overcome the anchor of inertia, he called: 'Enough! Finish. Rest.'

He had been taught a lesson.

But he knew, too, that she had looked into his sensibility only by virtue of her own. She had *known* that he would feel the needle danger at his back. By looking into his mind, she had opened a window on her own. He had been right about her.

Then he became angry. Soon she would be lost to the Capital. For what purpose did he press her further than he had ever thought it worthwhile to press Sammy?

He mounted the slopes, angry with whatever it was in her that invoked havoc in him.

He was shocked when he saw her face.

She sat on a hummock, delivering rounds into her spare magazine – *maintaining her fire potential* – and she looked grey. He said,

'You did well.'

'Indeed?'

'Good as I've seen, first time.'

'Be careful, I may believe you.'

'You think I'd lie about that?'

She considered the proposition.

'About that, no.'

'Well, then.'

She changed magazines, tested the lock.

'Somewhat after the manner of a dog walking on his hind legs?'

The remark baffled him.

'What?'

She waved him away.

'No matter.'

He knew that he had been insulted, but not how. He said,

'*But.*'

'Ah.'

Then his attention was recalled to her palms.

'Show me your hands.'

She coiled them instinctively.

'They're fine.'

'Show me.'

Patches of glistering flesh were rimed about by grime. He said, 'Have you got a clean handkerchief?'

She pulled one from her fatigues. He withdrew a water bottle. 'Hold them out.'

She barely flinched when he clattered water on her wounds.

'Dry them. Sarah'll fix them, when you get in.'

In a little, she said,

'*But?*'

'When the time comes – which it will.' He knew in that moment, beyond doubt, that death lay in their path. 'You'll have to aim at another human being. Stay up yourself, make him go down. Win the fire fight. Kill him.' He looked at her then. 'I don't know if you can do that. No one does. I can show you *how* to do it –'

She said,

'I understand.'

'Do you?'

'. . . In my mind, I do.'

At least she knew there was a difference.

'Look, you can do this. You've got good hands. Good instincts –'

She smiled then.

'You enjoy this, don't you?'

'. . . What?'

She gestured down the hill.

'All of this.'

'It's what I do.'

'Is it what Cassie does?'

'. . . Mostly.'

Her training would not go as deep as Anne's. She said,

'She having had on-the-job training?'

'. . . What?'

'You killed them all. That's what she said. You *and she*, killed them all.'

'She was the one who got raped.'

'She's a thirteen-year-old girl – !'

'When it happens to you, you can decide!'

He was beginning to be annoyed. She looked away, made a curious sound of ambiguity and frustration.

'Perhaps it's as well we'll soon be at the Capital.'

'You can say that again.'

Now she mocked him.

'Oh dear. Do we spoil it for you, Mr Savage?'

'What?'

'Now that you have a world to your taste. Few civilians; and those there are, cowed and in need of your protection.'

He stared at her.

'You think I want this?'

'Why not? Mr Savage in his glory!'

'You stupid – !'

'Woman?'

He turned away, for fear that he might strike her. She said, 'Child?'

It was inconceivable to him that anyone could suppose he might glory in the loss of the very civilisation he was covenanted to uphold.

Or derive pleasure from the liquefying grotesques who haunted his consciousness. She said,

'We have always been slow to appreciate the benefits of destruction.'

He wanted to hurt her, as she had hurt him. But he would not grant her the victory. He said,

'Zeroing the weapon.'

He took her to his 'range', the relatively straight stretch of lane where it was possible to fire over a measured one hundred yards at a target fixed to an open gate. Her first group was low and left. When he had made the minor adjustment of sights necessary to accommodate to her eye relief and physical configuration and having tested her again, still he smarted. As they returned to the house, he said,

'Anyway, you'll be at the Capital soon, like you said. You'll be able to make all the decisions for both of you, then.'

She regarded him with a droll expression.

'I take it you are an unconscious ironist, Mr Savage?'

He did not understand her, but did not doubt that again he had been insulted.

Inside the house, Cassie exhibited jealousy; but Savage had lost patience with them all. The matter had been resolved with Madge's death.

He retreated to his fastness in the tower.

Perhaps it was his fault. He had allowed a hope, without possibility of fulfilment, to fester in the group for too long, from lack of courage to extirpate it.

He would do so now.

They ate at midday. With pre-dawn rising and much to do before light failed, they had taken to eating their main meal at noon and sleeping shortly after dusk. Whether they saw it or not, the sun governed their days.

At table, Alice said,

'You leave in the morning?'

Savage hesitated.

'Yes.'

Cassie said,

'We're going to the Capital.'

Sammy said,

'When will you be back?'

There it was. Before Savage could speak, Cassie said,

'You won't be coming back, will you, Mr Savage?'

Sarah was patronising: 'I hardly think that Mr Savage –'

Savage said,

'No.'

It was as simple a way as any to achieve his objective. Cassie muttered:

'See.'

The animosity between the two was undiminished. Alice said,

'. . . Never?'

'Never.'

He glanced at Martin. Sarah said,

'You'll be back.'

'No.'

Cassie said,

'He's staying at the Capital with us.'

Sarah laughed.

'Now I know there's nothing to worry about.'
Sammy said,
'What about us?'
'Come with me.'
At once, in a sharp tone, Sarah said,
'No.'
Alice said,
'Mebbe it would be best.'
Again, Sarah said,
'*No.*'
Alice, at least, seemed to have learned the lesson of Madge's death. Martin said,
'What if we don't come?'
'The Army will be here soon enough.'
Martin knew better than anyone the advantage to Savage in returning to the house. He said,
'How soon?'
Savage shrugged.
'A week, ten days.'
It would need to be before the rains came. Sarah said,
'I won't go with you, John. Not to that place.'
Cassie said,
'How can you stay here, on your own?'
Sarah was offensively disdainful.
'I don't remember that you were invited to comment.'
Sammy murmured:
'Sarah . . .'
Savage would not have the child attacked.
'This has nothing to do with her; it's my idea.'
'Really? What are you going to do – retire? Not even she can be that stupid.'
Indeed, she could not. But before Savage could address the danger, Anne said,
'Yours is not the only pain.'
Alice said,
'*That's enough!*'
Sarah scraped back from the table.
'I haven't the stomach for this.' She leaned over Savage. 'I'll

never go with you, John. Never. But when you come back. Which you will.'

'No.'

'I'll be ready.' She smiled over-brightly. 'I'm sure you've heard. Converts make the best zealots.'

She left the room. When Alice made as though to follow, Sammy said,

'Leave her.'

It was plain that he could no more resolve Sarah's distress than he could his own. Cassie said,

'She hates me.'

Alice reached out a hand.

'She's having a bad time, that's all.'

But the child drew back.

'No. She hates me. Because it happened to me, too.'

She was watching Savage now with a deepening suspicion. He said,

'We'd better get out there soon.'

Alice said,

'That's it, then? Over.'

'Yes.'

Sammy said,

'I always hoped, you know, there was a chance.'

'No. There was never a chance.'

Bitterly, Alice said,

'Why train us, then?'

'Defence.'

But even this was not entirely true; more than ever, he regretted his compunction regarding Madge. Alice said,

'I can't leave here now, not the way she is.'

Sammy said,

'Nor I.'

'I understand that.'

Martin remained expressionless. Sammy said,

'When must we decide?'

'Tomorrow morning.'

Alice, sharply:

'We en't worth more time than that?'

114

Martin said,

'It isn't time, Alice, it's timing.'

'Oh aye?'

When he saw Anne watching, as though she had some special knowledge of him, Savage rose abruptly. To Cassie, he said,

'Come on. Training.'

Alice said,

'Oh, let her eat up. Why not? Last Supper.'

He wondered if she knew what she said.

Cassie, in training, was as he expected. A stubborn, effortful determination to get it right. Yet if she lacked Anne's fluency, as a shot she was remarkable. She could not miss. Throughout zeroing and a modified tactical phase her score was flawless.

And she had the ability to kill.

But she was wary of him; mistrustful. And when they came to rest, he said,

'What's wrong, Cassie?'

As though he did not know. She looked down the hill.

'Nothing.'

'Oh, come on.'

She would not look at him.

'You're not going to stay with us, are you?'

He hesitated.

'. . . I said I wouldn't betray you.'

He hated to lie to her.

'I won't stay there.'

'You said that.'

Abruptly, she rose, looked at the house and then out over the valley.

'I won't stay at that place. Or any place.' She took a handful of stilted paces, as though she were a bird on the brink of flight. 'Not *inside*. *Trapped*, like that.'

He was shocked. He saw suddenly what he should, perhaps, have seen earlier. That in one important respect she was like him. She had become habituated to the outside. She suffered the same suffocating dread of confinement as he did.

He was filled with apprehension. To betray her would be to betray himself. He said,

'Look. I won't betray you.'

But he did not know how it could be otherwise. He felt airless, turned to stone.

Abruptly, the child looked up the hill.

'*She'll* make you.'

Looking up, he saw Sarah, in fatigues and carrying a rifle, looking down.

'My turn,' she said. Beyond, Sammy stood guard. Savage seized the child's shoulders.

'She won't. Cassie, she won't.'

He saw that his sincerity communicated itself to the child, yet still she looked no less bewildered by their predicament than himself. He said,

'Tell Sammy you're to boil out your rifle. Anne, too. He'll show you what to do.'

In a moment, she nodded and ran up the hill, giving Sarah a wide berth. When she spoke to Sammy, he put an arm about her shoulders, as though glad to comfort someone.

Sarah looked down, with her mildly unbalanced smile.

'If I am to go it alone, I've much to catch up on.'

He said,

'They won't let you get away. They'll kill you first.'

She was amused.

'I rather think they'll kill us all, in the end, John.'

He saw no point to argument.

'Which rifle is that?'

'The one you tried to force – oops, issue to me before. We'll probably need to blow the cobwebs off.'

But she did not smile and neither did he.

'Let's begin.'

He took her through the basics: maintenance, aiming, firing, zeroing; movement. Her relationship to the weapon was one of unsympathy and the expression of contained rage. When he had done all that he thought practical to do, he said:

'In any meaningful sense, this is a waste of time.'

She smiled.

'It may be, John, that I know you better than you know yourself.'

He was weary of people possessed of that opinion: he had, besides, an appointment with Martin which might require daylight. He said,

'Time to get in.'

As they retraced their steps, she said,

'I don't want you to worry, John. I shall practise assiduously, while you are away.'

Martin had a 'workshop' in the old game larder behind the kitchen and a second bench in one of the alcoves in the cellars. It was to this that he and Savage now withdrew. As they crossed the flagstones, Savage said,

'What are you using?'

'Toy cars.'

'. . . You're serious?'

'See for yourself. Radio-controlled toy cars.'

They placed the lamps they were carrying at either end of the workbench and set down their rifles beside them.

At the centre of the work surface, a flat, rectangular tin box, approximately the size of a cigar box, had been set up on edge and was supported by four spindly struts (cut from umbrella spokes) so that its larger surfaces faced left and right along the workbench, as though it were a miniature billboard.

Savage had given the tin to Martin to represent the Claymore AP mine (which similarly stood on scissor legs) and had asked him to adapt it, if possible, for truly remote radio operation.

Beside the 'mine' were two small plastic boxes, neither larger than a cigarette packet. One plainly had been purpose-manufactured in the past. It had a telescopic aerial in the top, a toggle joystick in the face and was, presumably, the transmitter (and original controller). The other, equally plainly, had been bodged together by Martin, using a 13 amp socket box and was, Savage supposed, the receiver unit.

On the top edge of the 'mine' a mini lamp holder had been mounted, with a torch bulb in situ and two wires depending from it.

Savage viewed the contrivance dubiously.

'How does it work?'

'Well, normally you fire the mine by sending an electrical impulse down two command wires which connect here and here' – he touched the dangling wires – 'where your triggering device is.'

Savage understood him to mean that the lamp holder represented the location of the detonator well and that the wires supposedly trailed from the blasting cap, which would be inserted into it.

'Go on.'

'Well, what we've got *here*' – he took up the receiver unit – 'is a little gubbins that will fire a pulse by remote control when it gets a signal from that.' He indicated the transmitter.

'How?'

'Inside is a battery; the receiver, servo motor and actuator arm from the original model. What *I've* done is to adapt these components so that, when you toggle the joystick on that thing' – he pointed to the transmitter – 'the actuator arm in here' – he patted his artefact – 'will deflect left or right, it doesn't matter which, and make with a contact which will complete the internal circuitry and blow the mine.'

The big man was not without pride, but Savage's dubiety continued.

'Show me.'

'First off, you've got to attach this to the back of the mine.'

'How?'

'Velcro.'

Martin turned the receiver unit over to show the patch adhering to its face – which would mate, Savage now recognised, with a similar patch on the rear of the mine. Martin united them, testing the bond with a firm tug.

'Simple as that.'

Savage did not trust velcro (although he had no reason not to) any more than he trusted zips, unless there were buttons, too. He resolved to use gaffer tape in addition. He said,

'It'll be raining.'

'You said. Makes velcro favourite.'

'What next?'

'You do whatever you do to arm the mine, then you connect your leads, here and here.'

In the top of the unit were two knurled screw contacts. Martin wrapped the bared end of one trail wire around each, screwing the collars down. He said,

'Next, you raise the antenna.'

On the receiver, this was a single strand of tempered wire, which sprang upright when released from its rubber band tether.

'Finally, you switch the thing on.'

In the back of the unit was a ridged nub which travelled in a slot. When Martin moved it across, there came from within the box a faint grunt, as though it were tensing for action. Savage said,

'And when I want to fire it?'

Martin took up the transmitter.

'You pull up the aerial' – which he did. 'Switch on.' He showed Savage the similar nub in the side of the controller, which he also activated. 'Then, whichever way you toggle the joystick' – he demonstrated – 'up she goes.'

With each tilt of the stick, there came from the box an intestinal growl and the lamp on top of the mine winked, to indicate the passage of current.

Savage's caution persisted. He took the controller and experimentally 'exploded' the mine himself.

'What range have I got on this?'

'Hard to say. Thirty yards? Forty? I can't test it outside.'

Savage had early warned Martin of the constant watch maintained by Other Force, at the time of their mutual discovery of the trap door. He set down the transmitter.

'Have we got two of these?'

He had just two Claymores.

'No. But we've got two of *these*.'

From under the bench, the big man produced a second receiver unit, this time built into a thermostat cover, as though he were a cook showing a dish he had prepared earlier. He said,

'Fortunately, they're on the same frequency.'

'So, if I set out the mines together, when I fire one, I fire both?'

Martin touched the transmitter.

'This may be directional, to some extent. Try pointing it. You've nothing to lose.'

Except my life, Savage thought. But when the first mine went off, the element of surprise would be lost. Besides, if ever his life came to depend solely on the mines, it would be forfeit.

Martin misinterpreted his silence.

'They'll work, Savage. Trust me.'

'I do.'

It was the simple truth. He did not recollect harvesting these particular toys; perhaps Sammy had. Martin said,

'Will I put velcro on the mines, then?'

'Yeah.'

He could make his final choice later. In a moment, the other said,

'You'll want them for morning . . .?'

'Why not?'

But Martin was more perceptive than that. Even if Savage took the mines now, he could not take the missile launchers. A return to the house was all but inevitable. He said,

'Let's get rid of the bodies, before nightfall.'

The fact was, it was to Savage's advantage to have survivors remain at the house until he had made good his escape.

The Boss at the Capital (whoever he was) would be determined to capture the group intact, because of the skills they harboured. It was for that reason that he had placed Other Force in the field. The members of the group were his priority.

But for The Other – the name by which, in his mind, Savage designated the leader of Other Force – Savage was the priority. Taking care of family business.

Yet, so long as there were survivors at the house, he must concern himself with them, too. His attention would be divided.

Once the Army came, or the survivors left, he could put his concentration entirely where he wished it to be: on Savage.

By virtue of their shared discovery of the trap door, Martin had become increasingly involved in Savage's preparations; and, for all their reciprocal taciturnity, Savage well knew that the big man had discerned for himself the fundamentals of Savage's predicament.

Although it was true that Savage could quit his ground at any time and from any location, it was overwhelmingly the case that the house offered the best prospect of success: for he must open a gulf between himself and Other Force, so rapidly and so deep, that pursuit would be pointless. For the Boss at the Capital, such a decision would be made purely on political grounds; so long as he had the members of the group, he would give up Savage. But for The Other, Savage knew, no distance would be great enough. He would pursue relentlessly. It was personal; family. Only impossibility would defeat him and he would not acknowledge that.

The reality was that, with the mines and missile launchers, Savage was seeking advantage in battle. But if ever he fought that battle, he would lose it.

No other outcome was possible.

As he and Martin manhandled the hay cart to rest beside the farmhouse, Savage said,

'I may come back.'

The big man nodded.

'No need of anyone else to know.'

'Might be best.'

When they had loaded the bodies of Sarah's persecutors onto the plastic-sheeted floor of the cart, they hauled it along the lane and up the diagonal track to the crest of the ridge, where they turned away from the house and trundled a further hundred yards to the modest opening to a deep shaft in the rock, which had become their graveyard. It was surrounded by a coronet of barbed wire, presumably to protect children from the lesser dangers of the past. They had never successfully plumbed its depths.

When Martin had spoken the prayers that he always insisted on, they let slip the bodies, one by one; and after them, the weapons and ammunition earmarked for disposal.

Savage was conscious of Other Force, watching them.

They turned the cart back towards the house. Alice and Cassie were chivvying in the last of their stock for night. Dusk was almost on them. Savage said,

'You'd better be ready to take command here.'

'Aye.'

'I'll make it formal, if you like.'

'No. I'll know what to do, when the time comes.'

Before they reached the stable entrance, Martin said,

'How about I patrol the house tonight? You'll need your sleep for morning.'

It was a mild enough and well-intentioned test of altered status and Savage accepted it with a nod.

'I'll relieve you at 0300 hours.'

He calculated that if he went 'to sleep' late enough, three hours was the limit of his tolerance of confinement in the tower.

Sammy turned from the tower window.

'. . . I don't know how to help her, Savage.'

' . . . You're not talking to an expert.'

Sammy smiled awkwardly:

'I love her, you see.' Savage said nothing.

'You'd think a man my age . . .' Savage supposed him to be forty. 'But it never happened before.' He looked at Savage. 'She's the one.' Savage acknowledged what he did not comprehend. 'If I can't help her now . . .' Sammy made a gesture, as though his fingers let slip hope.

Savage said, 'You couldn't have prevented this.'

'Then what use was anything we did?'

The unanswerable question. You can train them, but you cannot live it for them. He said,

'I'd better get down. Stand to.'

'Yes. I don't mean to embarrass you.'

But Savage was not so much embarrassed as under-equipped. It was as well, he thought again, that the group had no further pretensions to viability.

In the kitchen, he said,

'Stand to.'

To Anne: 'Take the tower, with Sammy.' To Cassie: 'Patrol the upper floors with Alice. Don't forget your rifles.' To Martin: 'Ground floor and door.' When the others had dispersed, he said to Sarah: 'I want you to make up a couple of packets – you know the sort of thing; medicines, drugs, emergency rations – for Cassie and Anne to take to the Capital with them.'

She gave him the look of one who believes that, no matter how many such egregious offerings he made, they would never outweigh the betrayal he intended. But at least she carried a weapon now and wore fatigues.

He slipped into the darkling night and Martin closed the plug behind him.

Savage ghosted down among the shadows, under the fold of the southern approaches and west along the tuck until he came to the fall of the ridge.

He knew that his progress was tracked by Other Force: and that they were aware of his awareness. It was part of the inevitable interaction between them – born of shared training, shared instincts and (once) shared aims.

He did not operate to the height of his capability. He allowed himself to be glimpsed. He made no attempt to locate their lying-up point or forward positions. Of course, he did nothing crassly inadequate; but if he could unfocus, even by a small degree, their assessment of his potential, one day it might serve him.

As a deception plan, it was puny: but then, the true deception lay elsewhere.

They were close. He sensed their acuity engage with his own. Gave no sign, moved on, patrolled north.

Down across the lane and east towards the bulk of Low Wood.

He judged Other Force to be four in number; a standard patrol. This was based on perceived level of activity; not least, when they shadowed Sammy and himself out along the Main Route and back via the Southern Forest and The Bottoms.

He believed them to be a self-formulated unit, extemporised from the remnants of other patrols on ops at the time of the Event. But although, as such, there would be no long-term personal commitment among the members, there would be an ingrained loyalty to the Regiment and to ideals which would leave no weakness to be exploited.

He stalked the rim of the copse and mounted the slopes to the crest again.

Other Force had manifested within forty-eight hours of word of his activities having first been carried to the Capital. No doubt, they had passed a 'survivor' through the house since then, to take a close look at him, the interior and the group which, unnoticed by himself, had grown up about him: but he had prevented penetration by accepting no volunteers who had not joined within the first ten days, before even the earliest refugees known to him could have reached the Capital.

Having completed his sweep, he settled against the swell of the southern slopes to watch the house from the south.

He thought, They can see me now. Whichever of the two in the tower, Sammy or Anne, has the night sight. And The Other.

What manner of man is he? How good?

It was a source of perverse pride to Savage that, notwithstanding night vision equipment, no member of the group had sighted a member of Other Force.

(He had himself eyeballed two near the Southern Forest, having misdirected them for that purpose, but had recognised neither.

Not that friendship – had he had friends – would serve him now.)

Who is he? Do I know him?

(It would make no difference.)

Savage had spent as much time seeking that man's mind as the other, doubtless, had devoted to his. He believed that he knew how The Other would dispose his force when the time came. But as to the man himself . . .

He had the sense of a man yearning to be free about his own occasions.

But he might, perhaps, merely be looking into himself.

He believed that he had two advantages, of which The Other was ignorant. Specialised knowledge of high-country weather. And a trap door. If, in either particular, he was mistaken, then he was already dead.

But the same might be true of them all.

Sarah stood in the medical bay, between the armoury and Martin's workbench. On the table before her were the packages he had requested, already wrapped in plastic, and a large weatherproof medical pannier. As he crossed to resupply his bergen with the items expended since his last visit to the house, she patted the pannier and said,

'Don't worry, John, I haven't disturbed it. I am a believer now.'

He had permitted the pannier to be prepared at the time of his weakness (as he had the packs) under pressure from Madge: and Sarah had participated in the process with the irony of one who had not yet forgiven him for refusing to release drugs in the early days to be 'wasted' on the dying – rather than from the conviction to which she now laid claim. He said nothing. She said,

'The rifle is a great prophylactic. You are my doctor now.'

'. . . If you say so.'

She touched the pannier again.

'Shall you be taking it with you?'

There was mockery as well as pain in this.

'I don't need it.'

She chuckled.

'No, I believe you could exist on air.'

'It's what I do.'

'And walk on water?'

He made no response to this, having none. She moved a few paces off.

'My husband would be amused.'

'Oh?'

This was not a person of whom Savage had heard, and he had no wish to now. She said,

'All my life, I have loathed imperfection. I was a termagant in the operating room. Put the fear of God into housemen and visiting specialists alike.'

'I'm sure that isn't true.'

He was certain that it was.

'A colleague told me once that I was a good cutter, but a bad doctor, because I lacked humanity. But there were few female surgeons. I had to be better than the best.'

When she did not continue, Savage said,

'People don't matter.'

He meant the opinion of others, to which he had never been subject. She said,

'Richard was a congeries of imperfections. God knows why I married him.' She smiled bleakly. 'Perhaps I thought some of it would rub off on me.' Savage waited. 'When I removed him from my life, I told him that it was no worse than the evacuation of a small quantity of foetal jelly. That was cruel.'

'Yes, it was.'

'But I had come to dread the smell of fear on him.'

This was a sentiment with which Savage could sympathise. Sarah broke from reverie.

'It seems that, after all, I'd have brought him joy, at the end.'

Savage was not acute in these matters, but even he could not miss the parallel that was being drawn between her present condition and that of imperfection. He said,

'Look, this isn't us.' He touched his body. 'It's like torture. They can hurt you, but they can't touch you. What makes you you is always yours. No one can take that from you. Not ever.'

She smiled at him then.

'But John. It *feels* as though they can.'

She appeared suspended between anguish and detachment. It was like watching an icon bleed. He said,

'Sarah, trust me in this.'

Abruptly, she reverted to briskness.

'And you, John. When you return. Trust me. I shall not embarrass you.'

She took up her rifle and left.

He was unsure what to make of her, except that her unstable state rendered her unreliable.

When they had finished supper, which Cassie transparently prolonged, Savage said,

'Bed.'

Alice said,

'Oh, let her stay up a while.'

'No.'

Anne rose:

'I'm going up, too. I'm whacked.'

Knowing how Cassie would fear reacquaintance with the night, Savage said,

'Take this.'

He handed her a lamp from the table. She said,

'You'll come and say goodnight?'

'I've got stuff for you.'

By the time Anne and the child had left, Sarah, too, had slipped away, Martin had gone to the cellar and Sammy to the animals. Savage gathered together the packets of supplies and extra clothing, which he meant to give to the women. From the sink, Alice said,

'If you harm the child, I'll not forgive you.'

Savage retired to the tower room, where he waited what he took to be an appropriate interval, before descending to the bedroom below.

The child sat at the head of the bed, in dressing-gown and pyjamas, with Anne, in a housecoat, at the foot. Savage said,

'I've got clean vests, shirts and socks here. Leave the dirty ones in the corridor, Alice'll wash them for store.' When the child made to scramble from the bed, he said, 'You get into bed. Anne'll do it.'

The woman took the small bundle of garments. He handed her in addition the two plastic-wrapped packages.

'These are extra supplies, drugs, that sort of thing, for when you get to the Capital.' He heard his words as they did, added quickly: 'When *we* do.' But the child looked up sharply; and Anne was dry, when she said:

'Thank you.'

Cassie said,

'Have you got yours?'

'Sure. In my kit. Always.'

She nodded, wormed under the covers.

He would have to be careful. She was alert to any hint of defection. He crossed to check that the shutters had been properly secured and that the fire was out. While Anne added items to Cassie's pack and substituted clothing, he moved to the girl, who appeared younger than ever in the great bed, her wasted frame barely displacing the blankets by which she was covered. He said,

'Time for sleep.'

She nodded.

On the bedside cabinet, the accessories of an older woman had yielded to those of a child. There was a bar of chocolate, a candle in a holder, a comb, boiled sweets, a torch, water, a Snoopy toy. Savage lit the candle, extinguished the butane lamp and carried it to the dressing table, where he set it down. When he returned to the girl, the candle flame put tottering shadows up the wall.

'You'll need to blow this out before you sleep.'

She nodded.

He sat on the edge of the bed.

'If you need me in the night, I'll come at once.'

Again, she nodded.

He checked that the torch beside her worked.

'Well . . .'

She said,

'Can I have a light?'

Not a lamp. Not a torch. He sighed. He did not want this to become a habit. But he took the beta light from about his neck and, when she leaned up, draped the cord about hers.

'Thank you.'

She lay back, clutching the holder.

'I'll want it back.'

She nodded.

He said,

'Goodnight.'

Before he could rise, she had reached up, kissed his cheek, blown out the candle and vanished into all but darkness.

He was shocked.

Worse, he was affronted.

He snatched up his rifle and made for the dimly limned doorway. Anne said,

'A moment, please, Mr Savage.'

'Outside.'

He stormed the corridor, in a rage.

Rubbed at the wet patch where she had touched him.

Wiped his hand violently on the front of his smock, as though he could wipe affection from himself, as he would horror.

He felt violated.

He knew that he should not feel such things. But he was as he was.

He would not change for her.

Such light as permeated the corridor came from Anne's room.

When she emerged from Cassie's bedroom, she indicated her door
and said,

'In here?'

'Why not?'

A lamp stood on the dressing table. The woman crossed to lay
rifle and extra clothing on the bed. Hefting the packet of supplies,
she said,

'How do you propose to contrive this . . . parting of the ways, Mr
Savage?'

'Quickly.'

'I imagine.' She tossed the package down. 'And, certainly, the
pay-off is generous.'

'You're getting what you want, aren't you? The child will be safe
at the Capital with you.'

And, to judge from her dread of confinement, miserable, he
thought. The woman said,

'Life is full of these ironies.'

He pointed at the supplies.

'They may give you some kind of edge. Something to bargain
with.'

He did not know what the Capital would offer, but there were
always opportunities for trade. She said,

'I have grasped the point, Mr Savage.'

'Okay. If she wakes, call me.'

He would in any event know. She said,

'We'll try not to disturb you.'

'Disturb me.'

She said,

'As you were kind enough to observe, I have had some experience
in these matters.'

'If she needs someone in the night, it'll be me.'

He felt disinclined to explain why. She said,

'Don't you think the sooner she learns *not* to need you, the better
– given what the future holds?'

But this was a path too steep to climb. He said,

'Do what you're told.'

And made for the door.

'Very well.'

As though the disregarding of good advice were only to be expected of him. Yet, when he was on the point of leaving, she said,

'I did not mean to add to your difficulties with her. In so far as I have, I apologise.'

He contemplated her.

'Just do the job on the road. Five AM.'

At Cassie's doorway, he paused. From the bed, came an over-elaborate sound of heavy breathing. He said,

'You're snoring.'

'I'm not!'

Her voice smiled. He hoped that the night, too, would smile on her.

Martin was waiting in the tower room, shutters lowered and lamp lit.

'I've put up the mines for you.' He indicated the issue pouches on the map table. 'The odd bits and bobs are in the bag.'

This referred to the 'clacker' generators, coils of firing wire and test sets normally issued with the weapon, which he had secured in a plastic bag.

Savage realised that he had already decided to rely on Martin's 'technology'. He could not hope to hide firing wires from men of the calibre of Other Force – least of all in the terrain in which he anticipated fighting them. His sole advantage lay in the fact that they would not expect the mines to be radio activated.

He inspected the devices meticulously, because he knew that it would please the big man (each component had been neatly 'weatherproofed' with improvised gaskets and gaffer tape). And he made great play of discarding the supplied firing systems.

'Won't need them.'

Martin said,

'There's fresh batteries in the kit and spare in the pouch.'

'You've done well. Thanks.'

The big man said,

'I wish I were going with you.'

'I know.'

For all his own solitary nature and the other's lack of deep training, Savage would not have scorned his company. Martin said,

'Well. Three AM.'

'Three AM.'

When he had checked and tested every aspect of his equipment, weapons and supplies; and had reviewed his routes and objectives for the morrow; and had thought of the child and betrayal; and had remembered Madge and had mourned her; and had lifted the shutters and looked into darkness; and had paced; and had listened ceaselessly for Cassie's cry in the night, Savage acknowledged that he had exhausted every legitimate source of delay and that he should attempt sleep, for in the morning he must work.

He melted down the stairs, peed at an oblique angle to the porcelain, so as not to reveal his presence, poured from the sluice bucket with equal caution and fled, as he had come, a shade.

Wake in thirty minutes (and all will be well).

Forces closed on him.

He came bolt upright, repressing his breathing, the room pulsing about him.

Alright, then.

Wake in twenty minutes (and all will be well).

This time it was Cassie who clamped a bony suffocating articulation.

He was on his feet, sweeping his area of proscription.

Straining for the child.

As though the invasion by demons of his own mind might grant conduit into hers.

The fancifulness of this notion angered him.

But he knew that he must rest.

And that he could not defeat this enemy with anger. Only by stealth.

Very well. Ten minutes.

And so he boxed around the night.

Slipping enemies on either hand.

Finding his thoroughfares.

Harvesting sleep where he could.

By two AM he had had enough. He went through his rituals of preparation and, before three, intercepted Martin on his rounds in the hall.

'Get your sleep now. Rise at five. Leave by six.'

'Right. Alice is just raking down the range.'

From the kitchen came the subdued clump of metal on metal.

It did not enter Savage's mind that Alice might be weeping. As he crossed to sup from the stew which she had always on the range, he said,

'Morning.'

'Morning.'

It was only when he turned, at the moment that she lifted the top aperture cover to shoot coal from a scoop, that he saw the tracks of her tears briefly illuminated. His instinct was to say nothing. Perhaps he hesitated too long on the brink of another betrayal, for she looked at him in an aggressive manner and said,

'*What?*'

'. . . You alright?'

'Why wouldn't I be?'

She banged down the scoop, took up an iron and probed the deeps of the fire with it. He moved to fill his water bottles at the kitchen pump. She dropped the front of the range and agitated the innards, sparking the room with intermittent gleams. Then she closed the apertures again, the fire gate and the top plate. Only the partly open draw shutter cast light across the floor. He had restored the second of his bottles to his belt kit and was on the point of making good his escape, when she said,

'I never said goodbye to him.' Her husband. 'Or to them.' Her children. 'That were your fault.'

He thought, It's been a long time coming.

'He wanted to spare you.'

'I know that.'

'That's why he sent you for water.'

'*I know that!*'

The thing that had been her husband had clawed at Savage's arm, *Help us*, a vile malodour issuing from his gape; had sought to support the weapon, to share the burden, that had dispatched what had been her children; had been, in monstrosity, undiminished of humanity.

She had come, splay-legged, letting fall the bucket.

What have you done?

Had pushed past him, defying reason.

He said now:

'In all you did, you said goodbye.'

Meaning that in their life together, they had honoured one another. But he had not words. She was a dark mass at the rail. She said,

'It should have been me did what you did.'

'No.'

'But I couldn't have done it for them.'

'No.'

In a moment she came and, to his surprise, held him.

'God go with you, Savage.'

'And you.'

He stood in embarrassed proximity to her. She stepped back, touched his cheek.

'Have a care what you do.'

He understood that he had been forgiven. But that was a matter of interest to her, not to him.

At five AM he woke the woman.

'It's morning.'

'*Morning?*'

She startled up, giving of herself an intimate smell, which he felt a thief for taking.

'One hour. Be ready.'

The child was already awake. When he lit the lamp, she said,

'Good morning, sir.'

'Good morning.'

She came from the bed.

'I slept like a log.'

'Good.'

He was forewarned; and this time, when she attempted to

embrace him, he stood his ground, so that she was obliged to kiss what she could reach, his shoulder. He said,

'One hour. Eat your breakfast. Go to the lavatory. Fresh water in your bottles. Be ready.'

'Yes, sir.'

Stand to.

The 'hidden exit', of which Other Force was aware.

Unlike the 'trap door', this had offered itself by implication. In the eastern chamber of the cellars, just below ceiling height, there was an iron door set in the stonework – which could only be coincident, Savage had inferred, with the service track outside. Indeed, when he had examined the external wall, he had found the door to be all but obliterated by the variegated creepers which clad the lower part of the eastern elevation.

At night he had slipped out and had meticulously cut through each trunk and branch, while leaving the scrub adherent to metal and stone, until he had freed the door to operate (noiselessly on oiled hinges) while remaining camouflaged when shut.

He had not expected to deceive Other Force. But it was a functioning aperture and they would have to cover it. For this reason he had done nothing to subdue the copse to which it gave immediately across the narrow track. If he could maintain the deception, then effectively he might reduce Other Force from four to three at a crucial time.

He passed through the opening now and Sammy shot the bolts soundlessly at his back.

Savage experienced a surge of gratification to be free of the house and in his element again. He crouched at the foot of the wall to tune in. Then he tipped across the track and into the trees, where his arrival was so delicate that it barely disturbed the creatures newly returned to the underbrush.

Abruptly he recognised that one of Other Force was *all but within arm's reach*.

But no move came.

Had the man been caught off his ground? At *dawn*? Never.

Was it mockery? Provocation?

An attempt to communicate?

Something . . . personal?

Savage moved on, settled to watch day come.

And as it breached, he realised that some significant movement had taken place during the night. More than ever, the sky was fibrous and *low*; the air fustian; the light glaucous. Their world had changed again.

Savage sensed that, in her motions now, nature came on faster than his capacity to outrun her.

Breakfast was not protracted. In farewell, Alice, who did not expect to see him again, was sombre. Martin had grown visibly in stature. Sarah, behind the smile, was falling free. And Sammy, at a loss how to hold her

Not for the first time, Savage wondered whether, after all, survival was merely an illusion; and that those who remained were simply taking longer to die than those who were gone.

The Main Route

WHEN they were clear of the house Savage brought them to a halt.

Inspection for task.

He made them jump up and down; adjusted straps; had them take off and open their packs. To Cassie, he said,

'You still got that stuff coming out of you?'

'It's not so bad now.'

'What are you doing about it?'

Anne said,

'Sanitary towels.'

'Show me.'

Anne exhibited disdain but the child dug into her pack readily enough. The folded pads reminded Savage of other dressings for other wounds.

'Is this enough?'

Anne said,

'I'm carrying spare.'

He returned the plastic packet to the child.

'Pack them nearer the top.'

'Yes, sir.'

To Anne:

'Hands.'

She proffered them with some reluctance. The blisters were tinted with some kind of tincture (presumably applied by Sarah) and in two places protected by plasters, but they were acceptably dry.

'Fresh water?'

Both nodded.

'Weapons.'

He inspected their rifles, the loading of their magazines and that their selector levers were correctly set to safe. Finally, he contemplated Cassie. But he saw, from the involuntary lifting of her hand to her breast, that she knew he was about to ask for the beta light. He said,

'When we get there.'

Her relief was great. He said,

'Pay attention. This isn't a democracy. It's a fighting patrol.'

Remembering past patrols and his vanished comrades, the words mocked him. But he had deployed less promising material than these two. Nor did their gender trouble him. On the columns south, it had been women, rather than men, who had proved the strength.

Besides, he had so far abused standard operating procedures in the service of civilians, that the Gods of War could hardly find worse to hold against him now. He said,

'You will do as I say. Immediately and without question.'

The child said,

'Yes, sir.'

Anne nodded. At least she was not his enemy in this.

'We'll patrol with me up front. Cassie in the middle. Anne at the rear. We cover one another at all times. We maintain all round watch. We maintain eye contact at all times.'

They nodded.

'If we make a contact, you go to ground, to nearest cover. Stay there. Don't get involved. It's my job to deal with it.'

Anne made as though she might object, but remained silent. Cassie said,

'Yes, sir.'

'If you lose eye contact, but you're safe, stay where you are. I'll find you.'

Again, they nodded.

'Two more things. On the Main Route, nothing is what it seems. *Trust no one*. Secondly, whatever you see, it's nothing to do with us. Don't get involved. It's their war, not ours.' If you can call a clearance a war, he thought. 'Our job is to get to the pick-up point, without anyone ever knowing we were there.'

The woman stirred, as though she had noticed his error; but the child merely said,

'Yes, sir.'

'For the first two days, we'll be in high ground. We rest once each hour for five minutes.' On the columns, he had permitted longer periods of rest, but he believed these women to be capable of a stiffer pace than that: he could always modify his intentions. 'At midday, we break for a light meal. Forty minutes. Main meal at dusk. We should achieve our day's objective by four PM. Any questions?'

Anne said,

'How long – to reach the Capital?'

Was she seeking to redress his mistake? He shrugged:

'Five days.'

– to reach the place, which inadvertently he had referred to as the 'pick-up point', where he could be rid of them. He looked at their altered sky. He had not five days now – never mind the time it would take him to return to the house.

The prospect of failure galled him.

'Let's move.'

For the first hour, he chivvied and harried them. But it rapidly became apparent that he had command of a disciplined force. Whenever he called a practice 'contact', Anne unerringly chose the optimum location, from which she could cover Cassie and maintain eye contact with her. And Cassie – perhaps, in unconscious competition with Anne – accommodated her angular body with increasing fluency to the ground. He might not choose to lead them into battle, but he did not disdain to be of their company.

On the hour, he said:

'Five minutes. Rest your load. Don't drink yet. Maintain all round watch.'

They were in the high ground between the Main Route to the east and the receding Bottoms to the west. He meant to remain in these accommodating hills until they reached a feature called The Cut – beyond which the height declined into a plain so rugged that he planned to avoid it, if he could. Depending on conditions along the Main Route, he hoped to lead them at that point onto the Route itself or even into the river meadows beyond – although these, with their availability of fresh water and small game, offered a prospect as attractive to the Scavengers as to themselves.

The women sat with their packs resting on hummocks behind them and watching outward. He said,

'Drink now. A small amount. And change boots.'

There was time enough to wear in the boots by degrees and each woman had been soundly shod when he had found her (to which footwear they now returned).

By midday, they were approaching the site designated for their meal break and Savage was pleased with progress. He signed the others to ground and moved forward to clear the position.

On the crest of a modest ridge before them was a cluster of open pens, their stone walls tumbled down in places and cast about; but the location was such that it offered visibility in every direction and, having swept the ridge and scanned the surrounding landscape, Savage drew the women to him.

The pens were associated with a small farmhouse tucked in a shallow valley some half mile ahead.

'Take off your packs and kit. Rest completely. Sleep, if you want. We eat in fifteen minutes.'

The child needed no further urging. Within moments, she was spreadeagled like a starfish.

'I'm *whacked*.'

But it was the woman who looked the more weary. Of course, she lacked the child's youth and her experience of the outside. Concerned that she might allow pride to inhibit her from necessary rest, Savage discarded his own load and, sitting back against a wall, pretended to close his eyes. It was not long, he noted, before the woman adopted a like pretence. Cassie said,

'The sky doesn't move now.'

Anne looked in her direction.

'What, darling?'

'The clouds. Like they used to.'

'They will.'

'Do you think so, Mr Savage?'

'Why not?'

But the world was so out of sorts he had no more certainty. Cassie said,

'We'll see the sun today.'

'Maybe.'

A tear had been developing in the lowered overcast from which a lozenge of rusted light now depended, although it did not reach the ground. Savage had found that, no matter where he placed himself, such flaws never quite offered a view into the vault of heaven. Anne said,

'The wonder of youth.'

Mouth agape, Cassie was fast asleep.

'She's learned the lesson.'

'Which lesson?'

'Always sleep when you can.'

After a moment, she said,

'And is that a lesson you have learned, Mr Savage?'

The question was either unpleasantly informed or fortuitously apt. He rose.

'Take your chance.'

He made a sweep. No more pretence. In a little, he came to stir Cassie with his boot.

'Wake up.'

She emerged with the vivacity of spring.

'Was I asleep?'

'Perish the thought.'

This she found hilarious. He distributed food: biscuits, chocolate, boiled sweets. Cassie said,

'Not biscuits again?'

And Anne:

'I can't say my palate's stimulated, either.'

'You'll eat what I tell you. When I tell you. Never stop eating. No matter how little you feel like it. You go down quicker than you think.'

The woman nodded, as though it were reasonable that he should instruct them in this fashion. The child said,

'Yes, sir.'

He made a brew. When they had finished eating, he made them

pick the site clean of all evidence of their passing, waste wrappers being stowed in their packs.

'Never leave sign.'

And then:

'Anyone want to pee?'

Cassie made play of hopping on one leg and clenching her thighs.

'Me, me.'

Smiling, Anne agreed. He said,

'Ladies, this end. Gents, that.'

It was while they were buckling on their loads that there came, at the edge of their silent world, a familiar but unexpected sound.

'Isn't that gunfire?'

'Get down. Spread out. Wait here.'

He patrolled forward, listening, assessing. The vicious popple was relatively distant, in the vicinity of the small farm, he thought.

It was inconceivable that the Army could already have advanced this far north; and hardly less unlikely that a group of Scavengers would have ventured so far from the Main Route. He could deduce nothing from the undistinguished nature of the exchanges, since he had no more respect for the fire discipline of the soldiers than he had for that of the Scavengers.

Fortunately, the ground so favoured him that he was able, by modest tacks from side to side, to command the landscape for a considerable distance. Nowhere could he see evidence of any further rogue force in the area (any within earshot, he knew, would be attracted by the prospect of spoils).

As he advanced, he drew the women after him, false crest by false crest, until they had come to a place, some seventy yards short of their objective, from which it was unmistakably apparent that the hidden conflict was centred on the farmhouse itself. Here, he sited the women in a natural defensive position and, having given his bergen into Anne's care, moved forward alone to reconnoitre.

He did not mean to become involved in the struggle ahead, but he certainly intended to find what manner of force he would be leaving at his back, if he chose to bypass them (and indeed to dispose of them swiftly, if that seemed the wiser course).

The feature in which the farmhouse was located was not imposing, more of a trough than a valley, along the floor of which a cart track ascended into the hills and westward across his front. Having made a final sweep of the surrounding terrain, Savage lay among the coarse vegetation at the rim of the cut and peered into the hollow beneath.

To his left were abandoned ditch diggings, from which two men, in the tatterdemalion of Scavengers, were engaging the farmhouse which stood, across an open farmyard, to his right. Beyond the yard and linking the diggings to the house, was a thick straggle of trees and brush, in which Savage now saw a third man stalking the far end of the house. It was evident that the two in the ditch were drawing the fire of the occupant (or occupants) of the house, while their companion sought to turn its flank and enter from the rear. And from the openly jeering manner in which the further of the two offered bursts of fire and mockery to an upstairs window (and from the single shots in return), Savage suspected that they were dealing with an enemy of one. The nearer of the two fiddled with some object below the lip of the trench and out of Savage's view.

Concluding that this squalid squabble was no concern of his and the force involved negligible, Savage turned and signalled to the women that they were to move to the right flank, where he would join them. When he was satisfied that they were complying with his order, he returned his attention to the farmyard.

And received a shock.

The one who had been fiddling below the rim of the ditch now brought up the object of his interest.

It was a hand-held anti-tank rocket launcher!

Savage was genuinely shocked.

Where had he got it? From the Army? Why would the Army have such weapons along the Main Route? Were they in use now?

He looked towards the women.

And saw how at once Anne grew still, reading his face. He knew that she apprehended his dismay and turned abruptly away from her, disturbed by her empathy.

What to do?

If such weapons were in play along the Main Route, he needed to know about it.

But already the spread was too wide. The one in the trees was more than two-thirds to the house. The one in the house (if indeed only one) was unpredictable. He needed prisoners. Two at least would get to cover and get shots off. He could not dominate them with certainty, unless . . .

He needed a second gun.

Instinctively, he looked again towards the women.

They were almost on him, Anne responding determinedly to a need that had not been expressed.

He waved them to ground.

How could he involve them?

But he needed the information.

And then his unaccustomed debilitation was snatched from him by the arrival of Cassie, prone at his side. He heard her gasp.

'What is it?'

She was staring down at the trench.

'It's *him*!'

'What?'

'The one who did it to Simon!' She hauled up her rifle. 'I'm going to kill him.'

'Wait!'

'That's Simmy's scarf!'

'Not yet!'

'*When?*'

Anne loomed under them.

'What's wrong?'

Savage felt the impetus tip from his grasp. To Cassie, he said:

'See the one in the trees?'

She turned.

'Going behind the house?'

'You've got to kill him first.'

Anne said,

'*What?*'

'Go along there.' He pointed west on the rim. 'Wait until I attack, if you can. But make sure he doesn't get into the house.'

Anne said,

'I can do that.'

'No.'

Cassie said,

'And then the other?'

'Yes – go!'

But as the child made to leave, Anne sought to restrain her.

'Wait a minute!'

'*No.*'

Savage seized the woman by the front of her webbing.

'Come with me.'

He all but dragged her, hands and knees, until she resisted forcefully.

'What are you *doing*?'

He knew that she referred to Cassie. He pressed her to the ground.

'If anyone shows at a window or fires, *fire back*. Cover me.'

He worked on, under the line of sight from the hollow.

Thinking: *This is a mistake! Stop it now!*

But the child would not miss. And he needed the information.

He wondered for a moment where his shadows from Other Force were, whether they were watching. (They would not intervene.)

The one with the launcher below had brought it to his shoulder, but now he lowered it again, as though uncertain of his set-up. The one beyond fired at the house. The man in the trees had already passed from view.

Savage thought, *Don't leave the child hanging.*

He dropped off the stoop, soundless and deadly.

At the last –

Savage thought he heard Cassie fire.

– the one with the launcher sensed his coming, part turned, involuntarily discharged the weapon.

There was a flare of flashback, a *whoosh* of release.

Savage thought wildly,

(He was among them, clubbing them down.)

What if it strikes the child?

When he glanced up, he saw her run behind the house, a smear of trail above.

Anne fired. He shouted:

'You in the house! Throw down your weapon!'

At that moment, there came from behind the house two distinct shots.

Cassie killing or being killed?

The rocket came anticly to ground.

He thought, *This is a shambles. A complete shambles.*

But he was possessed of dread for the child. He shouted:

'Do it now!'

And to the two stirring at his feet:

'How many in the house?'

'Just the one . . .'

A rifle speared from the upstairs window.

Where was the child?

'Out the front door! *Now!*'

Movement at his feet.

'Move and I'll kill you.'

'Mister —'

'Shut up.'

In spite of himself, he could not resist shouting:

'*Cassie!*'

She came from behind the house, carrying two weapons, unconsciously strutting. Enraged by relief, he shouted:

'Are you on a stroll? Take cover!'

A man in rags came from the front door, arms raised.

'I want to surrender!'

'On the ground! Spread your arms and legs!' To Anne: 'Check him for weapons. Don't get in my line of sight.' To Cassie: 'If he moves, kill him.'

The man lifted up his head:

'I haven't —'

'Shut up!'

As expected, he had no further weapons. To Anne, Savage said:

'Make a sweep. If you see anyone, or anything, tell me at once.' She nodded, moved up the slope. To Cassie: 'If he does anything you don't like, shoot him.'

She took station beside the diesel tank. He turned to the two before him.

'Out of the ditch. Spread yourselves.'

148

He wanted the business ended. He saw how his sense of the vulnerability of the women had tilted things and he needed to resolve that. He needed, too, to be free of the obscuring walls by which the hollow confined them.

The men had no hidden weapons. He dealt with rocket man first.

'Where did you get this?'

He kicked the expended tube of the launcher.

'Mordred give them us.'

'*Mordred*?'

The one at MacKenzie's Farm who had played no part in the rape of Cassie (although he had not prevented it); who had preferred weapons maintenance.

'Aye.'

'How many did he give you?'

'Three or four, I think.'

'When was this?'

They had not been deployed against his safe house.

'About two weeks ago.'

'Are there others of these along the Track?'

'He said, aye.'

'Who's your boss?'

'They call him Rufus.'

Savage had eavesdropped on Rufus. He was nothing special.

'What about this Mordred – who's he?'

'We never saw him before.'

Nor had Savage caught word of him (although his interest in the Main Route had declined of late).

'He give you anything else?'

'Mines.'

'*Mines*!'

'. . . Aye.'

'What type of mines?'

'I don't know nothing about mines!'

Savage did not want fear to become incoherence.

'What did they look like?'

'. . . Cans of soup.'

'That size and shape?'

'With something sticking out the top.'

'Like what?'

'. . . A Christmas tree.'

Anti-personnel.

'How many of these mines?'

'Four.'

And how many others along the Main Route?

'Was there anything else?'

Like artillery, Savage thought sourly. Tanks?

'No, no.'

What had Mordred been? An entrepreneur? An agent seeding the Main Route on behalf of some boss?

The man said,

'You're Savage, aren't you?'

Savage said,

'Where's Rufus now?'

'I don't know. We come after *him*.' He contrived with his head to indicate the man who lay before the farmhouse; added hurriedly: 'Look, that attack on your place weren't nothing to do with us.'

'But you know about it.'

The man's eyes slid sideways.

'I heard.'

His companion, who had not yet spoken, proffered an egregious smile.

'Not from me.'

But the boy's scarf clanged like a bell about his neck. The woman had returned stealthily to Savage's side. He said,

'Well?'

'Nothing.'

She was regarding his prisoners with an ambiguity which they, Savage knew, would pick up on readily. He said,

'Fetch my pack. Stand watch at the top.'

He realised that he did not know how she would react to the end of this. The man at his feet said:

'Look, we got no quarrel with you, this is private business —'

'Why are you so far from the Track?'

'Chasing *him*!'

The one in front of the house again.

'Why?'

150

'He stole our stash!'
The other shouted:
'It were mine, too!'
'*Shut up*!'
From Cassie. Savage said,
'Stash of what?'
'Money! Jewels! What we found!'
Savage stared at him.
'You were fighting over *money*?'
'It were ours!'
'Mine, too!'
'What were you going to *buy* with it?'
'A way in, mebbe.'
'To what?'
'The Capital.'
'You're joking.'
'They won't let us surrender! They're just killing us!'
The other took up the plaint:
'It's true! They're hunting us down like dogs!'
Savage knew it to be true. He said,
'Don't tell me your troubles.'
'You could help us.'
'No chance.'
'You've helped others.'
'They made their choice, you made yours.'
Rocket man said,
'Well, let us go then, take our chances, we're nothing to you.'
This, indeed, was what Savage intended. With the exception of
one. He seized the second man by the scarf about his neck.
'Where did you get this?'
The man gasped:
'I found it!'
Cassie said,
'*No*! He's the one who did it to Simon!'
'Stand your ground! Watch your prisoner!'
'I want my chance!'
'In a minute!'
The man was craning to see his accuser. Cassie returned

reluctantly to her task. The woman, at the top of the shallow slope, was now thoroughly alerted. And rocket man was swift to grasp the implications of guilt by association:

'Look, he en't nothing to do with me! I never saw him before yesterday!'

'I know that.'

Scarf man understood among whom he had fallen. He keened against Savage's hand.

'Oh God, oh God . . .'

Savage said,

'Why come south again?'

'. . . What?'

The man was glazed with apprehension.

'Why not go north with the others?'

And spare me this.

'. . . My son.'

'Your what?'

'I heard my boy were still alive.'

Your *boy*? Savage thought. Yet you rape the children of others?

Disgusted with the entire business, Savage released the man and stepped back. To Anne, he said,

'Guard the prisoner.'

– indicating the man before the house. And to Cassie:

'Do it.'

All might yet have been well; two might have lived, had it not been for the intervention of Anne. As Cassie came forward, Anne moved to intercept her.

'Cassie – don't do this!'

'Leave me alone!'

And in the moment it took for Savage to shout for order and for them to fall to pushing and tugging at one another, scarf man was up and stumbling over the heaped sods. Rocket man, too, took to his heels (although he had no reason to). And beyond the baulking tangle of Cassie and Anne, Savage saw the third prisoner bolt for the trees. He shouted:

'*Get down!*'

He went about his business, killing them methodically. Even

Cassie got shots off. Then, in a rage of shame and disgust, he shouted:

'Fetch your packs! We're getting out of here!'

He thought: what if *they* had watched? What if Other Force had witnessed this grotesque parody of soldiering?

They would mock him. They would think the less of him.

He led the women from the pit, barely able to bring himself to look at them.

. . . Yet it had been his fault.

If he could find no better way to accommodate their presence, then he would bring them all low.

When he looked back, he saw that they, too, were preoccupied with the immediate past and he shouted:

'*Concentrate!*'

Time enough later to vent his spleen.

Whenever they stopped for rest, he embarked on unnecessary sweeps, not to be with them. Returning from one such, he caught Anne's comforting arm dashed off by Cassie with the words:

'You're not my mother!'

In a sharp tone, he said,

'Work together, or you die.'

Anne favoured him with a droll look.

'There's a thought.'

He knew that his own lowering mien oppressed them.

By the time they sighted their day's objective, the sky had become as though it were an earth-clogged rooting system viewed from beneath and the light dimmed early. Savage led them to the isolated barn set on the high plateau.

'Make ready for night. Stand to, fifteen minutes.'

He swept the approaches; chopped out a latrine sufficient for their requirements. When he re-entered the barn, the interior had darkened appreciably. The women had laid out their bedding rolls – apart from one another. He said,

'Hang your gear on the nails.' Driven by Sammy and himself into the woodwork, some five feet above the floor. 'And don't forget to cover your faces with scrim, when you sleep tonight.'

Anne said,

'Rats.'

Both women had been on the outside long enough to know that rats had returned as readily as rabbits. Cassie shuddered.

'I *hate* rats.'

He said,

'I'll watch, while you sleep.'

He could not deny the rats entry, due to the open nature of the barn. It was not a regular way station on their route south, being too far from the Main Route, but had served Sammy and himself often. He rapidly laid a fire in their previously prepared shallow pit, using branches and kindling stored on their last visit. When Anne remarked on his preparedness, he said,

'Stand to.'

He made them select their own positions, which he criticised; and kept them on alert throughout an extended period of false dusk.

When they returned to the barn, he lit the fire. He had no compunction about showing light in their new dark age. None moved at night.

He lit, too, the small candle lamp which, habitually, he carried in his pack. He preferred its light to that of torches or cyalume sticks and had found in the past that it comforted the fearful.

From their supplies, Anne chose steak and onion casserole; Cassie and himself, steak and kidney pudding; with beans in tomato sauce for all and fruit salad to follow. He drew also from his bergen an additional container of water; sachets of instant soup; powdered milk, sugar and tea; biscuits and chocolate, boiled sweets and dextrose tablets. As he cooked in their mess tins over stones, he neutralised conversation with instruction:

Pierce the lid twice, stand the tin part submerged in boiling water for ten minutes.

'*Never* drink the water. It'll be tainted with zinc. If you want a brew, clean your mess tin, start from scratch.'

On the soup:

'Ignore the instructions. Mix it with *cold* water first. Then heat or add to hot.'

154

Measuring:

'Fill your small mess tin to the lower rivet. That's one pint.'

Anne said,

'Remarkable.'

He made them consume everything. And when their eating irons and mess tins had been cleaned and stowed away; and the empty tins flattened for disposal in the latrine; and all waste gathered; and their rifles cleaned and lightly oiled, he said to Cassie:

'You want to use the latrine first?'

She rose.

'I'll be a few minutes.'

She took a gauze pad from where her pack hung on a nail. Anne said,

'Would you like me to come?'

'No.'

Savage said,

'You want a torch?'

She gave him a look as though he should know better.

'I'm not afraid of the dark.'

Perhaps, like him, she had come to prefer it.

With the child gone, Anne said,

'Do say it, Mr Savage. It's like waiting for the second boot to drop.'

Her flippancy reignited his anger.

'If you ever interfere in a battle again, I'll kill you myself.'

He turned embers to encourage extinction. She said,

'The battle, surely, was over?'

'How would you know?'

'The enemy were flat on their faces.'

'How do you know they were the enemy? How do you know they didn't have weapons – or support – that we didn't find? How do you know there was only one in the house?' Presumably because, like him, she had smelled the truth in the fear. He said, 'If I can't trust you, you're a liability. You'll kill us both, her and me.'

After a moment, the woman nodded.

'I was wrong.'

'You were.'

'But what, in the name of God, are you doing to Cassie?'

'I'm teaching her to survive.'

'What survives? A Cassie made in your image and likeness?'

'She's alive.'

'Is she? How many times can a child kill, without being – ?'

'Nobody's a child any more!'

Irony stalked him.

'Then what's the point of survival? If there are no children, there is no future.'

Cassie would, in any event, have killed the man, he thought. He said,

'He was the one who did it to her brother.'

'And the other two? Did they have to die?'

'Not until you intervened.'

She emitted a harsh bark.

'I see.'

He had not intended to say it. He said,

'I'd probably have done it, anyway.'

But this they both knew to be a lie. She leaned across the pit.

'Give her a chance to be what she is. A young woman. If you don't step back, she'll become you. Surely, she deserves better than that?' The woman looked contemptuously away: 'Surely anyone does.'

Coldness stilled Savage.

'I keep her alive. Anything else . . .' He made a gesture, as though to say: When you get to the Capital, she's in your hands. At that moment, Cassie said,

'Mr Savage is right.' She stepped in from the darkness. He wondered what she had heard (and what he had said). She could not yet have finished in the latrine. She said, 'The only thing that matters is to stay alive.'

The woman was unmoved by her reappearance.

'I'd like to think that isn't true, Cassie.'

'But it is.'

Savage found himself saying:

'. . . It isn't that simple.'

Why had he spoken? The child said,

'They deserved to die.'

'Yes, they did.'

'Well, then?'

'. . . We don't do it for . . . gain. Or revenge.'

'Why, then?'

He foundered on explication.

'. . . So the evil don't triumph.'

He imagined the woman mocking him. Cassie said,

'They were evil.'

'Yes.'

And helpless.

'. . . Are you saying that what I did was wrong?'

Anne said,

'It's not a case of right or –'

'I'm not asking you! I'm asking Mr Savage!'

'I can't tell you what's right or wrong! I'm not a priest, I'm a soldier!'

Implication snagged at him. The child said,

'You did it.'

'Yes, I did.'

Anne said,

'. . . It's over now. Why don't we – ?'

Savage said,

'There's always a price to pay, Cassie. When you do it to them, you do it to yourself.'

He saw her incomprehension.

'I don't understand that.'

He turned away, fumbling for words:

'You have to . . . step away from that.'

He recognised the echo of the woman's words. The child said,

'Yes, when we get to the Capital. It'll be different then.'

Yes indeed, Savage thought. That longed-for treachery. In a firm tone, Anne said,

'We must get to sleep. We've much to do tomorrow.'

It was as though, having drawn blood, she now regretted it. Savage seized the cue.

'Put your beds together. You'll need shared body heat in the night.'

He turned to leave. Cassie said,

'What about you?'

'I'm going to make a sweep. I'll be back before you sleep.'

He hoped not.

His confusion was no less than hers.

He could not teach the child what she should be. If the woman wanted a division of the labour, he was entirely happy that it should be so.

He yielded to silence and stealth and they comforted him.

He wondered where the two from Other Force had harboured for the night.

They were secure in their role in a way which he now could never be.

(And he did not know who was the loser for it.)

When he returned to the barn, the child was mourning her lost parents.

'I miss them so much . . .'

'I know, darling . . .'

The soft click of a kiss.

'*Why did all this have to happen?*'

'I wish I could answer you.'

Savage showed himself at the periphery of the light and, in spite of the woman's admonitory shake of the head, spoke (for he needed to have done with them):

'Goodnight, Cassie.'

The child looked up from where she lay in the woman's embrace.

'Goodnight, Mr Savage.'

To the woman, he said,

'I'll be outside.'

She said,

'Will you be warm enough?'

Why? Would they share body heat?

'I'll be fine.'

He settled just out of earshot. In a little, he thought he heard them giggle together; but then, he did not understand women.

There were few rats in the night and no demons.

He woke them before first light.

'Stand to.'

The child rose from sleep in exceptional good humour, as though the grief of night had purged her. She managed to plant a kiss on his cheek before he could evade her and he saw the mischief in it.

'*Outside.*'

Dawn brought an unnaturally heavy dew and a more than ever stalactitic overcast. The air was cooler without being more fresh and the light contrarily bright.

It was as though the weather had lost the code for the seasons and was trying each element in turn. When the conundrum was resolved, Savage did not doubt what that would bring: deluge.

But not apparently yet.

(Give me time.)

When they had breakfasted and had used the latrine and had buried all sign of their passing, Savage led them on.

He had revised his intentions.

If there was the smallest possibility that they might encounter AP mines or rocket launchers along the Main Route, then he meant to reconnoitre the track before he took the women onto it. They would harbour for night short of The Cut, in a cottage he had used before, which would allow him time to observe; to move down onto the roadway (if practicable); to eavesdrop; to test the temper of the Track.

To be denied the Main Route would be a disaster.

They would alter course SE at 11.00 hours.

They had been on the move barely twenty minutes when Savage heard a sharp whistle from Cassie and, looking back, saw that she crouched beside a stricken Anne. He ran to them:

'What is it? What's wrong?'

Anne spoke, but he did not understand her.

'What?'

She said,

'*Wind.*'

As though by way of demonstration, she discharged spectacularly. Cassie clapped a hand to her mouth.

'Crikey! *Anne*!'

The woman gasped:

'Oh God! I'm sorry!'

And fired again. The women were helpless with laughter. Savage said,

'Better out than in.'

Anne said,

'It seems to be trapped.'

'Not any longer.'

Whatever he said served merely to provoke renewed laughter and virtuosity. But their robustness of attitude spoke well for their future. He said,

'We'll take a short break.' What was funny about *that*? 'I'll stand upwind, if it's all the same to you.'

In short order, they were on their way again.

The day went well. It became apparent that, perhaps as a result of their exchanges during the night, a new intimacy had grown up between Cassie and Anne. They touched and smiled with a fondness which plainly was reciprocal. Nor did this rapport exclude Savage. They regarded him with at least as much affection as they did mockery; and they obeyed him promptly.

It was a development which he should welcome. And he did. He did. It would make his abandonment of them the easier.

They reached the target cottage with one hour of daylight remaining.

Savage lay on the height, looking down on the Main Route, the trees by which it was bordered, and into the river meadows beyond. The women covered his back.

The silence was absolute. In fifteen minutes, he had discerned not the faintest hint of animation on any quarter; not in the fields, the trees, nor anywhere along the track. It was eerie. He had never known the Route so devoid of life. He turned to the women.

'I'm going down.' They looked as though they, too, had

apprehended a strangeness. 'If anyone comes near you, open fire. I'll return at once.'

They nodded.

He worked down to level ground and turned south along the narrow track.

The Main Route had never been important, nor the river which ran nearby. Too many more attractive options had been available and urban and industrial development had taken place to the east, to the north and, especially, in the West. Savage's ground had always been rural and, of late, increasingly abandoned. Nor had the brief significance which the Track had attained immediately following the Event done anything to improve its crumbling state, which since had deteriorated further. Only minor hamlets were to be found along its length.

As he patrolled south, exposing new ground, Savage expected at any moment to see Scavengers, bedding down among the trees or fishing at the river. But he saw none.

And in a little he came to know that he would not.

The place reeked of death. It was as though dread had become trapped between the trees to his left and the rock wall to his right. He was on killing ground. Yet he could not have passed through the Army pursuit.

The very suspension drew him on – further from the women than he had intended. He passed the skeletons of cars, dismembered luggage, the liquescing detritus of flight. But this was old death, nothing newly killed.

And then, as though a hand had reached to a gas lamp, the light was extinguished. He turned at once to high ground and made for the women. He had instituted no night recognition procedure, believing that he would return before darkness came. If they shot him, it would be no more than he deserved. Their presence induced error.

He was almost on them when he heard it.

A remote *crack*, followed by a high doppler shriek, as though a bat had been felled in flight. He knew what it was.

And cursed.

He listened with such intensity it was as though the edge of his sensibility fluttered. But no further sound came, no locating sussurus.

Where had she been? North of him; south? In the fields? The trees? How far?

There was nothing he could do. It was already full night below. Get the women to harbour.

As he approached, he raised his rifle in both hands above his head, for he knew that, from where they lay, they would see him against the remainder of the sky; and he said,

'It's Savage.'

The woman said,

'What was that just now?'

'Maybe a rabbit.'

He did not need her face to experience her contempt.

'It was a *woman*.'

'There's nothing we can do.'

'There must be something!'

'No.'

Cassie said,

'Was that a mine?'

'Yeah.'

Anne said,

'She may be *alone*.'

'Women are never alone.'

Too valuable a commodity in their altered world.

'We can't just *ignore* her . . .!'

'It could take *hours* to find her! I'm not going to play Blind Man's Buff with trip wires! Even with night vision, they're impossible to see.'

Cassie said,

'Trip wires?'

He said,

'. . . Even if I find her, there's nothing I can do.'

Anne said,

'There's one thing.'

'Maybe whoever's with her has done that.'

If they had, they had done it soundlessly.

The women were subdued as they ate their evening meal.

The fortified cottage was secure, as he and Sammy had left it, all apertures permanently sealed except for those designated by Savage. He was damping the fire in the grate, when he sensed encroachment:

'Someone's coming.' He blew out the candle lamp. 'Don't open the door unless I say.'

There came a clamorous beating at his door:

'Savage, let me in! My wife's hurt!'

But Savage was gone, deploying the exits and entrances to which his safe houses were prone, and in a moment was on the roof, commanding the terrain in every direction via the glowing green smear of his night scope. No one was in view other than the desperate man at his door – and the shape slumped at the man's feet.

Savage dropped behind him and forced him against the door.

'Stand still!'

'Savage, help us . . .!'

'Shut up!'

He cast aside the rifle which the man wore slung across his shoulders and palpated him for further weapons.

'My wife set off a mine!'

'How many are you?'

'What?'

'How many?'

'Just the two! We fled the others weeks ago!'

'Face the door.'

'We've been looking for *you*! Trying to –'

'Shut up. Face the door.'

Savage maintained a physical presence on the man, when he crouched to the woman. The man said,

'Save her, Savage. Don't matter about me.'

His voice cracked. Savage encountered at once the tacky ruination of the woman's body. He bumped the door panels.

'Open up.'

'Thanks.'

'Straight in, on your face, spread yourself.'

'Anything, only look to her.'

The door opened.

'*Go.*'

By the faint emanation from the embers, Savage saw the man prostrate himself before Cassie's rifle. To Anne, he said,

'Torch. Not yet.'

He carried the woman in, immediately conscious of the infelicity of her limbs.

'Bar the door.'

Anne did so. As he laid the woman down, a quavering sigh issued from her. The man said,

'Help her, Savage. She's in pain.'

Savage thought her past pain. To Anne, he said,

'Let's have a look.'

The torch came on. When he lifted the woman's rags, there escaped from Anne a choking cough and the beam wavered. Savage said,

'Light the lamp.'

He was enraged by the needless suffering to which the woman had been subject on her portage to him. The man said,

'Save her, Savage! We're together now!'

He had crabbed round in the urgency of his appeal. Savage said,

'When did this happen?'

But he knew – as the other (he saw) knew, but could not acknowledge, the fatal nature of his 'wife's' injuries. Anne had lighted the candle and now extinguished the purposeless cruelty of the torch. Savage lifted his identity discs from about his neck. The woman's hand came like paper on his.

'. . . Don't . . . blame . . . him . . .'

She appeared transparent. The man, as though encouraged by this evidence of animation, scrambled to his knees.

'See, you'll be fine now, love! Savage'll fix you up!'

Savage wanted to punch him. The woman sighed.

'Oh, Jack . . .'

Her pain was all for him. Savage stripped the syrettes of morphine from his name tags.

'Say goodbye to your wife.'

The man said,

'No! You can save her!'

'Do it.'

Anne said,

'Savage.'

The woman had relapsed. Savage seized the man by the front and hauled him upright.

'Your wife is dying.'

'*No*!'

'Let her die with dignity!'

Anne said,

'John.'

And he heard the woman murmur:

'Please . . . Please . . .'

Anne's use of his given name stayed Savage. He crouched again to the woman. She said,

'All we've got is one another.'

Savage nodded as though he understood. Anne said,

'Kneel here.'

She vacated her place at the woman's side, indicating to the man that he should take it. When he did so, it was apparent that his crisis had passed. He took the woman's hand in both of his and, in so far as she was able, she reciprocated. He said,

'I'm sorry, love . . .'

'No.'

'It's just . . . I don't know what I'll do . . .'

He lowered his head to hers. She said,

'We'll always be together . . .'

'Aye.'

He seemed to derive strength from her words. Savage waited. The woman said,

'You gave me life again . . .'

'No, it was you gave me . . .'

'Shh . . .'

She made as though to touch him, but the effort was beyond her. She looked to Savage.

'Mr Savage can take you in now . . .'

'Don't say that . . .'

'Please . . .'

'I won't hear this . . .'

She said again to Savage:

'*Please* . . .'

He nodded.

'Sure.'

He did not doubt that the man would be unwelcome at the Capital. A force surged through the woman. She reached for her 'husband'.

'*Jack! I love you . . .!*'

And he, now conversant with the truth, gathered her to him and in litany repeated:

'I will always love you, I will always love you . . .'

Savage injected the first syrette of morphine into the woman's system and then the second. Anne showed that, with irritating prescience, she had withdrawn a sealed medical pack from her kit, but he shook his head. No more would be needed. Indeed, the woman slipped at once through an open door. Savage collected his waste for disposal. In a moment, the man said,

'Is it over?'

'Yes.'

'I'll bury her.'

'Want help?'

'No.'

But the man sat on, cradling his wife. Then he said,

'We waited for you. We thought you'd come. When we broke from the others . . . What they did to her. What I did. She made me what I could be. I'd have died for her. We looked to one another.' He turned to Anne. 'Could you open the door, please?'

Before Anne could move, Cassie sprang up.

'I'll do it.'

'Thanks.'

When he was on the point of departing with his burden, she said,

'Would you like me to come?'

The man contemplated her.

'No. Thank you.'

And after he had stepped into darkness.

'I'll pray for her.'

His voice came back:

'Pray for us both.'

Savage knew what would happen. He had not, after all, searched the woman and it would be she, logically, who would carry their second weapon, if they had one. Cassie hunched by the waning fire.

'He really loved her.'

Anne said,

'One had almost forgotten love.'

Savage said,

'Get to sleep.'

Cassie wrapped her arms about her knees.

'Are there many mines on the road?'

She had seen the ruined woman. He said,

'I'll keep you clear of them.'

Anne said,

'There's blood here.'

She touched the floor.

'I'll deal with it!'

She looked up, sharply:

'*I'll* deal with it!'

As though she were houseproud. He said,

'Don't waste water.'

'Why not? We've got a *river* of water.'

It was as though she were furious with him. But it was Cassie who shocked him, by saying, in a small voice:

'Please don't quarrel.'

Anne moved at once to embrace her.

'We're not quarrelling, darling. What would we have to quarrel about?'

Savage asked himself the same question, embarked, nonetheless, on a profound unease. Then they heard the shot.

The man had made a sufficient job of dispatching himself. Savage gathered the revolver (for disposal with the man's rifle). Then he laid them in one another's arms, as he supposed they would wish to be.

It was a horrible way to die.
People die.
I'm glad they're together.

At last, the child slept. Savage taped fresh syrettes to his identity discs. Anne said,

'The Scavengers are the victims now.'

'They deserve to be.'

'Even her?'

'Go to sleep.'

'You don't believe in redemption?'

'Goodnight, Anne.'

'You should sleep, too.'

'I sleep.'

'Not enough.'

'How would you know?'

'Cassie says you never sleep.'

'Everybody sleeps.'

'Perhaps, she meant you never rest.'

When you rest, you die. He blew out the candle. In a little, she said,

'There was nothing you could do for them.'

'I know that.'

'I know you know that.'

She sounded sad. He said,

'Goodnight.'

She said,

'They're only words, Mr Savage.'

Enemies.

When demons came in the night, it was to Anne that Cassie clung, while Savage maintained watch.

Morning.

An intense white vapour, which beaded eyelashes and hair with a constantly-regenerated supply of moisture baubles. But fog was not rain. Nor did it daunt Savage as it would, he knew, cow the Scavengers. To him, it was just another form of navigable night.

Within an hour, in high ground still and in close formation, they achieved The Cut.

Effectively, they were at a crossroads, where the western track, following the course of a substantial gully in the hills, crossed from the right to encounter the Main Route (where it ceased).

This was not visible. Indeed, where they lay on the rim of the gully, they floated in milky insubstantiality.

The Cut consisted of a multiplicity of slices, cleft from the opposing hillside, which yielded an interplay of facets and planes over a distance of some four hundred yards – although since, to the best of Savage's knowledge, the rock was of no serviceable material, he was at a loss to understand what once had been harvested there.

Beyond The Cut, the heights continued in a series of 'steps', divided by deeply-riven, lateral fissures (which rendered them unnegotiable), until, by degrees, the ground descended to an intermittently-wooded, coarse grassland and ultimately to the inhospitable terrain which extended all the way to the Southern Forest. This was territory which Savage meant to avoid at all reasonable cost.

He decided to commit to the Main Route. He was satisfied that the women had the discipline and the resolution to cope with any contact that the Scavengers might offer. When he explained this to them, Cassie said,

'But what about the mines?'

Their potency haunted her. He said,

'We've more than enough light to deal with them.'

They made steady progress.

He was impressed again by the patience which the women had developed so quickly.

Patrol slowly.

Perhaps women were patient.

They heard nothing. They saw no one. They passed among wraiths. In fifty minutes, they rested.

The fog exhibited signs of tearing in patches. They were, from time to time, vouchsafed glimpses down rolling corridors of visibility – over the water meadows, along the Track: and although the swags folded always together again, it was unmistakably the case that the cavern in which they travelled expanded steadily. Soon, he would move to higher ground to take stock.

They had left the hills behind and were skirting the grassland, no more than twelve feet above them now and to their right, at the crest of a coarse embankment.

Thirty minutes should tell the tale.

It did. As they lay among the grasses, it became evident to Savage that whatever dispersal had been in train had ceased. Indeed, from the lumbering herds at the periphery of the fog, it was apparent that soon their environment would compress again. Visibility had stabilised for a moment at between fifty and seventy yards. They had a partial view of the grassland and of clustered trees. They could see further than hitherto along the Track. And they had sight of the meadows, although not of the river itself.

Of the sky, nothing; but Savage felt a weight of water over him.

Twice, faintly, they had heard gunfire and on one occasion had seen Scavengers, like ghosts in the field.

'Time to move on.'

They began to pass bodies with increasing frequency (although not in number). These were newly dead, by gunshot or, occasionally, from mines. Yet still there was no evidence of Army pursuit.

And then, as they came to a place where a substantial copse spilled across the Main Route from the right, they heard voices call to one another in the grassland above and, from a separate location, the stinging scythe of sustained automatic weapons fire.

They went to ground. Savage signed to the women. All-round defence. He shucked his bergen and snaked up the embankment, checking behind him, although his modestly increased elevation showed him nothing he did not already know.

The sustained fire continued – gratuitously, Savage suspected, since he could detect no return fire. He did not doubt what he was listening to: not to battle, but to slaughter.

Someone had sprung a trap.

After a last sweep to his rear, he advanced his face until he could peer between the stalks.

The gunfire had ceased, cut off by angry commands. Savage looked from ground level into a vaporous chamber, some sixty yards deep, which was demarced to the left by the bulk of the copse and to the right, above and behind by a cyclorama of fog. At the heart of this space a struggle was taking place.

It was plain what had occurred. A party of Scavengers, whose corpses lay about, had been ambushed. And the sole survivor, a woman (spared, unquestionably, by design), was the object of predatory sexual assault by her captors.

Savage counted them. Two, three. Five. Seven. One searching the bodies. Eight.

Their violence was soundless, the woman's cries countered by blows.

Savage thought: *I can't let this happen.*

Too late for reason now.

The course to which his spirit drove him was neither logical nor sensible.

He signed the women to him.

(Think of them as firepower.)

But there was a problem.

The enemy were not Scavengers, but Army. His 'own side' (had he had one).

(How close, the follow-up?)

Anne, who had come beside him, said:

'Can't we do something?'

He said,

'Kill them all.'

'. . . What?'

'*No witnesses*! Kill them all!'

It had been intended as a command to both and, even as he saw dubiety in Anne's face, Cassie, beyond her, took aim and fired and he realised that indeed they had themselves come under fire.

It was the one who had been searching the bodies.

He and Cassie fired together.

The man went down.

But already, among the others, was a fatal disintegration. For all their inadequacy, they were trained soldiers; and as they scattered outwards, they took instinctive advantage of posture and the vagaries of ground. They were going down under his and the women's fire but, given the closeness of the fog, not quickly enough.

Two had broken for the trees.

Savage sprang up. He knew that he could not cut them off, but he could not afford to lose contact with them, either.

To his right, as he ran, he saw two others make into the fog.

A shot was discharged from behind him and one of the two reeled sideways and went down.

Glancing back, he saw that Cassie had stepped forward.

And that Anne, in that moment, snatched down her rifle and stared at him, as though shocked by recognition.

A further discharge to his front.

The second of the two reared up, as though he had been shot out of the fog.

Savage's quarry had all but reached the trees. He tried for a snap shot but missed and then they were into the smother and himself a moment after.

The copse was more dense than he had remembered and fat with fog.

He crouched. Listened.

There it was. The fluster of flight.

Then he heard a shot. A second. And silence.

He knew what had occurred. Their trackers from Other Force. Perhaps, in his heart, he had counted on it: that a residue of shared belief would draw them to his cause.

A voice in the trees said:

'Savage. I'm coming out.'

He saw the rifle first, at arm's length. Then the man, well set yet compact, with red hair and beard.

'Approach?'

Savage nodded, lowered his own weapon. The man advanced with a familiar, bulky delicacy, until they confronted one another, alike in stance and accoutrements. Savage said,

'Where's your oppo?'

But of course he knew, glancing behind him as the other replied:

'Taking care of business.'

Savage saw the woman who had been victim clothing and arming herself from the fallen soldiers and, beyond, a spectral sentinel at the edge of the world. The fog had grown appreciably thicker. By taking two paces, he brought Cassie and Anne into view, seated on the grass, their backs to him, talking to one another. The red-headed man said,

'Wouldn't want anyone telling tales out of school.'

Savage turned.

'No.'

The other contemplated the weeping trees.

'Macclesfield on a wet Saturday.'

Savage waited. The man regarded him.

'Give it up, Savage. Sparrow won't have it. He'll dust you, one way or the other.' So. Savage knew the man had not dropped the name from carelessness. It was Sparrow. Other Force was Sparrow Force.

He had seen Sparrow, never met him. Knew what they said. But then, he had never met the red-headed man and he knew him.

The other grew restive.

'I mean, What's the point? What are you after? Who do you serve now? Yourself?'

These were fair questions, to which Savage had no answer: except that he sensed it was not himself that he served. He said,

'I don't know.'

Exasperated, the other said,

'You've no chance.'

Savage said,

'You could help.'

'Don't think it. It won't happen.'

'It happened here.'

'Nothing happened here.'

Savage nodded.

'How close, the Army now?'

'Day and a half. Two, maybe.'

Savage calculated without pleasure.

'This lot?'

He indicated the fallen. The red-headed man scowled his contempt.

'"Advance patrols." Death squads. Cleaners.' It was no surprise. He said, 'Best not linger.' And then, looking past Savage, his expression altered:

173

'I think one of your people is down.'

Savage turned, shocked. For the first time, he saw how Anne sat, splay-legged, Cassie kneeling in attendance. Had she been hit? Surely, they would have called him? As he made to run, he turned back to the red-headed man. Not without shame, he said,

'Cover me?'

The other nodded.

Cassie rose to Savage's approach. She said,

'Anne's had a baby.'

He stared at her. Anne said,

'Hardly that, Mr Savage. A miscarriage. A common enough experience. Not least, in our new dawn.'

Her legs were parted and her bloodied trousers about her ankles. He skittered for a place to look.

'You should have told me.'

'You're not the father.'

'It isn't funny.'

'I'm not joking.'

He was at a loss to grasp the moment. She said,

'Perhaps you'd be kind enough to dispose of this?'

She handed to him a small plastic bag which appeared to contain condensation and a nest of grass. Her pack was open beside her and there was blood on her fingers. He said,

'You'd better clean up.'

'What a good idea.'

It was the weightlessness that repelled him. He ran back along the track as though he were skinless, seeking cracks that lately they had passed and possessed of a shrieking need to be rid of the thing. His mind resisted images of the woman colliding with the ground under the impact of his training. The moment he came to a suitable fissure, he thrust the object down and buried and buried it, as though by such means he could separate it from himself.

He was mortified. Yet, too, he felt betrayed.

And by the time he returned, having collected his bergen from the foot of the slope, anger had begun to stir in him again.

Anne had changed and was bundling soiled clothing in a plastic bag into her pack. He said,

'Why didn't you tell me?'

'What good would that have done?'

'Do you think I'd have had you charging up and down the hill?'

'Then I shouldn't have been trained.'

'*You're not trained now!*'

But this was irrelevant anger. She said,

'The loss was mine, Mr Savage, not yours.'

He was less certain. Cassie said,

'It was a boy.'

Anne said,

'Would have been. It was a foetus, not come to term.'

Savage said,

'It was a life.'

Anne said,

'A life already lost. The child was dead.'

Savage was not comforted. Anne said,

'You are not responsible, Mr Savage.'

But he felt responsible. What he was experiencing, he realised, was an inexplicable grief. Unable to comprehend it, he said,

'We'd better get out of here.'

The fog closed ever more oppressively about them. The red-headed man had been obliged all but to quit the trees, in order to maintain the contact that he had promised. Anne said,

'I'm ready.'

Savage said,

'Don't be stupid. I'll carry you.'

'*Carry* me?'

'How far do you think you can march?'

'How far can you carry me?'

'Far enough.'

'For what? I'm perfectly capable —'

'*Do you have to argue about everything?*' His venom shocked them both. Yet, as she looked away, he saw indeed how wasted she was. She said,

'Not everything, no.'

He said,

'We have to move. We've attracted attention.'

'I understand.'

To Cassie, he said,

'You carry Anne's rifle and pack.'

While they occupied themselves with preparation, he made covert eye contact with the red-headed man and indicated his intention. The other nodded. They would have cover, front and rear, for the next part of their journey. As he improvised a paracord sling for his rifle, he noticed that the woman victim had disappeared.

'What happened to the woman who was attacked? Do you know?' Anne said,

'We only realised just now that she'd gone.'

He hitched up his bergen.

'Maybe she couldn't tell one uniform from another.'

'I hope that isn't true.'

She would have been offered her options by the red-headed man's oppo; would have made her choices.

Nothing is ever what it seems along the Main Route.

To Cassie, he said,

'You take the lead.' And, seeing her dubiety: 'The mines aren't a problem now. Not behind the soldiers.'

He would not tell them the true cause of their security.

Perhaps sensing his awkwardness, Anne placed a hand on his shoulder and he lifted her into his arms. She was heavier than he had expected. But then he did not mean to carry her for long, although he thought it wise not to tell her the reason in advance. He said,

'One more thing. Nothing happened here. You saw nothing, you heard nothing, you were never here.' They nodded. To Cassie, he said,

'Go.'

The woman fell asleep, or pretended to, and by this simple artifice spared him much of the embarrassment to which enforced intimacy might have given rise. He smelled her sweat and her blood, but neither was an odour unfamiliar to him.

The fog achieved such density that Cassie, patrolling a short distance ahead, was obliged on occasion to close the gap to as little as fifteen feet – although they retained sight of the left-hand verge, which was important; for the object which Savage sought (one of many such that he and Sammy had 'hidden' in plain sight along the Main Route) was located on that side.

To carry Anne any distance was impossible. Already his arms had the rigidity of overstressed metal.

He was looking for a garden bin on wheels, with cast iron draw handles, which currently lay, upended and wheelless, amid the litter of flight. When Anne saw him disinter the wheels from the sealed plastic bucket in which they had been buried and oil and mount them, she said,

'You're kidding.'

He looked at her.

'We must reach the standby house by nightfall.'

In fact, already he had abandoned any prospect of achieving his day's objective (and with it, in all probability, his chance of making a clean break from his ground). If the woman did not understand his circumstances, it was plain that she understood her own. She smiled slightly and shrugged:

'It could have been a wheelbarrow.'

She surrendered herself to the bin with, he was obliged to concede, undiminished dignity.

It was Cassie who next surprised him. She signed for stillness and ran lightly back to them:

'There's someone ahead of us.'

Savage had not expected it. In the stutter of their stop and start, the red-headed man must momentarily have lost the rhythm and been glimpsed or heard. Savage was amused and was proud of Cassie; but he had no inclination to explain.

'It's not a problem.'

Anne, who had risen to quit the bin, said:

'Why not?'

Cassie said,

'Is he a friend?'

'Sort of.'

Anne said,

'Army?'

He said,

'We must get on.'

For the moment, they accepted it; but then there came from the fog a *cheep* of alarm. Savage said,

'Off the track. That side. Lie flat.'

He passed the warning back and, having thrust the bin in among the trees, rejoined the women to the right of the track, where the recession of ground had put up a low embankment, against which they lay. In a short time, an Army patrol slovened past above them. When the all-clear sounded, they moved on.

In a little, Anne said,

'They're other men like you, aren't they?'

Once, he thought. He said,

'Something like.'

'Are they on our side?'

'For now.'

She looked into the fog. Obscurely, she said,

'The way will be hard.'

That it will, he thought.

They came to a place of rest and Savage called a halt.

He did not know to what extent Anne might be haemorrhaging (although the rutted surface could not help). Perhaps, to a woman, the loss of an infant was no greater a matter than Anne had made of it; but Savage suspected otherwise. A comfortable two hours ahead, there was a cottage which he and Sammy had used in the past. Here, they could build a fire and eat a proper meal; and Anne would be able to bathe in the river and to rest for much of the afternoon as well as the night. (Security would hardly be a problem, given the escort they had acquired.) He would brook no argument.

There was a wayside shelter where they had stopped and here they settled, while he broke out hard tack and set about making a brew. The fog was unrelenting. Anne said,

'I'll need to change again.'

'Now?'

He made to rise.

'No hurry.'

He said,

'Are you . . . Is there much bleeding?'

She shook her head.

'No worse than a heavy curse.'

Lacking a long-term intimacy with a woman, he found the analogy unsympathetic.

'Right.'

In a moment, Cassie said,

'Anne?'

'Yes, darling?'

'You're sure it can't happen to me?'

It was a moment before the woman understood.

'Absolutely. This was from before.' She stroked the child's hair. 'Besides, you're ours now. We'll take care of you, whatever happens.'

The child was transfigured by these words.

'Yes,' she said, of them both. 'Oh yes.'

Savage was shocked; not merely by the woman's expropriation of himself, but by her callousness; for she knew, as the child did not, that soon he would desert them. He concentrated on his brew. When they had finished eating, Cassie said,

'Would your friend like a cup of tea?'

'No. Let them stand stag.' Savage chopped out a shallow pit. The woman, he noticed, took from her pack the spare packet of dressings that she had brought for the child. He drifted along their back track, but the red-headed man's oppo did not manifest himself.

As they progressed, they passed for a brief time increasing numbers of bodies at the periphery of their sulphurous tunnel; and then, none. Beyond this point, the cleansing had been accomplished.

When they came to the narrow path off the Track, he signalled his change of direction and turned towards the cottage. It was, as he expected, secure. At once he led the women, Anne on foot now, to the nearby inlet.

'You want to take the chance to have a bath?'

Anne said,

'Thank you.'

Immediately, she began to strip and he turned his back. Cassie said,

'Me, too?'

'Sure.'

There came a popping of buckles, a susurration of material and then the entry of the women, Cassie explosively, into the water. This was followed by squeals and a dashing up of spray until Anne cried:

'Enough! We're here for a purpose.'

'Sorry.'

But neither could keep the fun from her tone and Savage smiled.

Anne well knew that she could be overlooked from the encroaching trees or from among the rearing festoons of fog, but she defied this possibility with the practicality of nature that he respected in her. He said,

'Don't forget to refill your water bottles and to wash your clothes.'

'Shall I do yours?'

'I'm fine.'

In a little, he heard the women quit the water, the vigorous friction of a towel, a tugging at garments and then:

'If you'd care to get in now, Mr Savage, Cassie and I will endeavour to avert our gaze.'

The child giggled; but Savage knew that he was not being mocked with malice and he took the woman at her word.

It was while he was reclothing himself on the bank and Anne rinsing washing at the water's edge and Cassie refilling their water bottles, that a voice said,

'This is nice, John. Very domesticated.'

Cassie reached for her rifle. Savage said,

'Be still.'

The voice said,

'Wouldn't want to kill her, John.'

The man formed out of the fog, effecting a theatricality of entrance (of which Savage had heard). His features were so daubed that it was impossible to reassemble the planes of his face or to ignore the extravagance of his smile. He seemed to move above the ground.

Anne said,

'Who are you?'

Savage said,

'Sparrow.'

She said,

'Indeed? And are you the one who has been following us with such clumsiness along the track?'

It was nice. Go for the throat. In Sparrow's case, pride of expertise. But the man merely continued to smile:

'What's this, John? Are you sending your women before, now?'

Anne said,

'You have a problem with women?'

'I have a problem with nobody.'

'You've mastered the secret of life.'

Sparrow looked to Savage.

'Won't you introduce me to your . . .?'

He made a mildly derogatory gesture in Anne's direction. She said,

'I have a tongue.'

'I noticed that.'

'I have a mind, too. I hope the concept isn't too revolutionary for you.'

Savage knew that he should intervene. Sparrow was not a man to be provoked. Yet the woman's distaste of him was plainly feral: and, by such means, Savage might learn of his adversary. But the other glanced at him and smiled afresh:

'Naughty, John.'

Already, they were in one another's minds. Savage said,

'Why are you here?'

Sparrow ignored the question, turned his attention to Cassie.

'And who's this?'

The shift was vulpine. The child said,

'I'm Cassie.'

At the same moment, Anne said,

'This is my daughter, Cassie.'

And Cassie said:

'We're a family now.'

Sparrow said,

'A family? Well.'

Savage sensed Anne's eyes on him and remained silent. Sparrow said,

'I don't know that men like us can afford to have families, John.'

Anne said,

'What manner of men might those be, Mr Sparrow?'

But Savage understood that Sparrow referred, not to men of their calling, but to those who, like Sparrow and himself, had become detached from the order of things.

Cassie said,

'You must have had a family once.'

Sparrow said,

'I have a family now.'

Anne chuckled. Her mockery was perceptive.

'Oh dear. Has Mr Savage broken the rules?'

Sparrow contemplated her.

'You take your chances, Mrs Savage.'

The appellation was bizarre. Anne said,

'That was your mistake. You left us nothing else.'

Savage said,

'What do you want here?'

Sparrow smiled.

'Debriefing.'

Anne said,

'What's that?'

'Back to the Capital. Questions. For him, not you.'

Savage wondered whether they meant to kill him now; or whether the Boss at the Capital proposed to offer, to himself as well as to Savage, the fig leaf of pretence that Savage had operated to his orders from the outset. Anne said,

'Do we go together?'

(Had she perceived the threat to Savage?)

'I wouldn't separate a man from his family, Mrs Savage.'

'You couldn't, if you wanted to.'

It was to be the fig leaf, then. Sparrow had not yet taken over (unless this were misdirection). Savage said,

'When?'

'First light.'

'Helicopter?'

'We wouldn't ask you to walk, John.'

To the women, Savage said:

'Take up your kit. We harbour in the cottage tonight.'

Sparrow said,

'You can leave the weapons where they are.'

Savage said,

'No. The weapons are yours. Give them up to no one.' And to Sparrow, without irony: 'I command this force, not you.'

Sparrow put up exculpatory hands.

'Wouldn't have it any other way, John.'

He turned to speak to the red-headed man, who had materialised at his side.

As the women gathered their equipment, they closed about Savage. Anne murmured:

'Is this your best chance?'

'What?'

'While we're still in the open?'

Against men of the calibre of Sparrow Force? With two unlocated? He said,

'No.'

But he was touched. Anne said,

'We'll do anything you say.'

Cassie was quick to agree:

'Anything.'

'I know.'

He was not comforted. Sparrow said,

'Ahem.'

He coughed delicately, as though he were a manservant fearful of overhearing his betters.

Savage was not deceived. Sparrow had come for one reason only: to read Savage close at hand. He had no fear of anything that Savage might concoct with the women; for Savage, he knew, would never put them at risk merely in his own interest, whereas Sparrow, if obliged to, would.

Savage hoped that this was the limit of Sparrow's perception, for certainly it was the sum of his own. To Cassie, he said,

'Take the lead.'

As they moved along the path towards the cottage, where the red-headed man now stood stag, Sparrow said,

'A word, John.'

Savage said,

'Stay in my sight.'

The women crouched, adopted positions of all-round defence. Sparrow said,

'They're in more danger from you, than they are from me.'

Savage faced him.

'They're safe, then.'

The fog baulked them about. Sparrow regarded him with dry interest.

'How did you come to this, John?'

'You don't know me well enough to call me John.'

Sparrow said,

'They won't let you go.'

'*They* can't stop me.'

Both knew who could. Sparrow said,

'You're one of us, John. Family, you might say. Our mess to clear.'

Savage nodded.

'We all make our choices.'

'No one has infinite choice.'

'I don't want infinite choice.'

'You do. You just don't know it.'

Savage shrugged.

'You must do what you think is right.'

Sparrow snorted. In a little, he said,

'Come in, John.'

'I can't do that.'

'Why not?'

Savage thought: because I can't go back; I can only go forward to Whatever it is.

He said,

'I don't know.'

There was a long silence. Sparrow said,

'Last chance.'

He sounded irritated by his own further offer. Savage said,

'No.'

Sparrow looked along the path.

'Go back to your family, John. You've lost your soul.'

It was an odd word to use, Savage thought, of a man who had never supposed that he had one.

In the cottage, Anne said,

'Sparrow trying to tempt you back into the fold?'

Savage said,

'Let's make up the fire. Eat.'

He showed them how to build a fire for night, with a mixture of dry to green growth, so that the former, gradually baking the latter, would sustain combustion over an extended period. He strung up their washing on paracord to dry. He instituted a buddy system for the latrine, so that neither woman would be obliged to visit it unaccompanied. He knew that Anne, for all her weariness, would wait for Cassie to sleep.

When that time came, she said,

'Is he right, Mr Savage? Is a family death, to a man like you?'

'It doesn't arise.'

'Ah.' There was silence. She said,

'Could you get away, without us?'

'Not from here.'

She looked at him keenly:

'From the Capital?'

'They won't kill me at the Capital.'

'Why not?'

'Too public. The Boss will want a private place.'

'I see.' There was now a much longer silence; and then she said,

'I must do what I think is best, for Cassie and myself.'

'Of course.' He made a gesture, intended to indicate training and all that had passed between them. 'That's what all this has been about.'

She nodded.

'Good. Well. Goodnight, Mr Savage.'

Sleep snared him in the night and out of Anne's innards there reached a weightless thing that clamped a suffocating claw about his face.

He woke, screaming.

There was no sign, on the apparently sleeping woman, that she had heard him.

He woke them an hour before dawn. He heard himself say:

'Show him what you can do.'

And they did. Within forty minutes, they had dressed, breakfasted, used the latrine, picked their site clean and made ready for march. As they waited for day, he said,

'You must take care of one another now.'

Cassie said,

'But you'll be with us, surely?'

Anne said,

'Mr Savage means, when we're not together. They may have separate sleeping quarters for men and women.'

'But they wouldn't break up a family, would they?'

Anne stroked the child's cheek.

'I'm sure not, darling.'

'Good.'

Savage could not quite abandon the enterprise on which he found himself embarked. He said,

'I won't always be with you.'

Cassie said,

'Of course, not every minute.'

Anne said,

'We'll know what to do, Mr Savage.'

He nodded. He thought that she might be angry but, when he caught her eye in the candle radiance, she smiled and he was confused.

He ordered them out for Stand-to. Sparrow tolerated this and, when light had come, he said,

'Time.'

They followed Sparrow a short distance along the Track, the red-headed man bringing up the rear, and then turned onto a coarse, level area to the right. Here, a third member of Sparrow Force stood, watching south, his radio antenna spiking up. Sparrow said,
  'Wait here.'

The thick fog had dispersed but everywhere was fustian and the overcast low: it was as though the weather shared Savage's perplexity as to its next course.

Sparrow threw down a canister which fulminated among the grasses and spewed smoke.

Then came the helicopter, at first leggy and delicate, abruptly overbearing in their quiet world, berating the air and dismissive of the smoke.

It came to earth. The power was cut to an idle *phwop-phwopping* of blades. There stepped down from the open cabin an erect, narrow man, dressed in hound's-tooth jacket, cavalry twill trousers and side-buckle boots. He spoke briefly to Sparrow and then advanced on Savage, hand and smile outstretched.

'Mr Savage? This is a pleasure. Truly.' Savage gripped the strong hand. 'But you must forgive me, I'm afraid I don't know your rank.'

Which was interesting, Savage thought. Sparrow must have chosen, for some game of his own, to plead ignorance. Savage said,
  'Mister's fine.'

The man said,
  'Myles Chilcott. Commissioner for the Outlands. South-Eastern Region.' He turned his charm on Anne:
  'And you are . . .?'

Sparrow said,
  'Ah, this is —'

But before he could finish, Anne put out a hand and said,
  'I'm Anne Savage. Mr Savage's wife.'

Sparrow appeared disconcerted to have his ace so unexpectedly trumped and gave Savage a strange look. Chilcott was delighted:
  'Oh, splendid.'

Anne continued:
  'And this is our daughter, Cassie.'

The child was transported to have her status affirmed. Chilcott bowed to her formally.

'A pleasure, my dear.'

'Me, too, sir.'

Savage was concerned. If Anne thought to draw protection on Cassie and herself by public association with him, she was mistaken. Yet she was not stupid and she well understood his circumstances. For the moment, he remained silent. Chilcott said,

'I think we should leave. I don't trust this weather.'

Nor me, Savage thought.

As they walked towards the helicopter, he tried to warn Anne with a look – and encountered an imperturbability so complex that the appalled possibility entered his mind that, far from seeking *his* protection, she sought to offer him her own.

He must disabuse her.

In the cabin, two pairs of bucket seats had been bolted down to face one another across a central companionway. Cassie sat, as a special treat, beside the pilot. When Chilcott and Savage had settled themselves across from Anne, the crew member said,

'I'll have to secure your weapons for take off, sir.'

From instinct, Savage hesitated. But what would he do? Close-quarter battle with the women on board was not an option. He would give up the long, but retain the Browning; and he would insist –

Chilcott said,

'They'll be returned to you before we land.'

Savage nodded. The rifles and bergens were secured against the rear bulkhead. After a final pre-flight check, the crew member stood before Chilcott.

'Both doors open again, sir?'

Chilcott looked to Anne.

'You don't mind?'

At once, Savage said,

'No.'

Anne shook her head.

Savage loathed the bumble flight of the helicopter, not least when he could not see. Chilcott, apparently, was of the same opinion, for he said,

'If God had intended helicopters to fly, he would have given them wings.' And, to the crew member: 'Please.'

'Take off, Commissioner?'

'Yes.'

Chilcott was the power here, but he was not the Boss.

The crew member strapped himself into a jump seat behind Cassie and tapped the pilot on the helmet. Cassie, herself wearing a flying helmet now, turned back from the co-pilot's seat to share her excitement with Savage and then was subsumed in animated colloquy with the pilot.

As the aircraft shuddered to achieve another dimension, Savage looked out through the open waist door. Impervious of the buffeting downdraught, Sparrow raised his rifle in salutation.

We shall meet again.

Savage did not doubt that it was true.

The Capital

FOR the first time, Savage saw his world from above; and he was shocked by the slenderness of the green thread by which (to the best of his knowledge) life clung to the earth; and by the seemingly limitless expanse of grey-black Ashland by which it was surrounded.

Chilcott raised his voice:

'It is impressive, isn't it?'

Conversation was made difficult by the fluster of air and the grinding of the rotor, but for a little they persisted. Anne appeared disdainful of Chilcott's comment, although it had seemed to Savage to contain irony. He said,

'Are there others?'

'Survivors?'

'Command Centres, like yours.'

'Not that we know of.'

Anne leaned across.

'*None?*'

Chilcott shook his head. Savage said,

'No contacts at all?'

'No.'

Nor had Savage picked up any transmissions, other than those from the Capital. Nothing from members of his patrol; nothing via satellite (all of which were masked). He said,

'What about the net?'

– by means of which, in theory, all Regional Centres would be linked by secure landline in the event of emergency. Chilcott said,

'Nothing.'

So much for theory. Anne said,

'How many are you?'

Chilcott hesitated. Looking up the script, Savage thought: what he was permitted to say, and what not to. Chilcott said,

'Approximately eleven hundred.'

Anne stared at him.

'That's *all*?'

The number seemed to Savage not unreasonable. Chilcott said, 'For the moment, yes.'

Anne turned away and they lapsed into silence – except that Chilcott leaned in to Savage and, in a voice plainly intended only for him, said:

'I am a friend, Mr Savage.'

Savage wondered who their mutual enemy might be; and what weapons Chilcott would bring to the coming struggle.

As they progressed south, Savage monitored the river; but there was no detectable increase in flow, no evidence yet that it was raining in the high country – although, even in the unsympathetic environment of the helicopter, he felt rain close: and he smelled the ocean, before Chilcott said:

'We're there.'

It was evident that the pilot had been instructed to afford them an overview of the Complex for, as they approached from the north, he flew out over the sea and in a slow circuit all about the installation, returning to hover at their point of entry.

The coastline at this place consisted of an imposing headland, which fell vertically to the ocean, on the landward side of which lay a valley, longer than it was wide and enclosed at either end by ridges which reached inland from the main feature. At the eastern end of the valley (and protected by the ridge), the river crossed the valley floor and ran for the sea through a gorge in the cliffs. At the foot of the reverse slope of the headland was located the main entrance to what, undoubtedly, was a substantial complex beneath.

All about the valley floor was activity and the graffiti of cultivation. There were ditches dug or digging. A matrix of irrigation channels leeched off from the river. In one place, even, construction. And everywhere, faces tipped up to them.

On the heights, Savage noted, local defence, much of it man-portable. Beyond the river, what was plainly a garbage pit leaked smoke. As he sighted along the coast, it seemed to Savage that only here was the land able to sup sufficiently of the ocean to green with its former conviction.

Not without pride, Chilcott said,

'Southern Area Command.'

Neither Savage nor Anne spoke.

'Shall we go down?'

Chilcott motioned to the crew member, but Savage said,

'First, our weapons.'

Chilcott made a gesture, as though to acknowledge that argument were pointless.

Anne said,

'And our packs.'

As the helicopter descended, there came into view a smart young woman in a blue jumpsuit with, on either side of her, an unarmed soldier in uniform. The moment the aircraft had settled, the pilot cut power, Anne rose and the young woman ran under the blades to salute Savage.

'Good morning, sir.'

Anne called:

'Cassie!'

But the child, only now dragging off her helmet, did not hear her. Chilcott, too, had risen:

'Lieutenant Smith, this is Mrs Savage.'

The young woman extended a hand, but before she could speak, Anne again called:

'Cassie!'

The child turned.

'Yes, Mother?'

'Put on your pack.'

'Just a sec.'

'*Now!*'

Anne's voice was imperious in the quieting space. Cassie, mortified, hurried back.

'Sorry.'

The young woman said,

'The soldiers are here to carry your kit, ma'am.'

'We'll carry our own.'

Savage recognised that Anne intended from the outset to establish the integrity of the little unit which she and Cassie comprised – and he thought her wise.

Silence prevailed while Savage, Cassie and Anne reaccoutred themselves. When Anne dropped down from the cabin, the pilot, behind her back, waggled surreptitious fingers of farewell at Cassie, but received the barest smile in return. Anne had put her mark on them all.

As they followed the young Lieutenant Smith towards the tunnel entrance, there were, all about them, survivors in overalls engaged on a variety of tasks. It was some moments before Savage realised what was happening.

Suddenly they pressed in on him from every side, reaching to touch him, clamouring for his attention:

'Mister Savage . . .!'

'Thank God you've come . . .'

'It's Mrs Clarke . . .'

'God bless you, Savage . . .'

'You saved us when . . .'

'We was at the house, remember . . .?'

He was shocked by their importunity, repelled by their touch, which seemed to him as the hooks of the dead. It was Chilcott who rescued him from suffocation:

'Ladies and gentlemen! Please! Mr Savage has only this moment arrived. He and his family have not yet seen their quarters.'

The word 'family' provoked murmuration and a curiosity directed at Cassie and Anne. Chilcott continued:

'Please, let us through. You'll have ample opportunity to question Mr Savage later.'

Savage hoped that this would not be the case. As they passed among the reluctant throng, Lieutenant Smith said,

'You have to understand, sir. To many here, you are a hero.'

But Savage did not feel nor wish to be a hero; and when he glanced uneasily at Anne, he found her watching him as though she had learned something of importance.

The duty guard had formed up at the entrance to salute Savage. Within, as his eyes adjusted to the gloom, he found that they were in a dank box tunnel, lit at intervals by industrial units housed in wire cages. Above their heads was a massive steel shutter, which had been rotated to lie against the ceiling; and which could be operated, he noted, either manually or by hydraulic power. Its function, he surmised, was not to seal against contamination, but to bar entry when lowered.

This supposition was confirmed within forty yards, when they came to a circular vault door which, when closed, would fit precisely into a gusseted coaming, as though it were the door to a domestic washing machine. Beyond, was an identical door, opening in the opposite direction, so that between the two was contained a small chamber, with cleansing alcoves on either side. Primary Decontamination. Beyond this were double steel swing doors, part glazed and flanged with rubber. And again beyond, the main reception area.

This was composed entirely of plastic, steel and tile and lit from above by 'shadowless' lighting, which Savage loathed. He smelled at once the inertness of processed air, devoid of all natural scents. It was not an environment in which he could ever be at ease.

Behind a counter stood a woman, dressed as though for the operating room, who wore also a surgical mask. Chilcott said,

'Good morning, Sister. May I introduce John Savage and family.'

The woman marked her clipboard with a pencil.

'If you would step into a cubicle and undress for routine decontamination and medical procedures.'

She indicated a row of stalls of a type, as it seemed to Savage, in which unwanted dogs are killed. Together, he and Chilcott said:

'What?'

It was apparent that Chilcott was the more surprised.

'There's no need for this.'

'You should know better than anyone, Commissioner, the requirement for all incomers to be processed.'

Chilcott walked behind the counter and lifted the handset from a unit on the wall. Savage was intrigued. Some battle was taking place here, of which thus far he knew nothing. Anne said,

'I'm curious. What would be the purpose of this processing?'

At the telephone, Chilcott said,

'Command.'

The woman examined Anne with eyes like currants from above the mask.

'That, surely, is evident.'

'But if we have acclimatised to the Outside, then you, surely, are more likely to contaminate us, than we, you.' Anne smiled. 'Unless, of course, we're speaking philosophically.'

In a sharp tone, Chilcott said,

'*Now.*'

He restored the receiver crisply to its rest. Anne turned to Cassie.

'Perhaps we should leave, darling.'

The woman contrived to vocalise a smirk:

'Nobody leaves.'

Anne grinned at Savage.

'It appears we may be setting all manner of precedents.'

At this point, a pleasant-faced, younger man entered from behind the counter (Savage had a powerful impression that he had been waiting for a cue). He was all apology: My fault entirely, Sister not informed, of course you may pass through. He added:

'I'm Doctor Boyce, by the way.'

They were ushered to a second set of swing doors, which replicated the first.

It was plain that Chilcott had been taught a lesson – and Savage, too – in the limitations of Chilcott's power. What interested Savage was that it had been judged necessary.

He knew, too, that his and Anne's reactions to the contrived incident had been watched with care. He must warn her that the interior in which they now found themselves was ideal for the placement of covert optics and microphones.

Beyond the doors, Chilcott said,

'Mary – Lieutenant Smith – will take over now. I'll see you at debriefing. One hour.'

It was clear that he smarted. He bowed and turned to a nearby stairwell, down which he descended rapidly from sight – to assess, no doubt, what damage he had sustained in the recent encounter. Mary said,

'Shall we?'

They walked along a corridor, more human in aspect, with green walls and marbled composition flooring; but still a working space. There were doors on either side, from above which projected stencilled signs: TOOLS, CLOTHING, MISSING PERSONS. Savage's ears detected the faint reverberation of turbines (driven from the sea?). Partway, they came to lifts, beside which stood an older man, in a dark blue boiler suit, who came to attention at Savage's approach:

'Good to have you with us at last, sir.'

He wore a sergeant's stripes on his sleeve, the ribbons of an old soldier on his chest and on his tunic a modest patch which read: POLICE. Savage said,

'Thank you.'

The policeman drew open the cage door, they stepped into the lift and he closed a plastic safety screen behind them.

The interior was crowded by their weapons and equipment. There was a digital keypad and a simple console, with Up, Down and Stop buttons. There was also a crank handle, for use in the event of power failure. Mary pressed the Up button. Savage counted – twelve seconds, against the descending shaft wall. But he was not so foolish as to suppose that, because they passed no landing stage, they had ascended only one level. He would learn only what the Boss wished him to learn.

They emerged into a discreetly-lit, plain green corridor, with coarse fibre carpet and doors along one wall. Mary turned them to the left. Anne said,

'Which level is this?'

'Executive accommodation.'

'Executive?'

'The ruling council.'

'Of course.'

They came to the last door but one. Savage had discerned by now that the doors were not, as he had supposed, of wood, but of laminated metal; and that they, too, seated in coamings. He was reminded of the accommodation on board ship. Perhaps flooding was a danger. Mary said,

'It's a suite made from adjoining rooms, I hope that'll be alright?'

Anne said,

'Entirely.'

'We thought you'd like to stay together, to begin with.'

Cassie said,

'We'd like to stay together all the time.'

'You might want to try bunking in with the other girls, Cassie. The dorms are tremendous fun.'

'No, thank you.'

Savage hated the room. It was a box in the rock. He felt isolated from all natural sign which oriented him. He could not tune in. He felt entombed. It was impossible that he should remain in this alien place.

He did not listen as Mary, in the doorway between the two rooms, expatiated on their quarters to Cassie and Anne.

There was box ducting in the angle of low ceiling and walls, with swivel air vents at intervals along it. The bunk unfolded from one wall. There were two upright plastic chairs and a formica work surface. A television set on a stand. And two curtained alcoves. Behind the plastic of one was a shower stall; in the other, a shiny thermal jumpsuit hung from a hanger, as though it were a human pelt.

There was in the room no living surface; and, in the shadowless lighting, nowhere that he could hide.

He would withdraw into himself; and, from there, watch.

He heard a curtain drawn aside and Mary said,

'Perhaps, you'd like to try one of our famous space suits.'

Anne said,

'I think not, thank you.'

'Actually, it's a thoroughly practical garment, for the controlled environment in which we live.'

'I'm sure.'

'Certainly, you won't need to wear uniform or carry weapons any longer.'

Cassie said,

'Does the television work?'

'Absolutely. There's Community News every night. Cartoons. Movies. The Executive believes it's tremendously important to keep people informed.'

Anne said,

'I imagine.'

'Oh, and there's a disco in the Rec Hall tonight, Cassie. I'm sure you'd like to go to that.'

Anne said,

'A *disco*?'

Her disbelief mirrored Savage's.

'Lots of young people, your own age.'

Cassie said,

'I'm not much interested in that sort of thing.'

But Savage thought: Shouldn't she be? He wondered what harm he might have done her.

Mary's bonhomie was on the wane. She appeared relieved when they declined further explication and said:

'Forty minutes, then. Debriefing.'

When she had left, Anne came to the intercommunicating doorway.

'You don't suppose we make them uncomfortable?'

Savage touched fingertips to eyes and ears and fanned his hands to indicate surveillance. To his surprise, Anne laughed:

'They do offer hostages to fortune, don't they?' This, Savage did not understand. She turned to Cassie. 'I vote we wear uniforms and carry weapons; it so obviously gets up their noses.'

Savage said,

'You must do what you think is right.'

She comprehended his meaning at once: your battles are your own now (and mine, mine). She grinned:

'Believe me, Mr Savage, I intend to.'

He sorted his kit, sewed what needed to be mended and emptied himself for battle. There came a knock at the door.

'Come in.'

Anne said,

'We arrived at a compromise.'

He was taken aback. He had seen her in civilian clothing before, but now she wore a severely-tailored suit, with skirt shorter than he would have anticipated (her legs were shapely and strong) and a jacket cleft in such fashion that, while it revealed nothing, seemed to reveal much. She appeared wholly in command of herself.

Cassie wore the pink dress that he had seen earlier, but this time she had tied about her head a flax of bright ribbons.

They looked intensely feminine; a mother and daughter – except that each held a combat rifle and carried, over one shoulder, belt kit.

He was shocked by what he had done to them; glad that soon it would be ended.

This time, with Chilcott, they descended in the lift; impossible to judge how far (twenty seconds); and emerged into a dimly-lit corridor with staff padding about and opened doors, designated OPS, COMMS, MAP ROOM, through which there emanated the phosphor glow of screens and the squawk of radio traffic.

Savage did not for a moment believe that he was being offered the heart of the machine.

At this level, he noted, Security was dressed in red; and was armed; and did not pretend to be police.

They crossed a T-junction at the end of the corridor and approached a single door, inscribed COMMAND.

Debriefing.

Close-quarter battle.

There were in the room four persons other than themselves. To the left, a young woman, alone at a conference table, a laptop computer before her. To the right, an older, smartly-dressed woman, who sat in a padded, armed chair and who, alone, did not rise at their entry. Half left, stood a man in the uniform of a Major-General. And half right, there came from behind an all but bare desk, a man of burnished appearance, who wore a fawn tunic, buttoned to the neck, and matching trousers. Chilcott said,

'This is our Chief Executive, George Trevelyan. John Savage. His wife, Anne. And their daughter, Cassie.'

The man extended a hand.

'This is an honour, Mr Savage.' They exchanged grips. 'I understand that you prefer the soubriquet "Mister"?' Savage nodded. 'I think it fair to say that, but for your efforts, our establishment would be one-third its present size. We are in awe of your accomplishments.'

Somehow the man's ease disguised his physical dimension. He was in every particular more imposing than Savage – who said now:

'Thank you.'

The man bowed to Anne.

'You, too, are most welcome, Mrs Savage.'

Anne nodded.

'And, ah, Cassie, is it?'

'Yes, sir.'

But this was not a man to forget a name, once given it. He was master of his circumstances.

This was the Boss. He gestured.

'Please, sit.'

Chairs had been arranged for them about a low, glass-topped table. After a glance at Savage, Cassie and Anne sat, while he remained standing. Trevelyan said,

'Let me introduce Doctor Lane.' The middle-aged woman in the armed chair. 'She will look to your medical needs, along with Doctor Boyce, whom I understand you've met.'

The woman smiled.

'Mrs Savage. Cassie. I hope we shall be friends.'

Savage understood that this was a doctor, not of the body, but of the mind. Trevelyan said,

'And this is General Strang, Commander-in-Chief, all Area Forces.'

Not my boss, Savage thought. But the man's decorations implied service other than behind a desk and in a moment he nodded:

'General.'

The other said,

'Why don't you use your rank? Are you ashamed of it?'

Immediately, Savage regretted his courtesy. But Trevelyan smiled:

'I'm sure that Mr Savage has the best of reasons, Michael.' He contrived to make this not sound a rebuke of Strang; the politician's skill. He indicated the young woman at the conference table, who, as Mary had, wore a jumpsuit. 'And this is my amanuensis, Norah.'

The young woman nodded.

'Good morning, sir.'

'Good morning.'

Trevelyan reseated himself behind his desk.

'I suggest that we speak to Mrs Savage and to Cassie first; and then, while they enjoy a tour of the Complex, we can turn to formal debriefing.'

In a pleasant tone, Anne said,

'I think we should prefer to be seen together.'

'Of course; but I'm sure you appreciate that aspects of Mr Savage's work are . . .'

'. . . Secure?'

She was faintly ironic.

'Precisely. Secure.'

Not least from you, Savage thought. He became aware that Anne was watching him: but he did not know what he was being asked; and he merely nodded. She said,

'Very well.'

There was a *dink* as Norah activated her computer. She said,

'What was your name before, Mrs Savage?'

'Why would you ask me that?'

'So that I can feed it into our data base.'

Anne transferred her smile to Trevelyan:

'Wouldn't it be sensible to see whether or not we decide to stay, before you alter your records?'

Savage was greatly taken by this pre-emptive strike. But for all Anne's need to establish her identity in a new environment, the weakness of her position was that she lacked any alternative. Trevelyan was at once gracious.

'You are perfectly correct, Mrs Savage. It is for us to persuade you.'

Savage thought: This is a dangerous man. He cares nothing for the appearance of victory. He will cede any ground in pursuit of his aims. Doctor Lane said,

'I think you misunderstand, Anne. It's to find whether other members of your family are still alive.'

It was evident that this was not a possibility that had occurred to Anne. Nor was she impressed by it.

'I think it unlikely. My husband and daughter were at the Old Capital. And my son died in my arms.'

Lane said,

'I'm sorry.'

Trevelyan turned sympathetically to Cassie:

'Perhaps, Cassie . . .?'

Anne took the child's hand.

'Cassie's with us now.'

And Cassie said,

'We're a family.'

Again, Trevelyan adroitly shifted his stance.

'You're absolutely right, Cassie. What matters now are new forms, new ties; the future, not the past.'

Anne said,

'Just so.'

There was a silence. Savage sat. Trevelyan said,

'Where are you from, Mrs Savage?'

'Lulford.'

'That's . . . a hundred miles north of where Mr Savage established his safe house?'

'Approximately.'

'How came you to survive?'

Anne chuckled.

'Now there's an intriguing speculation.'

Trevelyan enjoyed her jest.

'Well, metaphysics aside, what were the practicalities of it?'

In a moment, Anne said,

'We were in the cellar. My son and I.' It was a common experience, Savage had found, that, like himself, survivors had been below ground level when the Event had occurred. Anne said, 'Some . . . passage passed across us. Some force. We both blacked out, for a moment.' This, too, had been a common recollection (although not of Savage's). She said, 'When we came to, there had been a partial collapse of the house. We were trapped in the cellar.'

'For how long?'

'Fortunately, the village was often cut off. By floods. Or snows. So we had laid in a supply of tinned food. And an emergency

cooker.' Most survivors had been possessed of some such serendipi-
tous cache. 'And the pump kept working.' Her face pinched.
'Survival was not a problem. And we heard your broadcasts. Stay
where you are. Wait for the Army to reach you.'

Strang said,

'Signal strength was satisfactory?'

'Oh, the *strength* was fine.'

Trevelyan said,

'What happened, Mrs Savage?'

'My son was ill. That's why he was away from school.'

Lane said,

'What was the trouble?'

'Some bronchial infection. But he grew worse.'

Trevelyan said,

'You decided to make a move.'

'I realised that if we didn't, he'd die. Waiting for the Army was
like waiting for snow in the Sahara.'

Strang bristled:

'We ventured north the moment it was practicable –'

'Oh, nonsense, General.' Anne sounded more weary than
angered. 'You didn't move until you were absolutely certain that the
dying were dead. And that you wouldn't have to clear up the mess
you'd made.'

'I don't know what you mean by – '

Trevelyan intervened:

'It's alright, Michael.' He looked at Anne. 'You're right, Mrs
Savage. We let the afflicted die. There was nothing we could do for
them. And I was not prepared to allow our facilities here to be
overwhelmed. Our priority was the living. But it was I who made
that decision, not General Strang. And I should do the same again.'

'I'm sure they're comforted.'

'No less comforted, I imagine, than by your husband's work.
Except that his, being the swifter sword, was the more merciful.'

Savage wondered for whom it had been the more merciful. In a
quiet tone, Anne said,

'But he, at least, was there.'

'We are all profoundly conscious of that fact. But to blame
General Strang for our present predicament is patently absurd.'

In a moment, Anne smiled.

'Who should we blame? You?'

Trevelyan spread innocent hands.

'I am a mere civil servant.'

'*Mere*?'

Her mild mockery was unconcealed; but Trevelyan said simply:

'There is a summary of the latest intelligence on the desk in your room.'

She contemplated him; then his team.

'You don't *know* what happened, do you?'

There was silence. She said,

'You haven't the faintest idea what caused this, any more than I have.'

Savage knew it to be the truth. Trevelyan said,

'All information has not yet been collated –'

She turned away with a soft laugh.

'Dear God. I thought at least there'd been a war. Or some environmental catastrophe to have orphaned us.'

Had there been a war, Savage would have been activated. Trevelyan said,

'Perhaps that is what occurred, but –'

'But you don't know.'

She continued to shake her head in amused wonder. Trevelyan said,

'I suggest that we abandon the delights of fantasy and return to the realities of survival.' Savage thought it a weakness, (as, plainly did Anne) that Trevelyan could not admit ignorance, as though he felt his authority threatened thereby. Trevelyan continued: 'Where, on the road, did you encounter Mr Savage?'

Savage said,

'Clay Cross.'

'How long had that taken?'

Anne said,

'Twenty-three days. And one half.'

'. . . That was a remarkable achievement.'

She shrugged.

'Timmy ordered everything. When to march. Eat. Hide. Sleep.

He knew that he was dying. But his spirit never yielded.' She smiled. 'One might say that he returned to me the gift of life.'

There was uncomfort in the room. Trevelyan murmured:

'If you would prefer to continue this later . . .?'

Anne smiled.

'Oh, take your chance. You may not get another.'

For the first time, Savage became concerned as to Anne's tactics. Trevelyan said,

'Mr Savage took you to his safe house?'

'Weren't you told?'

So Anne had deduced that, far from picking them up on the road, Sparrow held a watching brief over the house. Trevelyan said,

'What about you, Cassie? Where were you, when the incident occurred?'

But, as she had before, Anne said,

'Cassie's with us now.'

Lane stirred.

'If we are to place Cassie in a class . . .'

Cassie exhibited alarm.

'Class . . .?'

Anne said,

'Any decisions regarding Cassie's future will be made only by Mr Savage and myself.'

She was building on untenable ground. Savage must warn her. In a gentle tone, Trevelyan said,

'We are not your enemy, Anne.'

Abruptly, she was openly derisive.

'You think not?'

Strang was stiff.

'Wouldn't it be fairer to know us, madam, before you judge us?'

'Thank you, General. Once was enough.'

It was as though, in a single, unregarded moment, Anne had embarked on a course of resolute disengagement – and the shocked Savage could not fathom where she supposed it might lead her. Chilcott said,

'I think that what Mrs Savage means –'

Trevelyan was dry.

'I fancy we can count on Mrs Savage to speak for herself.'

Anne laughed. Trevelyan looked to Savage.

'Where did you find Cassie?'

But Anne had not finished.

'That, too, is surely well known to you? Or has Mr Sparrow been naughty again?'

Now that the conflict was overt, she was applying her scalpel to a sensitive place. Plainly, she understood that Sparrow had witnessed – and had chosen not to prevent – the capture of Cassie (and of the others). And she posed, by implication, two questions of Trevelyan: How much are you told? How much do you approve? Strang said,

'We need to gather intelligence –'

But Trevelyan was too practised to pursue a line potentially obliquitous of himself. He said,

'Tell us about your journey from the safe house.'

Anne said,

'What about it?'

'Did you encounter difficulties?'

'Of what type?'

Strang was becoming impatient.

'With Scavengers. Armed men.'

'Which, General?'

'I'm sorry?'

'Soldiers are armed men.'

This was dangerous ground. Strang scowled.

'Clearly, they fall into a different category.'

'Really? How can you tell?'

Trevelyan was swift to the implication.

'Are you saying that you had trouble with soldiers?'

But Anne was alert to the threat that the dead patrol represented for them.

'Only with their artefacts.'

'Their artefacts?'

'Mines, General.'

'*Mines?*' Strang's puzzlement was transparently genuine. 'Why would my people lay mines against a retreating enemy? They would be a menace only to themselves.'

'We've developed some remarkable fauna, then.'

Trevelyan was watching Savage.

'You encountered mines?'

It was impossible to read his face. But the speculation turned in Savage's mind that Mordred might have acted as provocateur for Trevelyan. He said,

'AP mines.'

Cassie said,

'They blow people to pieces.'

There was silence. Trevelyan frowned.

'You shouldn't have had to see that, Cassie. I'm sorry.'

Anne expressed distaste for sympathy from such a source, but the child said simply:

'It doesn't matter.'

'It matters.' Trevelyan rose abruptly and came from behind his desk. 'You've both been extremely patient. Thank you.' Savage realised, to his surprise, that for the women the interview was ended. Trevelyan looked to the back of the room: 'Please, show Mrs Savage and Cassie anything they wish to see, Mary. Anything.'

Savage had not heard the young lieutenant enter behind them. Anne extended a hand to Trevelyan.

'I'll say goodbye, then. It seems unlikely that we shall meet again.'

He took her hand gravely.

'Well, if not you, Mrs Savage, perhaps we can persuade young Cassie here.'

When he made to place a hand on the child's shoulder, she recoiled with such violence that it shocked the room.

'*No*! We stick together!'

Trevelyan's smile became a rictus.

'Of course.'

But he had suffered damage.

All the same, Savage was convinced that Anne had chosen the wrong battle on the wrong ground: he must warn her as soon as he was able.

Not that it had not been a pleasure to witness others on the end of her tongue. And certainly it was the case that, on their present battleground, she was far better equipped to prevail than he.

With edge, Mary said,

'Shall we, Mrs Savage?'

As they made to leave, Cassie holding fast to Anne's hand, Anne paused, where Savage stood. She said,

'Alright?'

Was he being asked whether he needed her help? He nodded dismissal. She fixed him with a look of the utmost unfathomability. At that moment, Cassie touched his fingers: it was as though there passed through her, from the woman to himself, a charge of extraordinary potency. Then Anne nodded decisively.

'Good.'

Her certainty baffled him.

There was silence after the women had gone. Trevelyan said,

'A remarkable woman.'

It amused Savage that no mention had been made of the weapons and equipment they carried. Trevelyan said,

'Perhaps, after all, you should take her with you, when you return to the house.'

What was being said to him? That he *would* return? That Trevelyan recognised a troublemaker when he met one? Trevelyan said,

'Thank you, Doctor.' Lane rose. 'Norah.' The young woman closed down her computer. 'Commissioner.' It was plain that Chilcott resented exclusion, but acquiesced in the requirements of 'security', for the sake of his dignity.

When this further exodus had taken place, Strang said,

'This is your formal debriefing.'

Savage said nothing. Trevelyan said,

'How did you survive?'

'I was in the ground.'

Strang said,

'In your team hide? At our dumps under the Southern Forest?'

Savage said,

'Operational details are restricted.'

Trevelyan was dry.

'Not, surely, from your Commanding Officer?'

'General Strang is not my C.O.'

Strang said,

'Are you saying you do not accept my authority?'

'Yes.'

Trevelyan spread hands.

'Whose, then? Mine?'

'You are the civil power here.'

Strang was sharp:

'And you – supposedly – are acting in aid of a civil power. Do so.'

'I have other work now.'

Trevelyan said,

'Of a covert nature, no doubt?'

'If you say it.'

Strang was contemptuous:

'Ah, don't dramatise yourself, man. Your tasks are no secret. To disrupt enemy lines of supply and communication. To destroy his chain and centres of command. To bring havoc to his efforts at reorganisation. But *also*. To help survivors. To dispose of the dead. To assist us in our efforts here to build order out of chaos. Have you forgotten that?'

Savage thought that he would never forget.

But how do you bring havoc to perfect disorder? How do you tell enemy from friend, when all are melted? How do you read the map of dissolution, when you can no longer find even yourself on it? Trevelyan said,

'Sparrow has experienced no difficulty in accepting our authority.'

Savage thought: You think not? He said,

'I am not Sparrow.'

But he wondered what he was. Strang said,

'Are you saying openly that you are a renegade?'

'If that's the word you want to use.'

He had not thought himself outside the law. Trevelyan said,

'What word would you choose?'

Savage said nothing. Strang said,

'Sparrow knew nothing of your presence on this ground.'

'I knew nothing of his.'

'But he was assigned to this area in time of emergency.'

'That only tells you what he was before, not what he is now.'

Trevelyan was quick:

'How interesting that you should put it in just those terms. Tell me, Savage. What were *you* before? And what are *you* now?'

Savage felt that he had said too much. Not unconscious of irony, he said,

'I can't answer such questions.'

Strang was impatient.

'This is a waste of time.'

But Trevelyan, plainly, was enjoying himself.

'What are you going to do about the people at the house?'

'Why would I do anything about them?'

'They are, after all, your people.'

'That's ridiculous.'

Strang said,

'They will do what you tell them.'

'They don't belong to me, any more than they do to you.'

Trevelyan was at him immediately:

'But they do *precisely* belong to us.' His passion, though subdued, was unmistakable. 'We have an absolute duty to gather them in. To provide for them here a place of order and safety and purpose.' He smiled then, as though in self-mockery. 'And we shall not abandon even one of our lambs, Savage. Not even one!'

Strang said, flatly:

'Least of all, a doctor, an engineer, a farmer . . .'

Savage said,

'I'm not trying to take them from you.'

Trevelyan said,

'The irony is, Savage, that I believe you. The question is, Do they?'

The man's perception troubled Savage. Of Sarah, he was unsure. Trevelyan said,

'I have a suggestion to make.' He was again droll. 'Why don't you return to the house? Tell them about us. Ensure a smooth handover. Do that last service, for them and for us. And then . . .' He made a gesture. 'You will be free to wander in whatever wilderness your spirit craves.'

Savage thought it ironic that Trevelyan, seeking to trap him at the house, guaranteed his best hope of escape. He said,

'I'll leave now.'

He turned away. Trevelyan chuckled:

'I'm afraid there'll be no flying until tomorrow. But at first light, I promise you.' Savage nodded. 'Besides, there are many here anxious to speak with you. You can spare them one meal. Midday. It is arranged.'

His tone brooked no argument. Remembering his reception on arrival, Savage grew uneasy.

'I won't sleep here.'

Strang said,

'You are not being given the option.'

'Not in the rock.'

If they thought it weakness, let them. Trevelyan shrugged.

'If you wish to sleep in the valley, I have no objection to that.'

Unexpectedly, Strang said,

'Stay with us.'

His tone held such simplicity that Savage looked at him.

'What?'

Trevelyan said,

'We need you, Savage. A future is not made merely of survival. But of decency; and honour; and integrity. Stay with us. Please.'

Savage had not expected an appeal of such naked sincerity and it disturbed him. But he knew, too, that for him it had come too late. Strang said,

'Your comrades are here.'

This, plainly, was a reference to Sparrow and his gang. Savage heard himself say:

'Not my comrades.'

He had not known that he was ready publicly to deny them; nor that it would hurt so much, when he did. Trevelyan said,

'Don't do it, Savage. Don't walk away from your own kind.'

Perhaps it was true: perhaps he had become . . . detached from his own species. But, for him, the future was not here. Whatever had shifted in him, had shifted irrevocably.

He could no longer . . . get back. He said,

'I can't stay here.'

Trevelyan sighed.

'Very well.'

He touched his desk and Chilcott came in.

'Show Mr Savage whatever he wishes to see.'

In spite of himself, Savage said,

'What about the woman?'

'Your wife?' The query was not entirely mocking. 'Does she know you mean to leave her here?'

'Yes.'

'And the child? Does she?'

Savage said nothing. Trevelyan said,

'I wonder if you know, Savage, what waters you dabble in?'

Savage quit the room. He felt that, in some sense he could not fathom, a defeat had been inflicted on him.

Chilcott said,

'What do you want to see first?'

Savage felt his disapproval.

'Does it matter?'

'In fact, all doors are open to you.'

Except, Savage thought, the one I want.

It was impossible not to be impressed.

In the OPS, COMMS and MAP rooms, nothing appeared hidden from him. On a vertical plotting table, he saw his house, encircled now by designated units (Sparrow Force, of course, was not identified). He listened to desultory, local radio traffic (Sparrow Force would not be on this net). Only in SECURITY – and then patently in defiance of orders – had half the banked monitor screens been shut down.

When they came to a main storage bay, Savage laughed: for such was its size and so comprehensively was it stacked with supplies of every description, that his concern that Anne should guard the puny stock he had given her seemed to him absurd. The facility, so Chilcott assured him, was one of three in the Complex.

As they approached the Rec Hall, they heard the spiky *ska* of electronic battle. Chilcott turned into the room. It was a plain space of acceptable dimensions with a rostrum stage at one end and, all about the cleared floor, tables for billiards, cards and other indoor activities. Immediately to the left of the door was a row of four arcade consoles, one of which had been activated. Before its display, two young faces flickered raptly in the emergency-lit room. Chilcott said,

'Why aren't you two at school?'

'Off sick, sir.'

'Space sickness?'

They grinned.

'Yes, sir.'

The dining hall was as large as a storage bay, its composition floor covered by a multitude of formica-topped tables, with four hardback chairs drawn up to each. Along the rear wall was a stainless steel serving counter with kitchens beyond, from which emanated an institutional smell which Savage loathed.

They had been in the room barely twenty seconds when there came from the kitchen first one and then another woman, wiping hands before taking Savage's own:

'How wonderful to see you again, Mr Savage . . .'

'Thank God you've come at last.'

He knew that he must leave this place as soon as he was able.

As they made to quit the room, he caught sight of a gallery of images beside the door. Snapshots. All of children. Hugging dogs. Holding hands with adults. Chilcott said,

'The Wailing Wall.'

'What?'

'That's what the women call it. A nostrum, one supposes, against grief. The lost children. No hope for them now.'

Savage remembered them.

Maddened by abuse, defeated by abandonment.

Those he had killed.

The one.

Chilcott said,

'Perhaps you would . . .?'

To his horror, Savage recognised one of them. Not so much the face, as the fate. He touched a photograph.

'This one's dead.'

'I'll tell the mother.' Chilcott read a name from the back. 'Mrs Langley. Any others?'

But Savage could bring himself to look no further.

'No. No.'

Child soup.

The sleeping accommodation was segregated by gender; and here some effort had been made to humanise the interior, with shaded lights, pictures, curtained cubicles. The children's quarters were on a separate level. Bold colours. Posters of past icons. A jukebox. Computer terminals. At one end, a 'den' for younger children, with soft toys and inflated animals. Savage said,

'Don't the kids want to live with their parents?'

'Most have none. Those who have, prefer the company of other children.' Chilcott frowned. 'Perhaps we made too much of them. But they *are* the future.' He looked along the children's world. 'I don't think they trust us any longer. They trust only one another.'

Savage shrugged.

'Haven't they always?'

But in his experience, children had proved no more trustworthy than adults. He had found his place in the interstices between the two.

For some reason, he had supposed that the hospital would be empty of patients.

The ward was a narrow space, white and steel, in which the beds pulled out on runners from the walls, as though they were mortuary drawers.

The moment he saw the boy, Savage thought: *Get out now.*

But he could not.

As he advanced down the aisle (not hearing what Doctor Boyce and Chilcott said), the boy came squarely into view. It was a look that Savage had seen so often: the ineffable vacancy of impending death. Because the boy was clutching the guard rail at his side while his eyes were yet directed emptily forward, there was across his collar bone a crease of flesh, as though his skin had become too loose for his frame (and that about his skull, too tight).

It was a spectacle that Savage had witnessed in so many places, he might have supposed it to be the natural condition of the young.

The boy exhibited no awareness of their presence. Savage said,

'What's wrong with him?'

Boyce said,

'Failure to thrive.'

'What's that?'

Boyce made a gesture, as of disavowal.

'He won't eat. Or sleep. Or . . . communicate.'

'Why not?'

Wasn't this a modern hospital? From close at hand, a female voice said:

'Survivor syndrome, Mr Savage.'

Doctor Lane had joined them. Chilcott said,

'It does have a ring, doesn't it?'

But his irony passed her by.

'Despite Myles's cynicism, it is, in fact, all too common. And takes many forms. Unprovoked aggression. Bedwetting. Fear of the Outside. Waking nightmares. Images of madness.' Did she, at that moment, peer keenly at Savage? 'We've helped many. But young Joshua, here . . .'

She stepped forward to ruffle the boy's hair. Savage wanted to dash her hand away. She said,

'He seems determined to elude us.'

Chilcott said,

'I fear we may have our first successful escapee.'

Boyce was uncomfortable.

'I wouldn't put it like that.'

Savage said,

'He's dying.'

'Oh, we can keep him *alive*. That's not the problem.'

'He's dying.'

Lane said,

'Perhaps you would speak to him.'

'. . . What?'

Chilcott said,

'That's enough of this.'

But the woman persisted.

'He must have passed through your hands. He may remember you.'

Savage did not trust her: but he understood now that this was why he had come to the boy's side.

He set down his rifle on the foot of the bed and sat near to him. At that moment, the woman obtruded with a put-on 'voice':

'You've got a visitor, Joshua.'

'*Shut up!*'

The violence of this caused her to step back.

The boy showed no sign. Savage contemplated him.

'Hullo, Joshua. Do you remember me? Mr Savage. At the house. John Savage.'

It was then that Savage remembered that he had offered his name as a light to another child in the darkness; and that he was on the point of betraying her. He thought: *Stay back! Don't come out!*

But the boy's eyelids fluttered and his eyes lolled glassily until the present rushed to fill them. Savage thought: *Dear God. What have I done?*

The boy peered at him as though along a tunnel of obscure kinship. He detached his hands and fastened them, one at a time, onto Savage's own. In a voice coarse with disuse, he said,

'Have you come to fetch me?'

The hair reared on Savage's neck.

'. . . What?'

The boy leaned forward to share the secret of his soul.

'I don't want to stay here.'

The unimaginable misery of Savage's own childhood welled through him: it was as though he were calling over time to himself from unfathomable desolation –

And then the woman deployed her 'voice' again:

'Oh, do stay with us, Joshua.'

A cry was wrenched from Savage. By the time he looked back, the boy had gone, clamped to the rail again, although his hands seemed still to hang as barbs in Savage's flesh. Savage said,

'Look.' He took the boy's sticks of arms in his awkward grasp. 'I'll come back!'

But when Lane said,

'To what purpose, Mr Savage?'

He knew that she was right. He was a purveyor of false hope. He took up his rifle and made for the door. Boyce said,

'He'll receive the best treatment.'

'Let him die.'

'I assure you –'

Savage shouted:

'Let him die!'

But this, too, was not what he wanted.

It was as though he were abandoning himself.

To Chilcott, he said,

'Get me out of here.'

'This way.'

But as they turned along another corridor, they passed Cassie and Anne outside the school. It was Mary Smith who spoke his name:

'Ah, Mr Savage.'

But it was the appeal in Cassie's eyes which slowed him – and the proprietorial concern with which Anne approached that angered him:

'Are you alright?'

'I'm fine.'

Mary Smith said,

'I was just showing Cassie and Anne the excellence of our school. Your daughter will receive a first-class education here.'

She laid possessive hands on Cassie, which were immediately shrugged off. From the child's expression, Savage suspected that the 'place' from which she had come had been a school or similar institution. Anne said,

'The relevance of the education is another matter.'

They stood in a small, open foyer, which afforded a view through glass-topped doors into one classroom before them and another behind. Mary said,

'The basis of a sound education, surely, never varies?'

At that moment, the door behind them opened and a female voice said:

'I wonder if you would say a few words to the boys, Mr Savage? It would mean so much to them.'

The teacher stood at the open doorway. Beyond, boys craned for a glimpse of Savage. Chilcott said,

'We've a lot to do.'

And Anne was at once beside Savage:

'You don't have to do this.'

Mary said,

'It's not a question of –'

The boys called:

'Do come in!'

'Please, sir. Come!'

Bizarrely, the teacher began to clap and the boys took it up. Anne gripped his arm:

'*You don't have to do this.*'

Perhaps it was her insistence on protecting him which goaded him forward.

Yet even as he advanced to the head of the class, he knew that he had made a mistake. To delay facing the children, he concentrated on a map which was attached to the wall before him. It consisted of cartridge sheets taped together and depicted, in line and wash, their vestigial, known world, against a vastness of terra incognita.

From a scuttering of footfalls at his back, Savage deduced that the girls, too, had been let into the room. To the teacher, he said,

'What do you want me to say to them?'

'Tell them of your exploits. Most have . . . encountered you before.'

Savage turned. The space was packed with young faces and bodies, which coalesced before him; at the front was a single, unoccupied desk, which he took to be the teacher's. To one side, Anne watched without expression. Quiet stilled the room.

He had nothing to say to them.

He thought: *What do you want of me?*

Anne stirred. Perhaps sensing his incapacity, the teacher said,

'Why don't you ask questions, Class?'

A boy said,

'Have you been engaging the enemy, sir?'

'. . . The enemy?'

Another said,

'The levellers, sir. The scum.'

The teacher murmured:

'The children know the Vandals from personal experience.'

Oh, the Scavengers.

'They're finished.'

Boys punched the air in triumph, which disgusted him. A girl said,

'Will you be staying with us now?'

He was unsure how he was supposed to respond to this. Again, the teacher rescued him.

'I don't imagine Mr Savage is free to discuss confidential orders.'

This met with approbation.

Suddenly, Savage understood.

The shunned place was *Joshua's.*

He missed the next question.

He felt sick. He said,

'Why don't you sit there?'

'Eugh!'

A boy made pantomime of sticking a finger down his throat and pretending to vomit.

'Joshua, sir.'

'. . . What?'

'He's a wet –'

'A wipe –'

'A *geek*, sir –'

Savage heard a shout:

'*What do you know?*'

It was inconceivable to him that after such time the enemy should remain unchanged. He heard a baying down the years.

Anne stood before him.

'That's enough.'

Deflecting the weapon that he had raised.

'. . . What?'

She took his sleeve.

'We've finished here.'

Beyond her, the children were cowed and uncomprehending. Savage wanted to kill them.

Outside the classroom, he said,

'Enough.'

But the corridor was crowded and a bell rang. Mary said,

'It's the midday meal.'

222

Anne was sharp:

'Not now!'

It was Chilcott who persuaded him, murmuring at his ear:

'Once it is done . . .'

Against Anne's protestations, he acquiesced. For a last time.

There was no space in the dining hall and chatter rang off a bright ceiling. As they followed Mary between the tables, recognition passed across the company and the entire assembly stood to applaud and to cheer him. When Savage hesitated, Chilcott urged him on:

'The sooner we sit . . .'

The more deeply they pressed into the throng, the more hands reached to touch him and he shrank from them. By the time they had come to a table at the centre of the concourse, whose surface was distinguished by white linen and glass and silver cutlery, Savage felt intolerably exposed.

Four young people waited to serve them – with whose help they draped belt kit over the backs of chairs and set rifles at their feet.

Savage saw now that at an adjacent table sat Trevelyan, Lane and Strang; and that Trevelyan regarded him with a benign disdain, as though to accentuate the napery and silver for the mockery they were.

A boy said,

'Will you take wine, sir?'

Savage shook his head.

'I drink water.'

Anne, too, declined and Cassie chose Coca-Cola. Children brought soup. Mary drew their attention to the menu: roast lamb, potatoes, peas; mousse; fresh bread, butter; cheese and biscuits to follow.

'When did you last have a freshly-cooked, four-course meal, Cassie?'

The girl said,

'Yesterday.'

Savage was cheered by this and Anne slyly entertained.

'When did *you*, lieutenant?'

Chilcott said,

'We try to make the main meal substantial every day.'

When the young people had withdrawn, Mary said,

'You may like to know that there was an embarrassment of volunteers to serve you, Mr Savage. We had to draw lots.'

Anne said,

'That was probably before your appearance in the classroom, John.'

Chilcott sought lightness.

'What did you make of our community, Mrs Savage?'

Anne shrugged.

'I am not an enthusiast of theme parks.'

Mary said,

'Mrs Savage believes we are merely re-creating the past here.'

'But the past, surely, is what people need. To build on. Where it may lead, we can't know.'

Anne was dry:

'Oh, I think we can say where it won't lead.'

'Where is that?'

'To a viable future.'

Savage's instinct was to agree. Chilcott said,

'You are too harsh.'

'With the same masters? The old agenda? I hardly think so.'

Mary said,

'Why don't you stand for the Executive, Mrs Savage? You could change things.'

Anne smiled.

'Perhaps Mr Savage should. From what I've seen, he'd be a shoo-in.'

Savage was not amused by this; nor was Chilcott:

'Surely, you understand – ?'

But Anne cut across him:

'I understand everything that's going on here. *Everything.*'

Savage knew that since the classroom Anne had sought to convey some meaning to him, but he was no longer prepared to listen: he meant to conclude the meal and be done with them all.

Perhaps Cassie sensed this, for she became taciturn; and Anne, tense.

As soon as they had finished eating, Savage said,

'I'm done here.'

But before he could act, he became aware that, at the next table, Trevelyan was bumping the bole of his knife for silence.

Trevelyan said,

'As you know, we have for our guest today a man to whom each of us owes an unpayable debt. I shall merely introduce him. Ladies and gentlemen, Mr John Savage.'

The ovation erupted again. Trevelyan motioned Savage to rise which, reluctantly, he did, taking up his rifle with him. He despised Trevelyan's artifice, by which he felt diminished. In a little, he glared about him until the tumult waned. Trevelyan said,

'Mr Savage has consented to answer your questions.'

And sat, complacent.

Questions came readily.

When would they be able to return to the Outside? Was life viable yet? Had growth re-established? He found himself embarked on a summation of his world:

'Rabbits and rats returned early. I've counted seven species of birds. Including thrushes. Finches. Blackbirds. The rivers are clear. I've landed roach. Bream. Trout, twice. I've found worms in the ground. Ants. Midges. Bluebottles, near water. Growth is superficial. But the rains should wash away the dust.'

They asked about individual villages. Loxton. Little Deasely. Cartonville.

He began to believe that, after all, the convocation would be painless. And then a woman, smartly dressed and wearing glasses, rose and said:

'Will you be staying here now?'

Immediately, Trevelyan stood.

'Mr Savage's first task, of course, will be to bring in our friends from the safe house.'

Cassie looked up at that; but Savage thought she would accept a brief return to the house, so long as she believed it genuine. The woman said,

'I take it your wife and daughter will be staying?'

There was something familiar about her, which confused Savage. Anne said,

'Why do you take that?'

Trevelyan was on his feet again:

'I have persuaded Mrs Savage and Cassie to return to the house, to speak of our achievements here.'

'. . . What?'

Savage stared at Anne – who murmured, urgently:

'Later.'

Trevelyan said,

'It will be for a morning only.'

Savage said,

'No, that's not right . . .'

But the woman spoke again:

'There's no truth in the rumour, then, that you plan to lead a party to the West?'

More than ever, Savage was confused.

'. . . What?'

Trevelyan said,

'I should explain.' He smiled on Savage, as though to share with him their lordly disdain of a foolish notion. 'There have been persistent rumours here that you intend to lead a party west, in pursuit of some fantastical, never-never future there.'

'. . . I see.'

Indeed, at last Savage was beginning to. The woman said,

'But that's not true?'

She was Trevelyan's stooge. Savage looked at Anne.

'I intend to take no one.'

Trevelyan said,

'Forgive me if I persist, but I'm sure you appreciate the importance of scotching rumour in a community such as ours?'

'Oh, yes.'

They meant not only to discredit Savage before the people, but to deny any future other than their own (before they killed him). Anne had known this but had chosen not to warn him; had plotted, rather, her own treachery. Trevelyan said,

'Have you at any time planned, or do you now plan, to lead an expedition to the West?'

The anticipation in the hall was suffocating. Savage said,

'No.'

It was as though the room died of loss. Trevelyan said,

'In your expert opinion, could such a venture succeed, or only fail?'

'It would fail.'

'Thank you.'

Trevelyan sat. Savage took his rifle and walked out. In that a stumble of applause accompanied him, it was that of bloodied stumps.

As the safety screen folded across the door to the lift, Cassie and Anne hurried forward. Savage said to Chilcott.

'Leave them.'

It had begun to rain, but Savage brushed aside the slicker proffered by the guard and walked out into the valley. Chilcott said,

'That shouldn't have happened.'

'*Not now!*'

As Savage strode on, Chilcott called:

'Don't leave the valley.'

Given the level of firepower on the heights, Savage snorted.

He had been betrayed. Twice. And had himself been used as the instrument of betrayal.

He wished only to be gone from this place.

He looked in his mind into the wilderness and yearned for whatever awaited him there.

The world was not for him.

And yet – to apply the balm of ritual, perhaps, to the hurts of betrayal – he found himself assessing the rain.

Not actually falling yet; seeping, rather, out of a soiled, low overcast.

When he looked along the valley, to gauge the flow of the river, a voice behind him said:

'You were mugged, Mr Savage.'

Anne wore a bright yellow oilskin and sou'wester, which beaded with accumulated fret. A short distance off, Cassie, similarly dressed, waited between Mary and Chilcott.

Savage thought, *Who by?*

Anne said,

'Imagine. All those weeks of people saying, It'll be different when Mr Savage gets here. They had to destroy you.'

'I'm not stupid.'

'I have never thought you so.'

Savage uttered a sound. She said,

'I should have warned you.'

'Against them? Or against you?'

She flared.

'You told me to do what's best for Cassie and myself. I intend to!'

'I will *not* take you with me!'

After a moment, she said,

'. . . That's your privilege.'

'That's right.'

'But how can you deny to others a choice you insist on making for yourself?'

'Have you any idea how little chance there is of success in this?'

She looked away.

'. . . I suppose not.'

'If you come with me, you'll die.'

Abruptly, drops smacked down like marbles between them and at once ceased, leaving over them a premonitory stillness. Anne said,

'Maybe we'd rather die there, than live here.'

Bravado infuriated him.

'What gives you the right to make that choice for *her*?'

'I'm her mother!'

He could not find it in him to deny this. She said,

'Why do you assume she's incapable of making that decision for herself?'

'She's a *child*!'

'So?'

'She needs an education! Give her a chance to be what you yourself called for. A fine young woman.'

Anne said,

'Anything she needs to know, she can learn from you.'

'That's ridiculous!'

He thought he was being mocked, but she said,

'Why don't we ask her?'

'What?'

She turned away.

'Cassie!'

The child started forward.

'Are you crazy?'

'You'll have to tell her sometime. Why not now?'

Ashamed, he said,

'. . . Couldn't you?'

Her contempt was withering.

'After you've gone?'

The child came to them.

'Yes, Mother?'

'Your father's got something to say to you.'

'Yes, Father?'

In the bright waterproofs, she looked seven. He said,

'You've got to have a proper education.'

She lowered her eyes.

'I understand.'

Of course, she did not; but Savage was a coward.

'Right, then.'

Anne said,

'Your father won't be here.'

He did not regard this as helpful. Cassie said,

'It won't take long to pick up the others from the house.'

Anne said,

'No. He has other work to do.'

The child understood at once.

'You promised!'

'Cassie, look –'

'You said we were together now!'

He struggled for explication:

'*I can't do this, Cassie* – !'

The child broke from them with extraordinary force.

'I won't stay here without you!'

At the same moment, the prefigured downpour burst over them.

Anne shouted,

'Wait here!'

And for all that he knew the deluge would be brief, such was its intensity that the fleeting Cassie and the pursuing Anne were reduced on the instant to vaporous wraiths; and then, as it eased, he saw them tug at one another in wet confusion. He could not hear what was said until Cassie shouted at him:

'You said we were a family now!'

Had he? He could no longer remember. Anne spoke to the child. Rain ceased. Cassie shouted:

'I hate you!'

He sought again to explain himself:

'I can't live this life!'

Anne shouted:

'Neither can we!'

Mary had joined them. Once more, the child cried:

'I hate you!'

And they were leaving, into renewed drizzle.

Savage remembered then that, unlike Anne but like himself, Cassie had become genuinely alienated from the inside life.

She could re-learn.

He had not.

But then, unlike Cassie, he had had no one like Anne to anchor him.

All the same, he wondered whether, in serving Cassie, he had in truth served only himself.

He felt that he had betrayed her twice.

The worst was behind him.

And yet, unaccountably, the unthinkable seemed suddenly less so.

To outrun confusion, he walked towards the river, conscious that Chilcott kept pace with him.

Already the new dug ditches were turning to mire and the grass was yielding underfoot. The construction to his right consisted of three wooden buildings, well on the way to completion, and two others, less so. All were temporarily 'roofed' with heavy-duty plastic sheeting and a power cable had been poled across from what plainly was a generator hut. The site was enclosed by nylon rope, threaded through the pigs-tail twists of metal stakes.

The weather had begun to establish a pattern: heavy showers penetrating an ever-deepening gloom. Yet when they came to the river, he saw no significant increase in its flow: rain was not yet falling in the high country.

When it did, there would be a brief window of opportunity. If he were not at the house – or if the rains broke before tomorrow – he would be dead.

Across the river, fumes seeping from the rubbish tip further fouled the murk. Chilcott said,

'She didn't mean what she said.'

'She was right. I made her a promise.'

'She's a child.'

'We don't keep promises to children?'

'Children don't know what they ask. But at what age are we qualified to make decisions affecting our entire lives – and deaths?'

Savage thought: *How about six?*

He had made his decisions at that age: that he would never – *never* – allow himself to be at the mercy of others again.

And he never had.

How could he deny that same right of choice to Cassie now?

Chilcott said,

'Let her go, Savage. There's a life for them here.'

'. . . Shouldn't that be their choice?'

'What choice is uninformed choice?'

'I can tell them.'

'Will they listen? Will they *hear*?'

Perhaps he could take them as far as the house; let events there settle the issue . . .

Chilcott said,

'If you harm them now, I don't believe you'll forgive yourself.'

'Ah.'

Forgiveness.

That was a large matter.

The rain began to fall with greater persistence. Savage was not concerned. He would anticipate more prolonged showers at this stage. Along the valley, figures hacked at the ditches again. Chilcott said,

'Speak to Trevelyan.'

'Why?'

'I don't think he's interested in you. So long as he has the others – all of them – I believe he'll turn a blind eye to your departure.'

Savage was sardonic:

'Will Sparrow turn a blind eye?'

'Oh, I'm confident you can deal with Sparrow. One might say that I count on it.'

'Everyone has their axe to grind?'

(Perhaps Mordred had been *Chilcott's* man). Chilcott said,

'I hardly think that Cassie has. Unless you judge . . . affection to be an axe.'

'Yet you want me to betray her, for my own gain.'

'It is preferable, surely, to her death?'

Anne did not think so. Chilcott said,

'Speak to Trevelyan. He's just along the valley.'

'Where?'

'In the ditch.'

'You're kidding.'

The stygian figures were indistinguishable from the mire in which they laboured.

'Oh, this is the democratic hour.' Savage fell in beside Chilcott, as they walked back along the valley. 'Our leader is a great believer in the axiom that all should take their turn at the coal face. Not least, the members of the Executive Committee.'

Indeed, as they approached, one of the creatures took on the aspect of the Chief Executive. Trevelyan stood waist deep in a trench, wearing a saturated and mud-boltered boiler suit and appearing entirely well pleased with himself (which Strang and Lane, in associated diggings, did not). He greeted Savage with droll expectation:

'An unlooked-for pleasure, Mr Savage. Shall you be joining us?'

The rain eased. Chilcott said,

'We need to speak.'

'Indeed?'

Trevelyan flopped up silt into a wheelbarrow held by a young man dressed like himself. Chilcott said,

'There is room for compromise here.'

'It would ill become me, as a politician, to forgo the delights of compromise.' He extended a hand. 'Andrew.'

The young man hauled him from the ditch with a lack of effort which implied exceptional strength and sureness of foot. This was a bodyguard. Trevelyan waved him a short distance off and waited, with ironic attentiveness, for Chilcott to speak. Chilcott said,

'I take it we agree that a man of Savage's ability, questing to the West, could be of inestimable service to us?'

'In what particular?'

Chilcott frowned.

'Gathering intelligence. Seeking other survivors. Further settlements, perhaps.'

'How will he convey this information to us?'

'Radio transmission is not unknown in that regard.'

Trevelyan lifted an eyebrow.

'Or, perhaps, the mobile telephone?'

It was evident that he placed as little faith in the propagation of radio signals as Savage – not least, now that communication had turned from merely imponderable to downright perverse. It was plain, too, that he was toying with Chilcott and that he had no intention of coming to accommodation with him. He said,

'Mr Savage would undertake this enterprise alone?'

'Naturally.'

'Have Cassie and Anne been apprised of this offer?'

Chilcott said,

'They have.'

But he knew as well as Savage (and, no doubt, Trevelyan) that the matter was unresolved. Trevelyan said,

'And they have agreed to it?'

Chilcott said,

'Mrs Savage is an intelligent woman.'

'Mr Savage?'

Savage said nothing. Trevelyan said,

'Let me put it to you another way. Are you prepared to sneak off, like a thief in the night, and abandon Cassie and Anne to their fate, regardless of their personal wishes in the matter?'

Chilcott said,

'I see no reason to put it –'

'*Be quiet*! Well, Mr Savage? Are you?'

The decision, Savage found, had already been taken.

'No.'

'No. And the others, at the house? Are you prepared to abandon them?'

'No.'

'No.'

Angrily, Savage said,

'They don't belong to you!'

'But followers are power.'

'I don't have followers!'

Trevelyan laughed.

'Do you know yourself so little?'

'They're entitled to make their own choices!'

'Ah. You believe in free will?'

'Yes, I do!'

Drops spotted them again. Chilcott said,

'There's no point to this.'

But Trevelyan was acid:

'And tell me, Savage. When you've led your people into the wilderness, what will you do with them then? What manner of Messiah are you?'

'. . . What?'

The word shocked Savage. Chilcott said,

'That's enough.'

But Trevelyan was scornful.

'You don't know yourself! How can you possibly know them?'

Chilcott said,

'Stop this now.'

Trevelyan said,

'You're a corrupt Christ, Savage! A twisted Jesus!'

The rain broke over them. Savage shouted in bewilderment:

'That isn't true!'

But Trevelyan's words pierced him as he had never known. Trevelyan shouted:

'Pursue your demons, by all means – but you shall not have *them*!' He turned away. 'Now get out of here, the pair of you! You make me sick!'

He snatched up his hoe and dropped again into the trench. Savage cried:

'It isn't true!'
But such was the rain and so certain Trevelyan's mockery:
'Look in the mirror, Savage! Your God is there!'
That he stumbled in darkness.

The moment he opened the door, Anne said,
'We must speak.'
'Not here.'
'Where?'
At the Complex entrance, they were given waterproofs again and,
by Chilcott, a lighted lamp.
'You'll need one of these.'
'So will you. You won't be with us.'
When they came to the stakes by which the building site was
demarced, Savage said,
'Out there.'
Chilcott carried his lamp out into the valley, while Savage ducked
under the rope and lit the women to the nearest building, where he
held aside the batten and polystyrene 'door' for them to enter. It
was by now all but full dark.
The interior sounded hollow, bounded by bare boards and
uncarcassed walls, as Savage set down the lamp and crossed to the
'window' – an unglazed aperture covered with rain-streaked
polythene, through which Chilcott appeared with his lamp as
though marooned in space. Savage said,
'I can't do this. It's over.'
Their silence oppressed him. They looked like matched dolls.
Anne said,
'Are you more likely to be killed?'
'What?'
'If we're with you.'
'That's not what we're talking about.'
'What, then?'
'Look, you can have a safe, ordered, *sensible* life here. Why don't
you take it?'
Anne said,
'It's not what we want.'
'What does that mean?'

She looked at the child.

'We've had an ordered, safe life. It was wonderful. We were happy.'

'Well, then!'

'We know what love is.'

Cassie said,

'We love you.'

Anne seemed for a moment as taken aback by this intervention as Savage; then she said,

'But it isn't here.'

'You don't know that.'

'We know what we don't want.' Her tone was hard. 'For myself, I shall *never* put myself in the hands of such people again.' Savage remembered his own vow. She said, 'What I have lost is worth more than that!'

Cassie said,

'Me, too.'

More than ever, the child appeared young. He said,

'Cassie, look, you can't know such things . . .'

Anne said,

'At her age? But at what age did *you* know, Mr Savage?'

She seemed to know precisely where to touch his doubt. He looked away.

'I can't be responsible for you.'

'Let us be responsible for ourselves.'

'It's not that simple . . .'

'It's never that simple. But why should you carry all of the burden? Let us share it.'

Cassie said,

'That's what families do.'

Exasperated, he shouted:

'We're not a – !'

But he could not bring himself to say it. Rain beat suddenly on the drum of their 'roof' as though on the top of his mind. Anne said,

'There isn't a trick, Mr Savage, that others know and you don't. We do what we can. So long as we do it honestly . . .'

He said,

'We can't get away.'

'. . . What?'

'It can't be done. We'll die.'

After a moment, she said,

'You can defeat Sparrow.'

'You're an expert in that now?'

'He talks too much. He doesn't know how to – disappear.'

This was perceptive; but:

'There are *four* of them, Anne!'

Cassie said,

'We can help.'

'*No*! *You must never fight these people*!' She shrank from him. 'They're the *best there is*! They'll wipe you like marks from a slate!'

She appeared frightened of him. Anne said,

'We'll do exactly what you tell us. We'll obey implicitly.'

'No.'

She said,

'And if you want us to go now – if that would be best for you – we'll do that, too.' A small sound escaped the child. 'Just tell us what you want, we'll do it.'

They stood before him. Then Cassie said,

'Only please don't.'

Anne chided, gently:

'Cassie . . .'

As though, by betraying emotion, Cassie had broken a compact between them. The child pushed at her cheek.

'Sorry.'

Savage turned away. He was utterly at a loss. Against all reason, he heard himself say:

'I could take you as far as the house.'

Anne said,

'Alright.'

He sensed the care she took not to sound triumphant. Possessed of a sudden rage, he rounded on them:

'But if there's nothing on there – that's it! Finish!'

Anne said,

'We understand.'

Cassie said,

'Yes, sir.'

She looked excited, as though she could not wait to die for him. He said,

'Get your packs. We'll spend the night up here.'

If nothing else, he could at least reestablish the integrity of his force. He set such a pace that Chilcott was obliged to run to catch up with them before they reached the Complex entrance:

'Is all resolved?'

Anne said,

'We leave with Mr Savage in the morning.'

'Is that sensible?'

Anne laughed.

'No.'

Savage said,

'We sleep up here tonight.'

'You'll be expected to attend the presentation first.'

Anne said,

'What presentation?'

'The people wish to express their gratitude to Mr Savage.'

Savage said,

'No.'

Over Chilcott's protestations, he pressed on along the tunnel.

He had been in the room barely a minute before Trevelyan entered.

'You will attend the presentation. It is not an option.'

Savage smiled.

'You won't kill me here.'

'That is merely a preference.'

'In your own living room?'

'If you soil my living room, I shall have no alternative. You know how the game is played. Your life depends on abiding by the rules. Embarrass me, I shall embarrass you. Terminally.'

The intercommunicating door opened and Anne said,

'Did you want something?'

The offer of help was transparent, much to Trevelyan's amusement. Savage said,

'No.'

She gave him a look and withdrew. Trevelyan said,

'Can you really be taming her?'

For the first time, Savage saw Trevelyan as over-confident, self-serving and false. He said,

'You never were on the Outside, were you?'

Trevelyan smiled.

'You are not, after all, going to tell me that there is some mystical beneficence to the wilderness life?'

'No, I mean, *never*. At risk. Always safe. Never the one to pay the price.'

Trevelyan spread his hands.

'Why keep a dog and bark oneself?'

Savage nodded.

'I would rather be dead than be you.'

Trevelyan was greatly entertained.

'So modest an ambition and so ready of achievement.'

Savage knew that he could not defeat the man on this ground. He turned, took up his bergen. Trevelyan said,

'While I think, I'm sending Chilcott with you. He deserves his chance to dissuade the others from foolishness, wouldn't you say?'

Savage thought that, if events went ill at the house, Chilcott's presence might afford the members of the group some measure of protection.

(Unless, of course, this was Trevelyan's method of disposing of Chilcott.)

At the door, Trevelyan said,

'Have a care, Savage. Adoration rots the soul.'

Music pulsed from the dim interior of the recreation hall and bright blades of light sliced colour through the gloom. From where he stood on the threshold, Savage saw figures hump at the centre while, all about the periphery, others dabbed at the walls, as though seeking escape. The impression was of Bedlam. Nor was Anne's reaction greatly dissimilar. She said,

'The disco from hell.'

Suddenly they were blanched by obliterating light. When he put up a hand to shield his eyes, Savage saw enemies loom at him, casting penumbrae before. One had a rocket launcher to the shoulder. Madness! He snatched up his rifle and a second put a stick grenade to his face and said,

'Just a few words before you set out, Mr Savage. Community Service Television News.'

Anne laughed:

'I don't believe this.'

The music had stopped. Through readjusting eyes, Savage saw that the 'launcher' was a camera, the 'grenade' a microphone and his interlocutor Trevelyan's stooge of lunchtime, the smart woman with the glasses. She smiled to the camera.

'But first, the presentation.'

It was made by a child.

What they gave him was himself. A graven image of a trooper, fashioned from wood and complete with rifle, bergen and faceless face – which he thought appropriate. He wanted to seize the head and *twist* the neck. He felt that his sinews would crack and his eyes pop out and his hurt cease. The mannikin filled him with revulsion. Goggles asked what he thought of his gift.

'Very fine.'

She became portentous.

'Tomorrow you set out to rescue the other survivors from the house?'

Rescue?

'Yes.'

'Will it be dangerous?'

Ah. Later she would say how prophetic his final words had proved to be. He played by the rules:

'It may be.'

Trevelyan clasped his hand, wished him Godspeed. The farewell for posterity.

When the television lights were extinguished, they sucked all darkness into the room.

In the partly-constructed house, a second lamp had been placed on the floor, along with a chemical latrine and containers of dry food and fresh water. Savage said,

'We supply ourselves. Field discipline from now on. Get back into uniform. Five minutes.'

He walked along the lightless valley. For the first time, rain fell with conviction. He must time the downpours now; duration and separation. A major shift was taking place. At the river, he crouched; but there was no significant increment yet.

He sensed, returning, how night-sights tracked him from the heights. Near the house, he stopped, stared into darkness.

He did not in truth understand the motive or purpose of his actions.

Trevelyan was right. He did not know these (or any) people. And in so far as he had any comprehensible image of the immediate future, he found himself concerned, not merely with how well they would withstand his environment, but how well it – and he – would bear their scrutiny.

Which made him angry.

He was a soldier!

That was what he did. What he would continue to do.

In that was certainty.

When they had eaten a frugal meal and were settling to sleep, Cassie said,

'Thank you for taking us with you, Father.'

He would dispose of the father business in the morning.

'Don't thank me. I've done you no favour.'

By midnight, he was troubled. Increasingly heavy downpours lengthened and the intervals between contracted. When he read the river again, for the first time he detected a burgeoning spate. Back in the house, he sat against the wall and checked both of his watches by pencil beam. It was happening too quickly. He needed seventeen hours.

He heard Anne stir and sensed her sit close.

'Are you timing the showers?'

'Yes.'

'Let me do it for an hour, while you sleep.'

'I am sleeping.'

As the rain eased, water rilled off the walls. She said,

'I want to tell you something.'

He thought, I don't want to hear it. She said,

'I loved my husband. And my children. But that life is gone forever. It will never come back. And I must see what lies beyond the life I lived before. I *must*.' He felt her face turn towards him. 'Not to find out would be a betrayal of my self. And of them. Of my soul.'

He did not feel qualified to speak of the soul. He said,

'What about Cassie?'

He heard her smile.

'You knew that before I did.'

Had he? He felt that he was on a treadmill of limitless moral confusion. Fortunately, at that moment the child cried out in sleep – horrors still stalked the edge of her night – and the woman went to comfort her.

In a little, she said,

'When you need my help, you must tell me, Mr Savage. Don't leave me to guess.'

But that day, he knew, would never come.

As dawn approached, his anxiety had turned through one hundred and eighty degrees. Far from being concerned by the accelerating rate of precipitation, he was shocked by an almost total lack of it. Perhaps, after all, Nature's weather had been overturned and he was relying on a climatic manifestation that never would occur.

Outside, the pilot was impatient to be airborne. Chilcott waited in the pervasive opaque, a Burberry over his tweeds. The river lapped at the sluice gates by which the irrigation system was controlled, but did not yet overspill them.

They climbed in silence into the helicopter. None bade them farewell, as had come to greet their arrival.

In the event, the pilot felt obliged to put down twice, on account of heavy showers; but there was far too little rain for Savage's purposes; nor was a monitoring of the river line encouraging.

When they came to the house, he ordered a wide sweep out over the valley, the hills and the trees. They would suppose, he knew, that he sought an overview of their troop dispositions – there were, indeed, soldiers now on every surrounding height – but it was in truth the valley floor which concerned him.

No hopeful (or telltale) signs yet. Over the intercom, he told the pilot to hover side-on to the southern tower window. Martin signalled All Clear. Savage pointed to the ground (Martin acknowledged); he then told the pilot to land as close as he was able, side-on to the ballroom entrance.

The moment the runners grounded, he dropped down into a clatter of blades and swirling grit; and when the engines cut to idle, he shouted to Chilcott:

'When I say Go – straight into the house!'

Chilcott nodded. Anne had adopted a position at the starboard door, covering the southern approaches. Cassie rose from the second seat, shook hands with the pilot and came aft to pull on her pack. The plug was hauled back and Sammy and Martin burst from the house to cover the flanks, east and west. Savage shouted:

'Go.'

Chilcott jumped to ground and strode into the interior.

'Cassie!'

As the child departed, the pilot said,

'Good luck, Cassie.'

'Anne!'

With his force inside, Savage called:

'Wait on the next ridge south!'

The pilot held up a finger.

'One hour.'

In the kitchen, Savage said,

'This is Commissioner Chilcott. He'll tell you about the Capital.' He scanned the room. 'Sarah's on watch?' Martin nodded. Savage said, 'I'll send her down.' Alice murmured:

'You'll find her changed.'

Sarah, indeed, looked changed. It was not that she wore uniform and carried a rifle, but that she did both familiarly and with conviction. He said,

'There's someone downstairs to tell you about the Capital.'

'I have no interest in the Capital.'

'Do it.'

She nodded with composed obedience. She offered no comment on his predicted return. In the manner of one issuing a report she said:

'The helicopter has landed to the south. There are soldiers on all high ground. We are surrounded.'

Savage was not concerned with the soldiers. They would play no part in the coming struggle. Sparrow would tolerate no extraneous elements on his ground. It was the weather which wholly preoccupied him.

For all that the sky by now melded nearly indistinguishably with the earth, still insufficient rain fell. The unnatural abeyance continued. Yet if no development occurred within two hours, or if the rains failed to break within three, then all his efforts would be vain.

He had only tonight.

Cassie said,

'They're ready for you, Father.'

In that their relationship was unlikely to be prolonged, what matter what she called him? He said,

'If anyone comes near the house – *anyone* – tell me at once.'

It was evident that the day had not gone to Chilcott. In a stiff manner, he said,

'Tell them what they face, Savage. They won't listen to me.'

Sarah said,

'We know what we face.'

'Do you?'

'You've told us about Sparrow. It transpires, indeed, that we've seen him in action. Or, rather, inaction.'

A bitter reference to rape. Chilcott said,

'But do you know *what* he is?'

Alice said,

'We know what Mr Savage is.'

Anne said,

'There's a difference.'

Savage wondered. So did Chilcott:

'Is there?'

Martin said,

'If you're so concerned for our welfare, how come there's an army outside?'

'To help you.'

Alice laughed:

'To make up our minds?'

'To get back to the Capital. Do you think it will be easy, when the rains come?'

Sarah said,

'It's only if you decline this kind offer that you'll be shot.'

'No one will be shot.'

Sammy said,

'Has anyone told Sparrow?'

Savage was out of patience with them all:

'This is your choice – make it! It doesn't concern me.'

Chilcott was scornful.

'You can't shrug off responsibility as easily as that.'

Sarah said,

'For us, he can. We are intelligent human beings, capable of independent function. For myself, it is simple. I go with Savage, or I go alone.'

Sammy said,

'Not alone.'

Alice:

'That's right.'

Martin:

'I go where Alice goes.'

Anne:

'You know how we feel, Cassie and I.'

Indeed, he did.

Sarah said,

'That would appear to make it unanimous, Commissioner.'

In a moment, Chilcott said,

'I can't dissuade you of this folly?'

Martin said,

'You can call off your dogs.'

'Thay are not mine to call.'

Sarah said,

'A basin for the Commissioner, Alice, to wash his hands.'

245

Sammy said,

'What they are, you are.'

Chilcott frowned.

'Not all rulers are the same.'

Anne said,

'Not all dogs are.'

Sarah made play of her watch.

'Time's up, Commissioner.'

As Martin stood ready to haul back the plug, Chilcott turned to Savage.

'You will kill Sparrow?'

'Or he'll kill me.'

Chilcott nodded.

'The world will be better, for either passing.'

It was a wish, Savage thought, unlikely to be long in the granting.

When he returned to the kitchen, the women all spoke together, but Savage overrode them:

'I don't want to hear it.' To Sarah: 'Prepare a second medical pannier. Make sure there are comprehensive instructions in each.' She nodded. If the party were to become divided, Sarah could not remain with both factions. To them all: 'Collect your packs now from the cellar. I'll inspect you – full kit, ready to depart – in one hour.' It grieved him that the packs, now so presciently prepared, would not serve their begetter. To Sammy, he said, 'We need to talk.'

In the tower room, Savage said,

'If you're not up to this, you'd better tell me now.'

Sammy said,

'I can do it.'

'That's not the question.' Sammy knew it was not. 'I need someone who can take over from me, when the time comes. Which it will.'

'I know.'

'Someone who's got the training and the experience. And *his mind on the job*.'

Sammy frowned.

'I won't fail you.'

Savage was blunt.

'What about this business with Sarah? You got that sorted?'

'Yes.'

'You sure?'

'We made love.' It was not what Savage had expected. 'She insisted. Commanded. She would not bow down to them, you see. She's . . . strong.'

There was in this much admiration. Savage said,

'She was always strong.'

He saw that indeed it was the case. Sammy said,

'So am I. In her.' He regarded Savage straightly. 'I'll be ready, when you need me. We both shall.'

Savage acknowledged the truth of it.

As to the other, Sarah was reclaiming her body, as he had his after torture. In their new world, there was no time for the niceties of recovery. You went on or you went down.

The first job with Martin was to open the 'trap door'.

They had uncovered it initially by accident. Needing to service the old boiler before they could fire it up, they had found, on inspecting its sheet metal housing, that the front panel was hinged on one side and pinned by iron bolts on the other. Supposing this to be an aid to maintenance (which it was), they had unscrewed the bolts and swung open the face of the housing. And although they had been obliged then to unbolt a heavy gate from the end of the cylinder, they had gained access to the interior.

The flue had proved another matter. It had seemed irremediably blocked. But there was space, between the curved flanks of the cylinder and the upright panels of the housing, sufficient to permit the passage of a man even of Martin's stature. And when they had worked back with torches, they had found that the venting pipe passed directly through the brickwork; and that, at waist level beneath, there was set in the wall a small iron door, which they had taken to be a sweep's access to the flue. Yet when they had opened it and shone in their torches, they had looked into a further arched chamber.

Or so at first they had supposed.

The finding of a 'secret passage' was not in itself unusual. This was a part of the continent in which few old houses would claim less. Nor was it a passage so much as a natural flaw in the rock, which (intriguingly) had been 'improved' by human agency. They had followed its gentle, downward course to the end (no great distance) and had come to a coarse, hand built, mortar-and-stone wall.

Savage had returned at once and had wormed a micro optic through the friable mortar. They had found themselves peering, from the rear of a cave, through tangled underbrush into trees.

Knowing that the bluff on which the house stood was not high and that their starting point had been the floor of deep cellars, they had realised that even the modest descent they had made must have carried them under the lane. Even so, it had taken days of deception, conscious of an ever-watchful Other Force, before they had been able to pinpoint the location of the cave.

The significance of their find had been evident to them both. It had placed Savage in the position of a player who, if he could not avoid the game, might yet manifest, unheralded, already on the board. From that moment, inevitably, Martin had become Savage's co-conspirator in preparation.

Savage kept the inspections brief, although thorough, and avoided all conversation. When they were concluded, he said,

'Rest now. You'll have plenty to do before nightfall.'

'Is that when we leave?'

Or never, he thought.

The question was answered within minutes. He had returned with Martin to the tower room, when a curtain descended over the world. Rain fell prodigiously and without cease. The opposing heights liquesced in indistinctness and, through binoculars, the soldiers on them adopted postures of timeless stoicism.

The rains proper had broken. Sparrow must close up his force now against day for night.

In the false chamber behind the boiler, Savage and Martin made

248

final preparation, adapting options exhaustively discussed weeks before: the expansion of the party from one to seven solved as many problems as it posed, since it eliminated all but a single alternative.

They pumped up the first dinghy. Into this they packed the second (sealed) inflatable; fuel and spare motor; the medical boxes; such general supplies as they were to take with them and Savage's specialist weapons. Food was to be carried on the person. They swaddled the load in a double layer of tarpaulin and secured the whole with an improvised rope net, which they passed also under the craft and by means of which they were able to contrive hand holds, sufficient for each member of the party to contribute to bearing the load to water.

They mounted the outboard. Martin had insisted that he could carry the rear of the dinghy with the motor in place and both knew that no later opportunity to mount it would occur. (A brief test satisfied Savage that Martin could do as he said.)

They checked their 'wet' clothing (the fatigue trousers and trainers, which they would wear into the water) and the plastic bags in which their boots, socks and DPM trousers would be stowed. They set tools and a working lamp before the coarse end wall. Finally, they returned to the cellars, where they assembled Savage Force.

Martin had contrived a practice 'dinghy' from a wine rack cut to size, with plywood hull and rope carrying handles. Savage explained its purpose. Then:

'This is our formation. Me, up front. Martin, at the rear. On the right, Anne; then Sarah. On the left, Cassie; then Alice; then Sammy. Let's begin.'

He led them a course through the cellars, from chamber to chamber, along the passages and back. In a little, with each circuit, he increased the weight; until at last they were carrying a load approximating that of the laden inflatable. But it was not until he felt them respond to one another as a unit that, after thirty minutes, he called a halt.

He sent Sammy to show himself at the tower windows and Alice to make smoke at the range. Not that any charade of normality would deceive Sparrow, but there was no reason to court unnecessary suspicion.

When they were again assembled, he said,

'Now, in the dark.'

'The *dark*?'

'When you do this, it will be pitch dark. And raining like you can't imagine. You'll be cold, deaf and blind.' He looked at them. 'You have only one another. You must work together. Feel one another through the ropes. If you are not one, you will fail.'

Martin extinguished the lamps. This time, Savage set them a harder course; abruptly doubling back; leading them over obstacles. But by degrees, he sensed in them the growth of a stubborn unity of purpose: the many-minded creature became one. Satisfied, he said,

'You've done well. Light.'

A further appearance in the tower having been concluded, he said:

'Now we practise embarkation and launching. You'll have three seconds to get into the boat.'

In fact, at best he hoped for ten; with the women scrambling aboard to drill order, followed by Sammy, Martin and himself.

'Remember to work your arms and legs under the ropes. Anyone lost then, is lost for good.'

He and Martin, embarking last, planned to spread themselves as widely as they were able and to secure the party aboard by brute strength, if they could.

The practice went well, by light and by darkness; and Savage was satisfied before Cassie, demonstrably wearying of his arrivals on top of her, demanded an answer to the obvious and already twice deferred question:

'But *how do we get to the river*?'

He said,

'We don't. The river will come to us.'

It had been Madge who had described to him the local phenomenon on which so much now depended.

When the rains first broke, so great was the release of water into the high country, that the gullies, creeks and ravines by which normally it was carried south could not cope. Within twelve hours, floods became established in the lowlands and equilibrium was restored. But during the initial period, a liquid anarchy prevailed, as the overspill, rushing south, sought any avenue of escape from the pressure of continuous rainfall.

One such avenue was the valley before Savage's house.

Due to the curvature at its eastern end, the overburdened East River naturally shot a substantial body of water into this inviting outlet, which then swirled along the valley until it encountered the rock wall at the western end, by which it was deflected north up the dried water course, past MacKenzie's Farm and into the powerful tow of the northern tributary, which turned it again eastward and so back to its point of origin.

This vast circular motion was the means by which, initially, Savage planned to elude the grasp of Sparrow Force.

He believed that Sparrow (who had operated on the coastal plain) was as ignorant of this phenomenon as he himself had been (having operated to the east). If he was mistaken, there was nothing he could do about it.

There was a second environmental transformation attendant on the onset of rains, of which Sparrow certainly would be aware: in a moment, it seemed, there sprang up, all across the flatlands north of the Desert, a matrix of temporary waterways, which joined the northern tributary to the great western river system, some hundred miles distant. Although brief in duration, this was a system of such complexity that it would be impossible, even given air time, for Sparrow to track them through it; and it provided a thoroughfare to the West.

Unhappily, Sparrow did not have to track them; for all ways led to a single destination: and it was here that he would await them.

Savage said,

'You are not soldiers. Do not fight these people. If we're bumped tonight, drop your weapons, put up your hands, do exactly what you're told. If you don't, you'll be shot.' They looked away or down. 'One more thing. It would be no disgrace to change your minds now. It would be only sensible. I tell you, we have almost no chance of success.'

None spoke or moved.

He sensed on them a fear that, if they offered the smallest occasion, he would desert them. He said,

'Any questions?'

He stood at the tower window, looking on a darkling world and, for a last time, parsed Sparrow's mind.

Sparrow must site a man to guard the 'hidden exit' (onto the service lane) – who, by virtue of Savage's failure to cull the copse, would be unable effectively to mount any other watch. He must cover the southern approaches. He must place a man in The Beard – not least, when the spill ran and he realised that it offered the only covered way to fast water. And he must site a man (himself, Savage believed) to cover the western slopes, Low Wood and the training ground.

Sparrow was not a fool. He would recognise at once the significance of the unsuspected spate, but he could not afford to seal one door at the expense of leaving others open.

His difficulties would be compounded by a darkness of absolute pitch; by rainfall so dense that it would amount virtually to being underwater; and by terrain so disrupted that he would find no location, high or low, from which he would be able to scan more than a third of the area at any time. He must patrol constantly. Yet with each move that he made, while he would disclose hidden ways, he would obscure others. There would always be alleys down which Savage might sneak.

Of course, Sparrow and his gang would be possessed of night vision equipment, but Savage well knew the limitations of such kit. He believed that, in the aquarium world in which they would be operating, they would find it increasingly difficult to distinguish one poppled green spectre from another.

Besides, if they were seen, they were seen.

Sparrow *knew* that Savage had a trick to play. Indeed, there was in Sparrow a streak which might induce him to risk all his force in the one place. But ultimately he must believe that, in order to play the game, Savage must leave the box. And the longer he watched doors, the more he looked where Savage would never be.

But Sparrow would smell it.

He would scent them on the ground.

In the last analysis, what happened this night would depend wholly on chance.

On a miscoincidence of timings which would grant them always to be where invisible eyes were not.

On his instinctive capacity, perhaps, to misalign the pulse of Sparrow's intuition and the metre of his own deception.

It was madness!

Who ever evaded his own image in the glass?

He turned from the window.

How had he come to this? That he must put civilians at hazard in order to serve them?

If, indeed, he would be serving them.

For in truth he no longer knew right from wrong in this matter.

He felt himself to be at a crossroads, between a past that had receded from him and a future beyond his capacity to envision.

And faced by an imponderable burden.

He did not know himself.

But he could not betray them.

And yet.

What would failure amount to? They would be taken to the Capital: no intolerable existence.

And success?

He would be able to fight the battle he could not avoid on his ground, rather than Sparrow's, in the place of still women and bus stops and eyeless cinemas.

Where he was fated to be.

Darkness deepened and in the netherworld of his binoculars he glimpsed only feints to paleness now as water charged the valley.

'It's time.'

He and Martin passed the party through the trap door into another place. Martin fired the boiler and, behind him, Savage secured the housing with purpose-machined bolts from the inside. They put on their wet clothing and stowed the dry and the party carried the dinghy like smugglers through the rock.

'Take your time. Help one another. Concentrate.'

They nodded. Savage extinguished the lamps, placed them behind his force and returned to the wall, where Martin waited, sledgehammer in hand, a pick nearby, should Savage need it.

'Begin.'

The sledgehammer soughed on the air and struck the stones with such violence that it spiked a flare in the darkness. Martin swung again; and once more, Savage had supposed that the old wall might prove stubborn of demolition, but at the fourth blow he heard the unmistakable shift of impending failure and, with the sixth, the implosion of substantial collapse.

At once an infusion of vegetable scents came from the trundling spate below and the rush of rain pressed closer at the opening. When Savage stooped to clear the spoil, Martin said,

'No need of help here. Best get on.'

The big man was right. The wall would not long withstand him. Savage took up heavy-duty bolt cutters and inserted himself through the gap into the cave beyond, where he set about cutting a swathe through the gnarled scrub, as close to the ground as he was able: he did not mean to face his people with an intractable obstacle at the outset of their journey. The tumult outside was more than sufficient to compensate for the thud of Martin's endeavours.

In a little, the big man joined him; and when they reached the mouth of the cave, they left a two-foot fringe of brush undisturbed, in the hope that it might serve some later, misdirecting purpose.

Returned to the party, Savage said,

'Take up the dinghy.'

And when he felt Martin's signal:

'Good luck.'

The moment they stepped out, rain fell on them tremendously. Savage felt the integrity of his unit founder under the sheer magnitude of the assault. But then the anchor of Martin took hold, they steadied themselves and, as Savage led on, followed him out of the unregarded tangle of brush between Low Wood and The Beard, hard left into dead ground.

He had wholly underestimated the volume of water running off the slopes. It snagged their ankles vertiginously, as though they were teetering across the grain of a tilted waterfall. The sound from the valley was extraordinary, turning from rumble to moan, the closer they blundered towards it. Darkness was absolute. They inhaled the very aqueous environment by which they were subsumed.

No fancy thoughts now of matching sensibilities with Sparrow. They were at the mercy of fate. Savage followed the memory of his feet.

Abruptly, he pecked at a rise and realised that they had come to the fissure which cleft the hillside from top to bottom. Hauling his party across the slope, he stumbled all but accidentally on the natural rock bridge by which he meant to cross the gap. Yet even as he edged forward, he was driven to his knees by the ferocity of spate which buffeted him: the fissure had been transformed into a chute, breaching where it could. Forcing the others down behind him, he crawled backwards through the torrent and, when he was satisfied that all were safely across, rose and turned and led them more swiftly on. They were beyond the training area but now they trod Sparrow's ground.

The moment he felt the dip beneath his feet, he turned along the shallow culvert and led towards the river.

As they descended, the vast motion of water before them took on a monumental quality, its reverberation so dense that it shook the ground and fluttered at the edge of defeating hearing. Savage, rainblind and bemused by this low-frequency vibration, lost orientation and plunged into the flood.

At once, his legs were snatched from him and he was immersed to the chin. Wrenching about, he shouted:

'Go! Go! Go!'

With each entry into the craft, the prow to which he clung pressed him more deeply in, but deprived of legs and unable to find purchase to help, he could only marvel at the magnitude of effort by which Martin held the dinghy against the forces which sought to possess it. Sammy shouted:

'All in!'

'*Go, Go!*'

Even now, the big man found strength to launch the vessel towards midstream. Power surged through the hull, but it was insufficient to wrest Savage from the undertow and, had it not been for the combined efforts of Anne and Martin, he would not have gained the interior.

Then the river had them.

Savage had supposed that, with his physical conditioning, he was prepared for what lay before them. His disabusement was total. The majesty of what owned them was awesome. They were taken up into a vast, giddying perturbation, by which they were whirled and tossed and cast on, as though they had no more integrity than a leaf in a mill race. They were utterly without capacity. And with each sickening revolution, it was borne in on Savage how fatally he had miscalculated, for they were being carried inexorably and with shocking speed towards the rock wall, against which they must be dashed. Indeed, even as he struggled to orientate himself, he sensed the mass loom ahead and spread himself over Cassie and Anne, as though he might spare them some measure of the impact.

And then he felt countervailing forces act on the dinghy, it reared up, began to tilt sideways and he realised that the mass of flow, encountering the intractable obstacle of rock, gave back a swell, an embankment of water, along which they now planed with increasing velocity as they were projected northward. Abruptly, they were flushed through the bottle-neck and on towards MacKenzie's Farm.

The debouchment was spectacular; almost at once came a slackening of the dreadful rotations and Savage was able to think again. How many minutes to MacKenzie's Farm? Three? Four? – before they must struggle to free themselves of the very tyranny which, to this moment, had served them with such fearsome authority.

They had not yet been in the water one minute.

Savage sensed relief in the boat as he drew up his night scope from where it hung about his neck. But after so entire a darkness, the sudden dash of phosphor bright was dizzying and he closed his eyes. At the second attempt, as he adjusted to the onrushing green ghostscape, he became conscious again how rain lashed at the already liquescing display.

As the dinghy skated on, Savage counted; waited. When he sighted recognition points to his left, he shouted:

'Stand by, motor!'

He knew that Martin would be already in position; but Cassie, as she had been instructed, confirmed the big man's acknowledgement by touch. And then, with the first significant diminution of heights to his right, Savage shouted:

'Start up!'

He did not expect the engine to bite yet; they lacked independent way. But when they approached the confluence of the northern tributary and the stream on which they now ran, he anticipated such a contradiction of currents and so relative a dissipation of pent force into level ground, that they should have a genuine prospect of beating across the pull of long water and escaping its traction. He meant to be up and running when the moment came. He was unsurprised to hear the motor bark up almost as he gave the order and before Cassie had time to acknowledge it. He hauled up the torch which, too, was suspended about his neck and by means of which he intended to communicate with Martin over the clamour of the outboard.

It happened suddenly, the loss of vigour in the roiling spate beneath the hull. The engine laboured, the screw burrowed and they acquired steerage way. As the ghost of MacKenzie's Farm danced towards them, Savage tipped back the torch to alert Martin and then dipped a steady beam to his left. Their heading swung as the big man put the tiller hard over and they butted into the broad rotational draw.

It took time. There was a period when, for all the efforts of the outboard and of Savage, with a paddle, to hold up the bow, they seemed fated to be dragged by the heels eastward. But then, in a moment, they slipped the noose of induction and beat northward into the teeth of rain and tide alike.

All that remained was to find a suitable opening into the waterways to the West. When, after three hours, this was achieved, Savage turned his party westward and they entered the Ashlands.

They had made good their escape.

For now.

The Wilderness

THE dinghy beat through the night, refuelled, beat on. At intervals, Savage and Martin exchanged tasks, the one at the tiller, the other with night vision at the prow, to revivify concentration. Rain fell unremittingly. The chill of his immersion had entered deeply into Savage, but he suspected that, since the launch, Martin had been no better off and they had agreed to endure discomfort in the interests of continuous movement. The others, by degrees, yielded to saturated sleep. But the run of the stream was no longer against them and, before midnight, they had achieved a water course broad enough to carry them all the distance to the great Fawkes river system.

Savage was not dissatisfied.

Dawn found them in another world, as yet barely hinted at, smudges only in a mist so pervasive it was as though they climbed the sky. For a moment, the rain had relented. Savage consulted watch and compass. They had sufficient visibility to shadow one or other bank of the waterway, but not both. In the boat was a stirring to raw wakefulness. Savage said,

'Breakfast. One hour.'

He needed to assess their morale. Rain fell again.

As drear light seeped in, the smother retreated somewhat and there was revealed about them a lifeless expanse, entirely composed in sepia and black. The effect was of a fixed, coarse, ebony sea, from which there rose in places obsidian shapes, like dark memories. It was as though a crystal world had melted down and turned to shellac; and off this bleak coral there leaked now skeins of silt into the water: a place at last washed, but not cleansed.

No one spoke. The others had not seen Ashland before; and Savage, who had, had nothing to say on it.

Near seven, he sighted a strand on the north bank, close to a ruined hut and suitable for landing; and although, in gaining the shore, he and Martin slithered about in rain-lashed surface mire, soon enough they had a spike driven, everyone ashore and the dinghy after them. Sarah clenched her thighs extravagantly:

'I've *got* to *go!*'

This provoked amused imitation among the women, who retired behind the nearest cover in high humour – which spoke well for their spirit. When the men had returned from a similar expedition, Savage and Martin, with Sammy's help, tugged out the spare tarpaulin from the dinghy and contrived a 'roof' between the standing walls of the hut. Then, while Sammy scraped the floor clear of silt with an entrenching tool, Martin and Savage set about inflating the second dinghy, which they inverted over the first, contenting themselves for the moment with roping the two together. Finally, they withdrew under the awning where (to ribald comment) they changed at last into dry clothing and ceased from their outboard-induced shouting.

When a hot meal had been consumed and under a streaming roof, Savage described what would happen next:

'We travel now in two boats. I'll be in the first, with Cassie and Anne.' He was aggravated to see the woman and child exchange a look, as though he had implied a relationship which emphatically he had not. 'In the second, will be Sammy, Sarah, Alice and Martin. Take turns at the tiller.' Sammy nodded. 'We travel all day. Harbour at dusk. Set out again at midnight. I estimate we'll reach The Gate before dawn tomorrow.'

They were surprised; but he pointed out that they had already travelled for twelve hours; that they had ten more at their disposal today and up to six the following morning. Even at five miles an hour, that represented a substantial distance and they had only a hundred miles to cover. He did not say that, if they failed to pass through The Gate before dawn, they would be finished. He said,

'I aim to enter the river system about two miles north of The

Gate.' At Devil's Point, he hoped. 'At that time, Sammy will take command and his boat will take the lead.' He was conscious of the keen look that Anne gave him. 'Martin will be at the tiller of the lead boat; Anne, of the second. You will run with the stream just before dawn, carry through The Gate and on to a designated rendezvous point, where I'll join you later in the day.' This provoked a stirring of unease among the group. It was Anne who said:

'What if you don't join us?'

'You must make your own decisions then.'

She was not happy:

'I don't like this.'

Alice said,

'Nor me.'

'You don't have a choice.'

Anne said,

'We could help you.'

'No.'

Martin said,

'Surely . . .'

'Not unless you want to get me killed.'

Anne said,

'I don't see that.'

'I need to know that everything on the ground is a target. If you foul the ground, you kill me.'

After a moment, Sarah said,

'Do you have to fight Sparrow?'

'Yes.'

'Couldn't we just slip away? We did last night.'

'Everything favoured us last night. We were stone lucky. It won't happen again. There's nowhere here to hide.'

They looked out at the wasteland by which they were surrounded and their faces reflected the truth of it. Martin said,

'But can he track us in *this*?' He indicated the weather. 'With a helicopter?'

'The rain will grow less in the coming hours. And he'll take every risk.' He'll have the best pilot, Savage thought. 'Besides, he doesn't have to track us. All ways lead to one place. He'll be there before us.'

Sarah said,

'That's good to hear.'

'You can give up. But you can't be free, unless you kill him.'

Alice said,

'Unless *you* kill him.'

'It's what I do.'

Anne was restive and angry:

'It's not right, this.'

Martin:

'No, it isn't.'

'It's what you agreed to.'

Sarah said,

'Perhaps we didn't know what we were agreeing to.'

'*It doesn't matter!*' He was sharp, but Anne continued to glare mutinously at him. To draw their concern, he said, 'It's what I'd be doing, anyway.'

Anne said,

'Not with us around your neck.'

'You won't be around my neck.'

There was to this more brutality than he had intended, but he did nothing to ameliorate it. Then Cassie said,

'But, Father, you might be *killed*.'

Her anguish hurt more than he would have imagined. He must guard himself. He said,

'We all might be killed, Cassie.'

The child was uncomforted; but when she looked to Anne, the woman was wrapped bleakly in herself, as though Savage had offered to her some private betrayal. He rose.

'Twenty minutes. It would help if you could all use the latrine before we start.'

With Martin and Sammy, Savage redistributed their supplies between the two dinghies, retaining his own weapons in the first boat. They mounted the second outboard, floated and tethered both craft and changed batteries in all powered kit. By the time Sarah had picked the site clear of sign, it was Savage who returned last from the latrine. Cassie had wandered along the bank and was fingering one of the obsidian memorials by which it was adorned. As he watched, she snapped off a jet protuberance and held it to her face for examination. He called:

'Time to go, Cassie.'

Turning, she cast down her souvenir.

'Were they trees?'

'People.'

They beat past the statuary watchers on the shore.

He had seen them first in water and had taken them for beasts. But as he had drawn closer, he had heard their lamentation and had seen the river choked with flopping limbs. It was as though Creation had dawned and failed experiments in humanity yet struggled to be.

Worst had been their eyes: a stricken recognition of what had come on them.

He had been unable either to help or to kill them all and had abandoned them to their primordial soup.

Others had come out of open country, limbs splayed as though they were blighted plants. And with them, a winnowing: the healthy few from (often loved) monstrosities; accomplished at first with an effort at consideration; soon, ruthlessly.

Finally, had come . . .

Things that had been human holding up things that had been children.

Killing for kindness, with all the confusion attendant thereon.

Until the boy had taken his hand.

And he had gone mad.

He found himself involuntarily wiping his hand on his streaming smock; but neither woman nor child appeared to have noticed his uncomfort.

He thought of them now, the icons on the bank, in terms that perhaps they never had fulfilled. Happy family groups. In the sunshine. Never hitting their children.

Never.

He felt joined to them by extensible bonds of steel and was content to fight his final battle at last among them.

He had learned nothing of what had occurred. One monstrosity had said, 'The sky blinked.' Another had spoken of the 'rush of day'. Most survivors referred to darkness; some to a 'shock' or 'pulse' of atmosphere. *None* had spoken of fire; or heat; or sound. Not one.

Savage held to one conviction: there had been no war. Whatever his species had done to itself, it had not been that.

At midday, he decreed a brief halt for further ablutions and a hot brew.

The weather had altered strangely in that, although there was no moderation in the weight of precipitation, unlooked-for periods of remission occurred, during which the tundra eerily yielded miasma and Savage thought: *Sparrow's up; running for The Gate; missing no opportunity*.

He had noted how Anne looked at him with resentment; but the clamour of the outboard, thank God, was continuous; and when they were on their way again, he dozed, as he had for much of the morning (as he had instructed Martin to), leaving navigation and boat management entirely to the women and dreaming no dreams in this place of the dead.

Dusk found them at harbour in a ruined farmhouse, at one end of which a segment of roof and partial walls remained and, at the other, sufficient of an outhouse to improvise a covered latrine. They had ported the dinghies into the middle section; and while they sat about a fire built from kindling and wood that they had brought with them and consumed a hot meal, Savage concluded his briefing for morning:

'The stream you'll enter will be nothing like as strong as last night.' He hoped. 'Just run south with the current, round the curve, through The Gate and on for about two miles. On the left bank, you'll see a dead village. Four hundred yards further, on the right, there's an old loading barn with river doors. Go in there. There's plenty of dry space up top. I'll join you later in the day.'

Rain fell into the uncovered part of their shelter. Sammy said, 'Do we use engines?'

'Sure. Sparrow won't collar you then. May show himself, just to let you know who's boss.' No one spoke. 'Any questions?' There were none. 'Clear up, then sleep. We leave at midnight.'

When housekeeping had been completed and they were settled, Cassie patted the space beside her ('Later'), but Anne turned her back, as though all words were traitors.

Savage prowled the deadlands. Not to keep watch: why would Sparrow pursue what inevitably must come to him with morning?

Anne's reproachfulness angered him. He had done all she sought. He owed her nothing.

Tomorrow he would fight those of whom he was, for the benefit of those of whom he was not.

And, in truth, he did not understand why.

It was as though he and Sparrow had the power to fight, but not the power not to fight.

As though it were destiny.

An outcome too long delayed.

He wondered whether Sparrow looked to morning with the same ambiguity as himself?

Or the red-headed man?

He found that he did not know.

'It's time.'

They set out into heavy rain, Anne with the night sight, Cassie at the tiller, Sammy maintaining close station behind.

The weather since afternoon had become increasingly volatile. It veered now between momentous downpours and intervals of cessation, some up to fifteen minutes in length; and from impenetrable fog to sliding drizzle.

The battlefield by morning would be utterly unpredictable.

It occurred at three AM, an alteration of drag under the hull, which indicated that they had passed from waters merely neutral into those which drew them subtly on. They had entered the influence of the Fawkes river. It was all he could do not to lift up his night scope in search of the *tricorne* shape of Devil's Point, which it was early yet to see.

Many rivers flowed from the Northern Highlands south through the heartland and into the great Fawkes river. They formed a vast inland delta. And it was by the most easterly (and feeblest) of these that Savage's people were to enter the system.

This, in the north-western corner of the Desert, was where Savage meant to make his stand.

The western perimeter of the Desert was demarced by a massive escarpment, which was cleft in only three places by gorges, of which the most imposing was The Gate. This name had been conferred by settlers, for whom indeed it had been the gateway to the West (and to plenty); and although this function had been overtaken by history and the place returned to wildness, its name persisted.

Savage loved this ungiving ground.

The tributary of which he intended to take advantage had been, at last sight, modest; and he did not believe that, even swollen by the rains, it would prove daunting.

The familiar coxcomb of rock had dinked and liquefied in his display for more than twenty minutes before Savage signalled STOP ENGINES and turned his attention to the greenly drifting southern bank. The hammer of silence and a temporary abeyance of rain were disquietingly exposing. In a moment, he sighted a suitable strand and, with paddles, they brought the dinghies to shore. He scrambled onto the dead plateau.

'Wait here. Twenty minutes.'

'Can we stretch our legs?'

'Stay together. Stand stag.'

He patrolled delicately westward, tuning in, until he came to the designated tributary, rather closer than he had intended. Rain fell again as he settled to assess its speed against the green rock mass at the foot of which it flowed across the bottle world of his night vision. The current was, as he had surmised, lively but not threatening. He estimated a drift time to The Gate of approximately twelve minutes.

He looked south along the great ghost of the escarpment, to where Sparrow waited, his force disposed, fuel cache established, helicopter bedded down. If nothing else, the ambiguous light of dawn might cause him some anxiety.

Finally, Savage looked eastward, towards the battleground, where the blight of Ashland, encountering the barren desert, had yielded to it in a series of declining, dark steppes.

The moment he made to return to his people, Savage realised how little he wished to.

Get it over.

He came on them soundlessly out of teeming rain:

'Steady the boat. I need my gear.'

With Martin and Sammy stabilising the lead dinghy, Savage drew out his two single-shot missile launchers, slung together for portage; a haversack containing two acquisition packs; and the pouches which held his modified Claymore mines. As he set about vesting himself of his equipment, he said,

'Pay attention.'

The faintest of pre-dawn had begun to manifest in the overhead and, in that the universal wetness gave back the meanest gleam, he discerned their shades about him. The rain had turned to drifting veils. He said,

'The river's about eight hundred yards ahead. Try to enter the stream at a quarter to the hour. Use engines for control, but don't run faster than the current. I want you in The Gate around dawn. Okay?' There was a murmuration of acknowledgement. He said, 'Good luck.'

As he shouldered the last of his load, Alice said,

'You'll be leaving us now?'

'You know what to do.'

Sammy said,

'Good luck, Savage.'

And Martin:

'Aye.'

Sarah put to his face a wet cheek, from which he recoiled.

'Thank you, John.'

In so far as she was able, the child wrapped arms about his middle.

'Goodbye, Father.'

'Best get in the boats.'

269

As soon as he detected movement in that direction, he slipped from them.

He had barely begun to run eastward, when he heard behind him:
'John!'
He turned; furious:
'*What do you want?*'
She was the merest presence.
'We need you.'
'I know that!'
He made to run again. She said,
'*I* need you.'
'*What?*'
'I need you.'
He thought that she would touch him and pushed out a hand.
'*Get away from me!*'
He had not intended it, but he glimpsed how she sprawled. He turned and ran. When he looked back, he saw with what fleetness she quit him and he was pierced by an aching sense of loss; of a terrible act committed. And when he ran on, it was as though he were joined to her and that – as with the bee which, stinging, dies – the entrails were hauled out of him and pegged like a butcher's skein across the landscape.

But what else could he do?'
Yet he sensed the enormity.
He stumbled through mothers and set children tumbling from the waist to dust.
He found himself straining for the last of her.
He knew that he ran from life to death: that he had scorned a gift of infinite grace. But he had no choice. The battle could not be denied.
It was his destiny.
And then, as he ran, it was borne in on him that the darkling plain, for all its ambiguity, grew every moment more substantial.
And that he was leaving sign.
And the part of him that never rested took command again and he turned, with appropriate care, towards the appointed place.
He scanned his counting mind: two minutes.

They were in the stream.

There was a chain of minor heights which backed to the waterways by which they had come and which, to the front, commanded a view over the tundra and into the desert. This was his chosen ground.

He ghosted up the rear slope of the first feature and shucked bergen and mines into the hollow which was to be his primary firing point. He then ran on along the crest, into and out of the col which joined it to the second and on to the far end of the third feature, some eighty yards distant, where he set down launchers and acquisition packs against later use.

As he ran back through the dank cavern contained by dimly manifesting overcast and dull sheen underfoot, he thought: Four minutes. Five. The rain continued in abeyance.

Returned to the firing point, he considered: Where to site the Claymores?

Sparrow was a subtle, expert opponent. There was, in Savage's miniature range of hills, a shallow re-entrant, just short of the nearest col, which snaked covertly into his position. It was all but impossible to discern from below and difficult to exploit; but given this very sneaky intractability, Savage fancied Sparrow for it.

He must, in any event, cover his east flank, for it was in that quarter that most dead ground and virtually all viable approaches were located.

He took up the first pouch and moved to the head of the draw. The rain had washed the dust off the rocks and had deposited it, in the form of silt, into every natural receptacle, including the re-entrant itself, which had tidal reaches on either side. He could not move in the gulley without leaving sign. At a time when he most needed speed, he was constrained to caution.

Dabbing before, testing the crepuscular surface, he worked down the rock face until he came to a place, some twelve feet below the crest, where the draw, rising and turning, would itself impose particular care on the intruder. Here, he lay flat and reached for the gulley floor.

There was at this point a cleft in the trough wall (one of many) and, under the silt collected in its sump, Savage felt the level platform of a ledge. It would serve.

271

He drew out the first mine, opened its scissor legs and settled it on the shelf. Working more rapidly, he then installed the blasting cap in the detonator well, attached the receiver to the back of the mine, released its tensile aerial and made good his contacts. Having aimed the weapon across and slightly up the draw, he switched it on. To his relief, there was no premature detonation.

As he checked to be sure he had left no sign, it occurred to him suddenly that he could follow his movements with unwonted clarity – and looking up, he saw to his dismay that, although distance vision had yet to be established, his surroundings materialised with unwelcome speed.

He peered at his watch.

Eight minutes!

It was a jolting shock.

Hobbled still by caution, he regained the crest and ran for his firing point, where he thrust the empty pouch into a fissure, took up the second mine and

hesitated.

For all his expertise, there was in Sparrow an element of the outrageous; of theatre. And for all that the cover was all to the east, Savage's instinct prompted him that it would be from the west – where cover was all but non-existent and the rock wall vertical and his own position dominant – that Sparrow would come.

Outrageousness was not necessarily a weakness.

Almost on impulse (and ignoring the need to guard his left rear against encirclement from the east), Savage drew back off the height and picked his way around the west face of his position, evading all too visible drifts of silt.

Dawn was almost on him. When he glanced westward, he saw the escarpment forming out of murk.

Near the conjunction of forward and lateral faces, there was a group of stalagmitic figures (failed at the last, perhaps, on their flight to water). Savage readied the mine, thrust it among the gumboots of children and legs of tired women and switched it on. It may be they would favour one of their own.

Returned to the crest, he set down the transmitter with his kit at the firing point and, rifle in hand, ran for his flank position, where he lay with the launchers, separated the tubes and mounted the first of his acquisition packs. Only then did he look up.

His battlefield had been born. And

There

There was the helicopter

Tiny and deadly

Hanging in The Gate

Dancing from view round the curve. Tracking them in the water.

What if he was wrong? What if Sparrow simply killed them now?

Dense rain obliterated his world.

But no, he thought; struggling to disentangle unaccustomed emotional perturbation from the sour logic of his position. Sparrow would not kill them now. If they were dead, Savage would be free. And Sparrow needed to kill Savage as badly as Savage needed to kill him.

Sparrow would come.

The power to kill but not the power not to kill.

For the first time, this struck Savage as grievously sad.

He knew what he had been offered. He was painfully conscious of the irony that now, when for the first time in his life he had desire and reason to live, his life must be forfeit.

Well. Too late to change his destiny now.

The rain ceased and water ran tunefully off the heights.

When next he sighted the helicopter, it was high over the escarpment and behind him. Having by now mounted the second acquisition pack, he switched on and showed the weapon the target. Almost at once, he heard the 'acquisition' tone. But he did not intend to fire at this range. Sparrow might not expect missiles, but certainly he would allow for them. To have any prospect of downing the chopper, Savage must find the moment which would afford the pilot the minimum reaction time – and that was likely to depend as much on luck as on judgement.

The instant he fired, he would betray his location – although that was hardly a secret. On his appreciation the evening before, Sparrow must have read the probabilities with ease. Indeed, this was confirmed when the helicopter, at a distance now, touched on the ridge and lifted off: Sparrow had sited a man overnight at Devil's Point.

Rain plunged again and Savage thought: *Down* the thing! *Swamp* it! But without expectation. He switched off the acquisition packs and wondered how his mines were faring.

When the rain lifted, the helicopter rose under its skirts.

It set a pattern over the waterways to his rear, gradually working eastward, drifting from time to time in his direction but always maintaining distance. He knew what was happening: he was being offered first shot. Show me yours, I'll show you mine.

Not yet.

At unpredictable intervals, the overcast emptied torrentially, but never, unhappily, to the detriment of the helicopter. And Savage could only marvel at the skill with which the pilot contrived not to present exhaust and engine heat directly to any potential seeker system in his vicinity.

He glanced at his watch. Thirty-seven minutes.

They would be in the barn by now. (He would not think of that.)

Although the chain of heights on which he lay was modest, it was substantial in length and a further twenty minutes had passed before the pilot had crabbed about its eastern end and set his pattern over the southern slopes and approaches.

Now was Savage's time. If he was to engage them, it was here that he wanted them, between the desert and himself. He switched on the acquisition packs and settled to his weapons, the one tube beside him, the other loosely in his grasp. The helicopter worked steadily towards him; squatted under rain; rose; squatted again; always drawing closer, always maintaining distance. Sparrow was not going to lose patience or taunt him a yard too near: there was no flaw there to be exploited. He must take any shot that offered, even at a thousand yards.

As the helicopter danced across his front, he brought the first launcher to the shoulder and heard the acquisition tone. But it was weak. He would wait until the aircraft had passed him, in the hope of capturing a stronger –

It happened without warning – the helicopter wallowing, as

though it had lost uplift, rotating about its vertical axis – the rising pitch of acquisition as heat presented.

Savage rose and fired. The pilot's reaction was startlingly adroit. The helicopter skated across the landscape, vomiting flares as though it were evacuating fright. Savage glanced down to change tubes and by the time he looked up again, he had lost the helicopter – and so had the missile, which speared the desert in pursuit of phantoms.

He realised that the pilot had cut back behind the rampart of heat he had erected in the sky, but when Savage sought to track him, his system was overwhelmed by the multiplicity of acquisitions. Then he saw that the helicopter was hovering and that Sparrow Force dropped from either door. Before he could react, his view was extinguished by teeming rain. As he groped amid the babel of contacts, he instinctively tracked onto a disengaging course and, when he acquired a powerful lock, he released the second missile. He then discarded the expended tube and, taking up his rifle, ran through the vertical twilight. He heard a muffled concussion followed by a bizarrely dustbin clang, which he took to be the helicopter coming to ground.

At the firing point, he settled to check his equipment.

They were down; but they were not reduced, even by one. The battle now was theirs.

He removed from his rifle the improvised paracord sling, since he wished above all, in what would follow, to be himself.

The helicopter did not appear badly damaged, although its rotor blades curled back and, through binoculars, Savage could see the face of the pilot, inert against the plexiglass. He hoped it was not Cassie's friend.

Of Sparrow Force, no sign; but they, he knew, were not far to seek: in cover, clear of their landing zone, they were discussing how best to dispose of him.

That should not long delay them.

The terrain over which he looked resembled nothing so much as a frozen, anthracite ocean, the turbulent water all to his left and front – with abundant troughs and peaks (and dead ground) attendant thereon – and, to his right, the gentler undulations of discharged seas: all of which he viewed from the crest of the tallest swell.

Rain possessed their world again.

And Sparrow Force drew closer.

Each downpour now was a drifting, aqueous smokescreen: unthinkable that they should not take advantage.

He sought to reconstitute in his mind the shapes abseiling from the helicopter. Rifles, certainly. Shotgun? Maybe. Grenade launchers? Minimi?

He sensed that Sparrow would seek advantage by other means.

Suddenly he had an intuition that he would never see them. That they would come and do the job and be gone.

Except that Sparrow

would need the moment of recognition.

This was family.

The rain eased and Savage lifted a protective hand from the small transmitter with which he hoped to detonate his mines. His personal radio was switched off: he did not expect Sparrow Force to break radio silence and his own people, although on listening watch, would not transmit before he did.

He thought of Anne.

She had offered him love, but in a form he had been incapable of recognising.

Not having experienced it, he had not known that love is defined as much by what is *taken*, as by what is given.

He had recognised Cassie's love (and had turned from it). Perhaps, he thought, we recognise only what we are capable of encompassing.

His grief was profound.

The world liquesced again.

But they would not come out of netherlight. Why operate in a milieu in which they could distinguish one another no better than they would see him?

And then, even as it started, the rain stopped. And he thought,

They're very close.

There was a stinging, airless suspension.

But he could not find them. They pricked at the bubble of his awareness, but he could not find them. Only ghosts.

He thought,

Goodbye, Anne.

The explosion took him completely by surprise.

How had they got there? How triggered the mine?

He tipped the lever to fire the second mine and dropped into the cauldron of reek and blood to his right

The standing man was momentarily distracted.

Savage fired twice.

The man went down.

Too late, Savage felt another behind him.

As he turned, the shotgun discharged.

His left arm snatched back, the world bolted bright with blood.

He realised that rain pounded on him and that he was *down*.

As he wallowed one-handed to bring his weapon to bear, it was as though the sky bled and he could not find the shooter.

Then he sensed death over him.

Looking up, Sparrow towered on the height, taking aim, rain breaking about his head.

Savage tried to roll, trailing his lifeless arm.

He hauled at his rifle, last engagement with the enemy. He thought,

I'm dead.

It made him angry.

Sparrow in spasm, performing a jig.

Shots.

Savage groped for the new danger.

Anne and Sammy ghosting out of mist.

Savage shouted:

'There's another! Shotgun!'

Labouring to point. Sammy said,

'He's dead.'

'. . . What?'

277

Indeed, as he regained insecure legs, Savage saw the shooter sprawled at the rear slope – and realised that, had the man not been shot in the act of firing, he would himself be dead. He looked up at Sparrow; and then, behind him: the ruination of a man, sundered at the waist by an outrush of projectiles; and an evident corpse. He said,

'Make sure the others are dead.'

Sparrow sat at the very rim of the crest, his bemused expression that of a marionette whose strings have been cut. Even as Savage watched, he dropped, in the sitting position, spilling his rifle, to encounter the ground with a fearsome impact, of which he appeared wholly unconscious, sitting blandly on. Anne said,

'Sarah, come in.'

Sammy fired a single shot. Anne said,

'Savage is hurt. Come.'

She was using her personal radio – and Savage realised that, in co-ordinating her approach, it must have been Anne who had triggered the mine with a rogue transmission. So comprehensively had he and Sparrow Force been absorbed in one another, that they had disregarded (with contempt) the only other force in the field: and now paid the price.

As he removed the short from Sparrow's holster, he saw the other watching him as though he shared Savage's mind. In a little, Sparrow said,

'Are they all dead?'

'Yes.'

Sparrow's eyes wandered to Sammy and Anne. It was apparent that his eyes were the only part of himself he still commanded. He smiled.

'Hearts and minds, Savage.'

'Yes.'

He looked at the pistol in Savage's hand and again to Sammy and Anne; but when Savage made to dismiss them, he found that already they had moved a distance off and had turned their backs.

Sparrow watched him. It was not an obligation that Savage relished, but he would not deny it. Sparrow fixed him with a look of ineffable transcendence.

'We were the best, John.'

'Yes, we were.'

But it did not seem to Savage now so great a thing.

Sparrow reclined at his ease.

'Now would be a good moment.'

Afterwards, Savage restored to Sparrow his weapons, against what battles may lie ahead. He saw, to his dismay, that it was the red-headed man who had been dismembered by the mine. Of the other two, he knew nothing.

They had compassed him about: it was fate decided the issue.

Sammy said,

'There's no joy in it.'

'No.' Savage regarded Anne. He did not doubt that she had been sole instigator of their critical intervention. He said, 'What are you doing here?'

Sammy said,

'We all backed her.'

She said,

'I'm sorry.'

'You were told to keep out of this.'

She lowered her head.

'Yes, I'm sorry.'

He did not know what to say to her. Nor did he understand why she should choose this moment to apologise to him. He was relieved of the need to find words by the impending approach of Cassie and Sarah across the tundra, Cassie vaulting ahead in her eagerness to reach him. He said,

'Cover them.' He indicated the worst of the gore. 'Use their smocks.'

They had barely time to impart small dignity to the dead before Cassie, headlong, halted at sight of Savage:

'Father! You're hurt!'

'I'm fine.'

He knew that his numb arm leaked, but he could not know from blood-steeped vision what ruin was in his face. She said,

'You're sure?'

'I'm sure.'

She flung at him and wrapped arms tightly about his neck.

'I love you! I didn't tell you! I love you!'

As he held her with his good arm, Savage experienced an exultation of the spirit such as he had never known. He was conscious that Anne watched him, but he could not in this moment hide from her. It was she, indeed, who turned away. This, too, he did not understand. But one mystery was as much as he could solve in a single day. Sarah said,

'Perhaps I could have my patient, before you do him further injury?'

Cassie stood back, grinning. Savage looked to Anne:

'Are you at the barn?'

'Alice and Martin went ahead. We've got a dinghy beached about a mile downstream.'

To Cassie, he said:

'Go with' – he hesitated – 'your mother. And Sammy. I'll join you soon.'

'Yes, Father.'

As they moved off, Anne placed an arm about Cassie's shoulders. Savage knew that he must speak. He said,

'Anne.' She looked back. 'You did well. Thank you.'

She nodded.

'So did you.'

Sarah's verdict was:

'No promises about the arm. The improved movement is a good sign.' He had regained some articulation in two fingers. 'But you will never recover full mobility.' Then, he thought, I'll teach myself another way. She said, 'I'm going to immobilise the arm for now and give you a jab.' She applied one field-dressing to the wound and used another to secure his arm against his body. She said, 'As to the eyes. You're badly bruised and you don't look any prettier.' She administered an injection. 'But I don't *think* there'll be permanent visual impairment. You were incredibly lucky.'

'The shooter was distracted.'

She viewed him up and down.

'You'll rattle when you walk. But you'll do.'

He said,

'I want to fetch the pilot.'

She looked across the tundra.

'You'll need help.'

There had been this boy.

This had-been boy.

And when, at the behest of his had-been parents, Savage had drawn his Browning

The boy had opened a gape of gratitude and had reached out a hand

But when Savage had taken it, it was as though the hand remained in his grasp and yet slid from him

And when he had looked, he had seen that the gauzy sheath had separated at the shoulder and that what he held in his hand was a case, as it were the ghost of an arm, trailing like a human glove

When he had sought to dash it from him, it had cleaved to his face

And when the boy had reached with an undressed arm

Savage had gone mad

And had killed the family

Many times

Until he had extinguished himself.

It does not sound much.

The pilot had been Cassie's friend. With Sarah's help, Savage hefted him to the shoulder and brought him to the others, where they laid them side by side. Sarah said,

'Do you want to bury them?'

He said,

'Perhaps, tomorrow.'

He would decide then what to take – and what from the bergen cache. Now, he could not rob them.

He grieved for them.

Then he mounted to the crest and checked that indeed the mine in the re-entrant had detonated, which it had. Martin would be pleased. By the time Savage had gathered his bergen and kit and had returned to Sarah, it had begun to rain heavily again. He said,

'Time to move on.'

281

And so they set out for the edge of the West, terra incognita, where his family waited.